THE
GOOD
WIDOW

ALSO BY
LIZ FENTON & LISA STEINKE

Your Perfect Life

The Status of All Things

The Year We Turned Forty

THE GOOD WIDOW

A NOVEL

LIZ FENTON & LISA STEINKE

Text copyright © 2017 by Liz Fenton & Lisa Steinke
All rights reserved.

No part of this book may be reproduced, or stored in a retrieval system, or transmitted in any form or by any means, electronic, mechanical, photocopying, recording, or otherwise, without express written permission of the publisher.

Published by Lake Union Publishing, Seattle

www.apub.com

Amazon, the Amazon logo, and Lake Union Publishing are trademarks of Amazon.com, Inc., or its affiliates.

ISBN-13: 9781503943445
ISBN-10: 1503943445

Cover design by Rachel Adam

Printed in the United States of America

To our fathers, for teaching us how to be strong.

She can kill with a smile
She can wound with her eyes
She can ruin your faith with her casual lies
And she only reveals what she wants you to see
She hides like a child
But she's always a woman to me

—Billy Joel

CHAPTER ONE

Before

His fingers slithered like a snake to find hers. She opened her palm and accepted them. There was something about the commanding way he reached for her. It felt like a statement. *You are mine.*

The reality was less clear. Because she was and she wasn't. And it was in this contradiction where their relationship lived, where it took its deep sighs and shallow breaths, where the highs felt like the top of the most beautiful mountain. Breathtaking. Exhilarating. Peaceful. And the lows felt like the La Brea Tar Pits she had visited as a child. Trapped. Anxious. Uncertain.

She ran her free hand through her hair, sticky from the wind that whipped through the rented Jeep after they'd decided to take the top down to feel the sun, the air, maybe even the spray of the ocean. They were both a bit quiet; it had been a long drive with so many turns, both on the road and in their relationship, so she leaned back and let the silence between them comfort her. She needed to confess something to him. And as long as the wind continued to swirl around them, as long as they kept winding their way slowly down the tortuous and twisty back side of the road to Hana, she could hold it on the tip of her tongue, where it had been resting for the last twenty-four hours. She squeezed his hand to check in, and her heart fluttered when he echoed it and made eye contact for a moment before looking back to the treacherous road.

There's something I need to tell you. She had attempted to force the words out several times since she'd found out. As they lay in bed, wound tightly together, their faces shamelessly close. He'd shared his own secrets, their lips brushing as he spoke. But when it had been her turn, the words would not come. She had not been ready for him to know. To face what might happen after.

The lush rain forest opened up and presented the ocean, the view so magnificent that she gasped slightly. He squeezed her hand, then pointed down below the cliffs they were navigating, the creases around his eyes deepening as he smiled, his hand leaving hers again only to downshift as they reached the top of a steep incline. She often wondered why he had chosen her. Why he'd risked so much to be with an average-looking woman, the owner of a nose that was a little too small for her face, lips that were just slightly too thin. A girl who worked hard but still hadn't found a career.

But in moments like these, this man's love, or lust, or even his *affection*—she was never quite sure what to call it—buoyed her. When he looked at her just like that, she knew that she'd do anything he asked. She might have even jumped off that bridge with him, as long as he'd held her hand on the way down. Granted, these thoughts of devotion were often fleeting. She questioned him almost as much as she revered him. But right then, in the Jeep hugging the side of this mountain, the unpaved road so riddled with potholes that she was getting carsick, she felt like they could overcome anything together. That the world could be theirs.

That's probably why she took off her seat belt. And decided to lean in close and breathe her secret into his ear. She could have simply called out her confession over the wind, but she needed to deliver the news gently. The rest of their lives together depended on it.

CHAPTER TWO

Jacks—after

I'm FaceTiming with Beth for the second time today when the police show up. I swing the door open, half listening to one of my sister's long-winded, albeit hilarious, stories about some moms at her children's elementary school who want to petition the school board to allow them to "manage" their kids' school projects. "They come out so much better when we're involved," one of them had said without a trace of irony in her voice.

"Are you Mrs. Morales? Wife of James Morales?"

I nod, dropping the phone to my side, my sister still speaking loudly as her view changes from my mud-brown hair and matching eyes to the dark denim of my jeans. I take in the static sound coming from the walkie-talkie on the female cop's slender hip, the handle of a gun protruding from the holster of her stout partner with a thick mustache, their squad car in the background.

She rattles off their names, which I immediately forget, then points to the olive-green front door, the only thing distinguishing our modest tract home from the others on the block. "May we come inside and speak with you?"

"Why? Is something wrong? Is James okay?" I ask as I study the knotted skin between the female officer's deep-set eyes, my mind clicking the pieces together.

"Mrs. Morales, may we come in, please?" she repeats, and I wonder, in a flash of annoyance as I stare at her partner's thick black hair, if they'd planned this. That *she'd* talk to me? Deliver the bad news I sensed was coming—woman to woman? She steps closer, and I jerk my body back, the heel of my shoe catching on the doormat. I lose my balance and grab onto her arm to steady myself. She offers me a sad smile, but still, I don't invite them inside. I want a few more seconds of not knowing.

"Jacks?" Beth says my nickname, and I silently turn the phone around so she can see the cops.

"Mrs. Morales?" The officer looks down, and I realize I'm still gripping the heavy fabric of her uniform, my knuckles bright white against the blue polyester. She puts her hand over mine, her skin cool and smooth. She guides me through the doorway, her partner easing the front door shut behind us. The three of us silently lower ourselves onto the red chenille couch. Ironically, it was purchased on one of my shopping binges when I tried to fill what my therapist had defined as the hole created by James's perpetual absences while traveling for work. I have a closet full of shoes, a bathroom filled with cosmetics, and a kitchen stacked with gadgets, all bought in the same mindset. Beth would come over to survey my latest haul, then give me one of her looks.

I stare at my sister on the screen of my phone resting in my palm, and together we hear the news that will seem surreal for weeks, like a bad dream I'm fighting to wake up from. May twenty-first. Maui. A car crash. The road to Hana. Cliffs. Lava rocks. A fire. His wallet with ID found several hundred yards from the car. Yes, they'd need his dental records to be absolutely sure, but they felt confident it had been him—confident enough to show up on my doorstep and tilt my world on its axis.

I try to process the words into separate thoughts, but they all blur together into one long rambling sentence. Beth starts to cry the kind of heavy tears I've always envied; my emotions have always been much harder to conjure. I know my sobs will come, but I won't have any idea when—just that my body will finally give.

The screen of my phone goes dark, and I know Beth has hung up and will be on my doorstep in just minutes—she lives only a mile and a half away. She will arrive with a tearstained face, staring at me incredulously when mine isn't like hers. It's hard to explain, but from the moment I hear he's dead, I'm both desperate for and afraid of feeling my husband's loss.

I stare at the two officers flanking me on the couch that has never been as comfortable as I wanted it to be, then eye the laundry basket filled with mismatched bath towels that I'd been folding earlier that morning. I wish it were five minutes earlier. Because five minutes ago, I was just a fourth grade teacher taking care of the dirty clothes that had piled up this week while I was cleaning out my classroom and getting ready for summer hiatus. Five minutes ago, I was laughing with my sister and making plans to meet her for lunch. Five minutes ago, I wasn't a widow.

I wonder what the officers will do when they leave my house. Will they think about me again? Or will I be quickly forgotten as they stop at Starbucks for iced caramel macchiatos on the way back to the station?

The male officer speaks for the first time since arriving, his baritone voice sounding out of context. "Is there anything we can do? Anyone we can call? I mean other than—" He doesn't finish his sentence; instead he motions toward my cell phone.

"My sister—she'll be here any minute," I say.

"Okay, good," he says, and scoots forward on the couch. "Do you have any questions?"

I stare into his eyes. They are kind—pale blue with errant flecks of brown dancing around the pupils. The truth is that there are so many things to do. And there is an overwhelming number of calls to make. I imagine breaking the news to all the people who loved James. I'll dial their numbers, then lean my head against the cold granite in the kitchen as they cry, in the same desperate, unbelieving way I haven't, but eventually will. Oh, how I will.

And of course, there are so many questions. But I only have the strength to ask the cop with the kind eyes the most important one.

"What the hell was my husband doing in Maui?"

CHAPTER THREE

JACKS—AFTER

It's ridiculous how your life doesn't need your permission to turn upside down. You think you have it under control. That you're good at handling the colossal disappointments: the ticket for the illegal U-turn, the late fee on your credit card that sends your APR through the roof, the dry cleaner's fuckup. Okay, maybe you weren't so good at dealing with that last one and would probably take back that terrible Yelp review you wrote. They'd refused to admit to ripping your favorite black pants that made your legs appear longer and leaner. You'd never find another pair that slimmed you that way again. It was a tragedy.

But then your husband dies, and you think how you'd beg for the apocalypse of the torn pants. Because now it's your life that has ripped apart at the seams you thought were so tightly sewn.

I've been binge watching *Shark Tank* because I can't sleep. And it reminds me of James—he'd always wanted to invent the next great thing. When the smug college freshman turns down Mr. Wonderful's fifty-thousand-dollar offer for his pointless collapsible hangers, I want to tell the kid that life is short. To take the damn deal. That he'll never miss the 5 percent of equity he's hanging on to like a life raft. James would have said yes, wrapped Mr. Wonderful in a tight bear hug, and thrown the hangers into the air in celebration while all the sharks erupted in laughter. James charmed people in the same way he took a deep breath: easily and without much thought.

Every day since James's memorial two weeks ago—still a blur of dark suits and tearstained faces—has started the same way. I haul myself out of bed a little after 10:30 a.m., the haze of the sleeping pill I took the night before still lingering. I pour a cup of dark coffee, add three lumps of sugar, turn on my laptop, and wait for the numbers on the digital clock to hit eleven—eight in Maui. I picture Officer Keoloha staring at his phone as it rings. I know from my Google Images search that he has a round face, thick brown hair speckled with gray, and a wide inviting smile. I can imagine his jolly expression shifting when my 949 area code illuminates on his caller ID and he debates sending me to voice mail. To his credit, he never does.

The first time I talked to him was the day after I found out James had died. After the female cop had pressed her card into my shaking hand with Officer Keoloha's name and number written on the back. After she and her partner had waited with me until Beth arrived. After Beth had thrown her arms around my shoulders and stroked my hair as if I were a little girl. After she had spent the night and held me in our guest bed as I fell in and out of sleep, the harsh reality of the news I'd been given hitting me all over again each time I woke.

Officer Keoloha listened as I told him my story. How I was shocked to find out James had been in Maui, because he was supposed to be in Kansas. I rambled about how we'd been married eight years, about how he'd never lied to me before—that I knew of. I was aware I sounded like a desperate widow not wanting to accept that her husband had secrets, but I couldn't stop talking. And it didn't help that he didn't try to fill the lulls. I think he knew I needed someone to understand that this wasn't supposed to be my life.

When I asked how he could be sure it had been my husband in the car, he gently walked me through much of what the officers who'd come to my house had already told me: How James's brown leather wallet with his driver's license and credit cards had been found not far from the wreckage; that they'd interviewed Heidi from the rental car company, who'd confirmed James had rented the Jeep and that the signature on the agreement matched the one on his ID. They'd also verified that James's name was on the manifest of a United Airlines flight from LAX to Maui. That he'd used the same Citibank Visa (which I had no idea existed) that had been in his wallet to pay for four nights and several sightseeing excursions at the Westin Resort and Spa in Ka'anapali.

His voice became tender when he reminded me about the next part, that because of the fire, the only way to be 100 percent sure it was James's body that had been in that car was for our dentist to confirm James's dental records. I couldn't bring myself to think about what that meant. So I held on to the sliver of hope that provided—that there was a possibility it had all been a huge misunderstanding, and James was in Kansas closing the software deal he had told me was so important.

But then our dentist, Dr. Matias, delivered bad news all over again.

So, it was confirmed. My husband was dead. But why had he died in Maui?

Every time I think of James tearing out of our house the morning he left, my insides ache. He was wearing a starched white button-down and gray trousers that rose up a bit too much when he sat. His light-brown hair was longer than usual, hitting the collar of his shirt, his five-o'clock shadow already in full force, dotting his deep-olive skin. Ironically, I had the thought that he looked more like a surfer going to the beach than a salesman on his way to a conference. He blew past me with a tight grip on his carry-on, muttering obscenities in Spanish, his worn black leather laptop bag slipping off his shoulder as his sturdy body barreled toward the driver parked out front. I could see a man with a short white beard watching us and could only imagine what he'd been thinking—how many of these types of scenes he'd witnessed in his amateur driving career. And the worst part? We'd had this fight before, so many times. And I knew we would again. Or at least I thought so.

Was that why he'd gone to Hawaii? Because I couldn't give him what he wanted? Because I'd let him believe that I could?

That, I was not ready to explore.

~

I've walked through our (my?) house day after day since I found out he died, looking for an answer I'm realizing I'll never find: why.

I've tried to find out why James wasn't in Kansas like he was supposed to be. But the answer eludes me, the same way his truth seemed to. So right now, I have decided to focus on something I can control, something manageable, mundane.

I'm trying to get the kitchen spout to stop leaking.

The water is almost therapeutic, causing a rhythmic echo as it hits the inside of the sink, reminding me of those drummers in the New York subway making music by hitting the top of a paint bucket. I turn the handle of the faucet to the right, remembering my father's instruction from when I was a little girl and he'd directed me to turn off the hose that was attached to the Slip'N Slide. Lefty Lucy, righty tighty.

It's funny the things that stick with you and the things that don't. Since James's death, I'm discovering that the mind works in strange ways. I can recall his smell without putting my nose to a single item of his clothing—because I can't bring myself to. I cannot even look at the sleeve of his crumpled pale-blue button-down shirt peering out from the top of the hamper, but the scent is there, as potent as when I buried my head in his shoulder and breathed him in on our first date, the sake

I'd drunk making me brave. His musky aroma is entangled in our bed-sheets; it's emanating off the last bath towel he used. It's clinging to my nose hairs like my grandmother's perfume, which she treated like a can of air freshener. It's a comfort but also a terrible burden, still smelling him. I've had moments where I've longed for hyposmia—the decreased ability to smell, a definition I only learned because I Googled it at 3:00 a.m. I'd been hugging James's pillow between my legs like an anchor and smelling him so strongly in the pillowcase that I could almost tell myself he'd just been lying there and had gotten up to go to the bathroom.

His scent assails me, while I try to make sense of remembering only some details about James and not others. Like the way his hands felt. I have no idea. Were they smooth? Calloused? Did I ever take the time to notice? I grabbed Beth's wrists when she came over this morning, trying to memorize each of her fingers. They felt soft, and as I touched the small scar on her palm from when she'd sliced through it while chopping tomatoes, I promised myself I wouldn't forget them.

I can't manage to remember the sound of his laugh. I've been trying, the way you do when that actor's name is on the tip of your tongue but you just can't spit it out, squinting hard as if the concentration will help me recall it. A few nights ago, after polishing off half a bottle of port—the only alcohol left in the house—I tore through a box of home videos, searching for the one from our wedding. I wanted that moment when, after Tom gave his best-man speech, James let out a belly laugh that rippled through the courtyard of the hotel. It was infectious, that laugh. And now I can't remember it. And I never did find the video.

James and I had eight years together, but in many ways we hadn't even made it out of the gate, like a racehorse that gets spooked by the sound of the gun. So many things had held us back. The loss of his job during our first year of marriage that led him to the one he has—had—that forced him to be out of town each week; my arrogance that we could wait years after getting married to start a family.

Which leads me back to the whys. Why did it end before it ever really began? Why were the last words we spoke to each other hostile? Why can't I forget how he blew past me out of the house and got into the Uber driver's rusted Toyota Camry without looking over his shoulder? Why can I still feel the way the house trembled after the front door slammed?

He shouldn't have died. He paid his taxes. He coached Beth's son's baseball team. He was thoughtful, once turning the car around to drive twenty minutes when he realized he'd forgotten to tip our server. Why had the knock from two police officers been on my door? Why not on the door of the awful woman from across the street, who once yelled at a group of gap-toothed kids in our neighborhood for placing their lemonade stand too close to her driveway? Why not hers?

~

After three glasses of sauvignon blanc at James's memorial, which Beth had planned without my even having to ask, I'd found the courage to ask his boss, Frank, if he knew James had been in Maui. My stomach churned as I studied Frank's bushy eyebrows and his bloodhound eyes, both wanting and not wanting to know if Frank had been covering for him—that I was the only one not in on the joke. It was incredible how many questions I wanted and didn't want the answers to. It felt like when I had learned to drive, the instructor jamming the passenger-side brake as I pumped the gas. But Frank shook his head vehemently. He knew only that James had requested a few days off, nothing more than that. And, oh yes, he was so very sorry.

Later that night—after Beth and I had said good-bye to James's mom, Isabella, and dad, Carlos, my parents, and a few other stragglers—Beth searched the house for clues. (She actually called them that. Like she was starring in a bad episode of *Law & Order*.) We started with his personal items that had been shipped back to me and arrived the day before. I unzipped his suitcase and sifted through his clothes, pulling out a mix of clean and dirty items, my hand resting on his favorite bathing suit, a pair of red board shorts with a frayed waistband. The same ones he'd worn on our honeymoon. I dug deeper, but there wasn't so much as a bar receipt. His cell phone and laptop proved to be just as unhelpful—every single password attempt denying me access to the man my husband had been. The thing was, I had naively—or stupidly, I don't know which at this point—never thought I'd need that access.

CHAPTER FOUR

Our conversations about where James was going on business always went something like this:

Him: I'm off to Des Moines (or another city name) tomorrow.

Me: Um, hmm. When will you be back?

Him: In a few days. I'll text you when I land.

Me: Okay. Can you pull the trash cans out before you go?

~

We were finishing our fettuccini Alfredo when he mentioned the Kansas trip. I looked up from my plate and watched the noodles swirling inside his mouth as he told me he'd be leaving the next morning and would be gone until Saturday. There was a dinner he couldn't get out of on Friday night. He went on about how the clients were impossible and closing this deal could potentially double his bonus check next quarter. I frowned, mentally canceling the reservations I'd just made at a new Italian spot down the street. Trying to convince myself that maybe the timing was good. I had a ton of prep work to do for the end-of-school-year open house in the fourth grade class I teach. That night was just a week away, and I still had to decide how to display the kids' essays about their heroes and come up with a creative idea of how to showcase their family-tree projects.

Noticing my face fall, James came around to my side of the table and kissed me softly, and my irritation began to dissolve, as it often did. We fell in and out of arguments easily, like that snap on your shirt that doesn't quite clasp. You think you've finally secured it and then, *bam*, ten minutes later it's popped open again.

~

Could I have asked him more about his trip to Kansas? Sure. But I wouldn't have. I had stopped doing that a long time ago. In the beginning of our marriage, I'd pepper him with questions about his job. But he would give me clipped answers, finally admitting he saw his job selling web conferencing software simply as a means to an end—a paycheck. One day, he'd leave and start his own business. He had ideas, ones that didn't involve the lack of legroom in seat seventeen C or the gate agent who loved to scold you if your carry-on was larger than twenty-two by sixteen by ten inches. He liked his job and was very good at what he did, but he hated all the travel that went along with it. So I learned not to ask about it. And definitely not to bring up his plans to leave.

I never thought he was lying about jaunting off to Sioux Falls or Wichita. I believed he would have much rather been home with me every night. Our marriage was far from perfect, but did I think he was cheating on me? Never. Not even in hindsight. Maybe that made me naive or stupid or a little bit of both, but I was happy I wasn't one of those wives with trust issues. I'd heard it all from friends whose husbands traveled—that they *required* their spouses to check in several times a day, to supply them with a full itinerary, to regale them with details about their trips when they returned back home. I didn't want to be like that. Requiring it. As if he were my employee.

I liked receiving the texts he sent on his own, which came frequently—quips about the sea of Nebraska Cornhusker shirts he saw in Omaha or the endless number of BMWs he spotted in Dallas. He'd text selfies while stuck on the tarmac. I could reach him whenever I needed to. So did I get his travel plans like those controlling wives I know? I didn't. Clearly, I should have. Those women obviously understand how the world works much better than I do. Their husbands may resent the hell out of them, but they are home safe, while mine has just been delivered to a columbarium at the Good Shepherd Cemetery.

So maybe if I'd been more checked in to my husband's life, I wouldn't have been so shocked by what Officer Keoloha told me when I called him the day after the memorial.

It turns out that James hadn't been alone when he died.

He'd been driving down the Hana Highway in a rented Jeep Wrangler with a twenty-four-year-old woman named Dylan Matthews.

And my first thought? I'd once asked him to rent a cherry-red one when we'd taken a road trip up to Monterey, and he'd scoffed at the price. I think my mind went there because it couldn't handle the reality of what I was hearing. That he'd been in Hawaii with someone who wasn't me.

According to the officer, Dylan's body had washed up on shore two weeks after the crash. At first they didn't put it together that she could have been with James in the accident. But after investigating, they'd found her name on the same flight manifest as his and at the Westin Ka'anapali, where they'd stayed; she'd shared the same room number as him and had charged a manicure and pedicure to it. Her signature was also on many of the slips from drinks and food they'd ordered at the hotel. And then there had been the surfers who'd watched James pull Dylan in and kiss her hard on the morning of the accident. Actually, the way *they'd* described it was "getting up on each other on the side of the Jeep." That detail stings. A lot. But not as much as imagining this woman getting her nails done on my husband's dime. Somehow that feels more intimate.

But that wasn't all. There were other sightings. The day they'd driven the road to Hana, they'd stopped at the Kuau Store, just past the town of Paia, on the Hana Highway. According to the cashier who had worked that shift, James and Dylan had just taken pictures at the famous surfboard fence and were laughing about how Dylan was posing for a selfie and fell back into the boards. And James's credit card charges confirmed he'd been there. He purchased goat cheese, salami, a bottle of wine, coconut water, banana bread, and a *Road to Hana* CD guide. As I listened to the officer rattle off the information, I couldn't decide which detail about their trip bothered me the most: the Jeep James wouldn't rent for me, the romantic picnic lunch I imagined them enjoying as they sat by a waterfall, or the CD. James and I had always laughed at the people who got all touristy and bought things like that. Had I known my husband at all?

But there was information I still wanted that Officer Keoloha couldn't uncover from credit card statements or the memories of store clerks. Why had they been in Maui together? How long had they been seeing each other? Did he love her?

Did he love her more than me?

Officer Keoloha tried to be empathetic but still said hugely unhelpful things, like, "I'm sorry," and, "If there's anything I can do," as I'd choked on my sobs, the tears finally falling hard—like the waterfalls I imagined James had hiked to with the woman who ruined my life.

CHAPTER FIVE

Jacks—after

Here are the things I now know about the road to Hana after obsessively Googling it:

It's 52 miles of highway.

It passes over 59 bridges.

There are more than 600 curves.

It carves into the cliffs of one of the most beautiful rain forests in the world.

Because of its many winding roads, blind turns, distracting views, one-lane roads, and tall cliffs, it is considered dangerous. (As one of the websites described: *It can bring you to God in more ways than one.*)

No shit.

Apparently there are multiple fatalities there every year from people falling off the 300- to 1,000-foot cliffs (some in cars, some on foot) and hitting the lava rocks below.

My husband and Dylan Matthews are now on that list.

～

Here's what my Google search didn't provide:

Any helpful information about Dylan Matthews.

I learned only that she graduated from a high school in a small town outside of Phoenix. She had no Facebook profile I could locate, no Twitter account. She wasn't on Instagram. A very poor millennial, if you ask Beth.

~

I'm pulled out of my thoughts by the doorbell. I squeeze my eyes and mentally will whoever is outside to leave. I can't face another well-meaning neighbor with a casserole. I've started to polish the already-gleaming stovetop when the knocking begins. The longer I ignore it, the more incessant it becomes. Finally I peer through the peephole and see the back of a man's head, his wavy hair not giving anything away as to who he might be. He turns and cocks his arm to knock again, and I take in his dark eyes and square jaw, not recognizing him. Is he one of James's friends? I received several emails, phone calls, and cards in the mail from old buddies of his who couldn't make the service; maybe this guy is one of them, in which case I can't leave him standing there. I open the door slightly, leaving the chain on.

"Hi," he starts. "Are you Jacqueline Morales?"

I hesitate, then nod. "Yes. Jacks to most."

I notice a motorcycle parked next to the curb.

"I'm Nick Ford."

I look at him as if to say, *And?*

He steps closer. "You don't know me, but I need to talk to you." He pauses as a woman walks by with her golden retriever. "It's about your husband."

I glance down at the welcome mat, his worn cowboy boots grazing the edge. "Okay?" I say as I look back up into his dark-gray eyes, which feel familiar to me somehow.

"Can I come in?"

I feel uncomfortable letting a stranger into my house, but there's something about his demeanor that's disarming. I remove the chain and step outside, closing the door behind me. "I'd rather talk out here." I smile slightly to let him know I'm not trying to be rude.

"I don't know how to say this. I had it all planned out, but now, looking at you, it just seems wrong. Maybe I shouldn't have come."

I stare down at my boyfriend jeans rolled at the ankles, my bare feet, the chipped pale-pink polish on my toes. I smooth my still-unbrushed hair, wondering what he means. Now that he's looking at me, it seems wrong? "How did you know James?"

"I didn't." He shoves his hands into the pockets of his jeans and takes a deep breath. "But my fiancée, Dylan Matthews, did. And I'm here to find out why she was in Maui with your husband."

CHAPTER SIX

JACKS—AFTER

My breathing is short and raspy; my lungs are burning. How do people do this? Run for sport? I see cars driving by, people walking their dogs, tiny faces pressed up against the windows inside a passing school bus. But I don't hear any sounds. It's like someone pushed the mute button on the world around me. My calves are on fire and my face is dripping with sweat and I have that damn ache in my side, but I push myself harder anyway. When did I grab my Nikes and lace them up? Leave the house? It's all such a blur since I told that Nick person to get the hell off my property.

I can picture the sleek black iPod that James gave me five (or was it six?) Christmases ago. He grinned like a goofy schoolboy with a crush when I opened it, launching into a spiel about how he knew I thought exercise was boring, how I'd never found a physical activity that I enjoyed, that maybe I should try running—an amazing endorphin releaser. But I would need music; that was the key. He'd even created a playlist for me—*Jacks's Workout Mix*—and he suggested an afternoon run. I eyed the bottle of wine we'd planned to open after presents but decided I'd do this for him.

But a few blocks into our jog, I was already losing pace with James. I tried to let Beyoncé's song about girls ruling the world propel me forward, but my breathing was all wrong, and I got a cramp. I finally had to stop and walk, and I told James to keep going. He refused, walking beside me as I huffed and puffed and even spit at one point—anything to get the offensive saliva out of my mouth.

He placed his arm around my sweaty shoulders, my shirt soaked through with perspiration, and we continued in silence until I finally begged him to not let me hold him back. He stopped when I said that. Right there in the middle of a busy four-way intersection. The red hand was blinking, but James wouldn't budge, cocking his head and frowning at me. "What?" I asked as an SUV inched into the crosswalk, ready to make a right turn, but we were blocking its path.

"You'd never hold me back, Jacks. We're in this together. We're a team. Haven't you figured that out by now?"

"I do know that," I said sheepishly, watching the red hand count down the seconds behind him.

The light turned green, and the driver of the SUV held his hand on his horn, the long blare jolting me. James grabbed my hand, tugged me onto the sidewalk, and kissed me on the forehead.

"I'll speed-walk race you home." He grinned.

I shook my head, suddenly determined to push myself out of my comfort zone. I slowly took my gait from a fast walk to a jog, James running beside me in disbelief. "You sure?" he said. "Don't feel like you have to run for me."

"I don't. We're a team, remember?"

And back then, we were. I didn't realize then the change that was coming. If I had, maybe I would have cherished that moment, *that* version of James more. But I didn't—I took for granted that he'd always stop and wait for me.

I was wrong.

I think that iPod ended up buried under half-sharpened pencils and incomplete decks of cards in the junk drawer later that month. But maybe it could have helped drown out my thoughts today as I sprint to Beth's house, because no matter how large my stride or how hard I pump my arms, I can't outrun them.

Dylan Matthews's fiancé, Nick, showed up on my doorstep like a Jehovah's Witness trying to convert me. And I let him preach; I allowed him to speculate about my husband's relationship with his fiancée. To ramble on about the things he needed to know to move on with his life. I listened to him as he paced in front of my house, shaking his head and saying that he just couldn't believe it. How could they do this to him? To us? I had all the same questions, but there was a part of me that was scared to find out the answers. It was so much easier living in denial, telling myself James had just been having a midlife crisis. That this woman, Dylan, meant nothing to him. I thought of the time I'd snuck downstairs when I was eight years old and peeled the Scotch tape carefully off my birthday gift to reveal the Teddy Ruxpin I'd begged for. Afterward, my chest had felt heavy with guilt; my greed had outweighed common sense. Listening to Nick's words reminded me of that night—my hunger for information causing me to ignore the obvious: finding out was going to hurt like hell.

But that's the problem with letting your curiosity overrule your conscience—you can't change your mind afterward. Nick told me he'd found emails they'd sent each other—did I want to see them? He said he needed to know if they had been serious. If they had loved each other. If they were going to leave us. That last one? It hadn't crossed my mind. Then it was all I could think about.

I turn onto Church Street and come to an abrupt stop in front of Beth's tan two-story home. I press my hands against my throbbing quads, trying to steady my breathing, hating that my ability to drive seems to be another casualty since James went over that cliff. Because getting behind the wheel would have been such an easier way to get here.

The front door opens. "My God, look at you!" Beth rushes down the steps and bends over me, her mud-brown hair that matches mine hanging around her creamy complexion dotted with light freckles.

"I know." I hold out my hand so she can pull me up. "Could use some water, please."

She gives me a once-over, her perfectly tweezed eyebrows arching over her light-brown eyes. "You ran here?"

I nod. "Because I couldn't . . ." I don't finish, but we both know what the rest of the sentence would be.

Get in a car.

I did attempt to drive, just a couple of days after I found out. I was going to buy wine. Many bottles of it, preparing to drink myself into a dreamless sleep—anything to stop the nightmares. I slid into the seat of my Mini Cooper and started it just like I would have any other day. But as the engine roared to life, I saw a flash of James's face, grimacing as he tried to steer the Jeep away from the cliff. My heart pounding out of my chest, I started gasping for air, my hands tingling so much I almost couldn't get the driver's door open. Then I laid my cheek against the cold, oil-stained garage floor and sobbed into the concrete until I managed to move myself into an upright position and call Beth, who came racing over, *again*. When she found me, resting against a bag of fertilizer, I looked at her and shook my head.

~

As I follow her inside now, I watch her nylon shorts start to slide down her slim hips, and she tugs them upward; I'm amazed that after birthing three children, she's been able to maintain her high school figure. She'd cheered—literally chanting a *Go! Fight! Win!*—after she'd found her red-white-and-black cheer uniform in a bin and zipped it up as if

24

she were still sixteen. But then again, she works at it. Without asking, I know she's already dropped her kids at summer camp, been to a 9:00 a.m. SoulCycle class, and blended a Paleo-approved shake. As a lover of processed foods—anything with that orange stuff they're trying to ban—I find eating like a caveman feels as unachievable as making the Olympic track team.

"Shoes," Beth calls over her shoulder. "I mean, if you don't mind," she adds quickly, turning her head and giving me a quick, toothless smile. It's funny how people hold their tongues when you go through something awful. I caught my neighbor, who spent years knotting her gray eyebrows together when my garbage cans were still sitting by the curb long after trash day, dragging them up our driveway last night, pulling forcefully as one wheel got stuck in a deep crack that appeared after the last earthquake. And Beth. She's been on her best behavior since James died—replacing her typical blunt opinions with kind and gentle responses that seem foreign coming from her. What she doesn't understand is that I wish she would go back to her normal personality, because I need her to be *her*. I need her unfiltered commentary about my life, her know-it-all attitude, her need to be right.

It's not just Beth who's been on first-date behavior. Before James died, my mom, who lives in Solana Beach, a sleepy beach town about an hour south of my neighborhood, would rarely made the trek "all the way up" to Aliso Viejo because northbound traffic is "just the worst on the weekends." And now she has miraculously gotten over her commuter issues and has been religiously making the "journey" once a week to check on me. She's never been a big believer in comfortable silences, so as she scrubs my spotless countertops and heats up some casserole we both know I'll never eat and fluffs pillows and opens windows, she relentlessly throws words my way, telling me stories about her book club or my dad's refusal to stop eating red meat, tiptoeing around me like I'm a land mine she might trigger.

What my mom doesn't get is that I don't need her to come to my house and rearrange my coffee table books. Just because James is gone, she doesn't need to change; she doesn't need to prove anything to me. It never bothered me that she didn't drive up to see us. James and I liked going down to visit her and my dad, the coastal setting making us feel like we were going on a staycation the minute we arrived. But Mom's unwillingness to come up north to see Beth and me, and our father's silent alignment with her, drove Beth insane. "Can't she do it for her *three* grandchildren? Doesn't she realize we have soccer and gymnastics and we are bu-sy? I swear it's Poochie Poo. She can't leave that dog for five minutes." I'd tell her that was crazy talk, that of course it wasn't about the dog, but she'd spit back that I was too agreeable, that I accepted things too easily. And she's right; I usually do. Part of me wonders if that's why I'm standing here now, with questions out-numbering answers.

I force my sneakers off without untying them.

Beth hands me a glass of water and sets my shoes neatly by the front door next to three pairs of soccer cleats in varying sizes, waiting for me to tell her why I'm here. She knows better than to ask if I'm okay or how I'm doing or if I slept last night. I've banned all questions like that.

I take a long drink and look at her, my eyes watering. "It's just a lot."

"Come here." Beth wraps her arms around me, and I stand there stiffly like a child being cuddled by a great-aunt she barely knows. I'm afraid if I hug her back, I'll dissolve into tears. That I won't be able to stop.

I pull out of her embrace. "I had a visitor."

Beth frowns, waiting for me to continue.

"A man; apparently he's Dylan's fiancé. Or was . . ."

"Wait, what?"

I tell her about Nick. How he felt so familiar to me even though I was sure I'd never met him. How he'd held out Dylan's driver's license, which the police had mailed back to him, to prove his connection to her. How I found myself staring into James's mistress's bright-blue eyes, her white-blonde hair resting on top of her shoulders in a simple blunt cut, her bangs swept to the side.

I had read over her description as Nick watched me: five foot two, 103 pounds, contact lenses, organ donor, lived in Irvine, birthdate July 7, 1992. I felt my stomach twisting into hard knots as my brain computed the differences between us.

Nine years younger.

Twenty-two pounds lighter.

Four inches shorter.

Blonder.

We sit and I explain to Beth what Nick said when he came to see me. That he hadn't been able to sleep since he found out his fiancée died, because he needed answers. He needed to understand more. About Dylan. About James. About the bond they had formed together, seemingly right under our noses. He wanted to travel to Hawaii to retrace their steps. It might sound crazy, but would I go with him?

"He asked you to do what?" Beth interrupts me.

"To go to Maui with him."

"A perfect stranger."

"Yes." But what I don't say is that we are connected by this event in a way that no longer makes us people who don't know each other. "He said I'm the only person who can understand what he's going through. That the simple police report, deeming the crash an accident, won't tell him the things he really needs to know: why his fiancée was cheating on him with another man and why she was in Maui with him. He thinks going there could help fill in the blanks."

"Honey." Beth puts her hand on my knee. "I don't mean this to sound harsh, because I love you and I'm so sorry you're going through this. But what good can come from taking *their* vacation?"

It's worth noting once more that preaccident Beth would have never prefaced anything with *I don't mean this to sound harsh*. She would have just said it, along with an eye roll and an impatient tone. So I know she'll bite her tongue rather than chastise me if I confess the rest—that he suggested retracing their *exact* steps: Had they eaten coconut shrimp? Sipped piña coladas as the sun set? Did they kick their shoes off and stroll down the beach? But still. I don't tell Beth this. Because I know she won't understand why there's a part of me that shares Nick's morbid curiosity. And that I would strongly consider running my hand across the bed they slept in, leaning over the railing of their lanai and taking in the same view, looking in the mirror over their bathroom sink to try to make sense of what he saw in her. Maybe that's exactly it. Going to Maui could help me understand why he was willing to risk the comfortable life we'd built. Because I can't ever ask him.

Beth's concern is obvious, and I get it, because I'm thinking it too—whatever answers I find might make it all worse. "Don't worry, I kicked him off my front steps," I say as I watch her face soften. She thinks this means I'm not going. But the problem is, I can't stop picturing his hunched shoulders as he walked to his bike; how he'd slowly slung his leg over the seat, then pulled his helmet on; how the sound of his motorcycle firing to life had startled me; how I'd watched him until he disappeared down the street.

"But?" Beth asks, sensing my thoughts. Only eleven months apart, we've always shared a bond, an intuition as strong as if we'd shared a uterus.

"But . . ." I pause, remembering his eyes filling with tears when I'd told him to go away, not recognizing the sound of my own voice. How do I explain to her that I both want and don't want to know more? I'm curious about the shrimp and the sunset strolls, but frightened to find out about the real emotions they might have shared. "But . . . what if he's right? What if going could help? I know it may sound crazy to you, but there's a part of me that understands exactly why he needs to go to Maui." I pull my long hair out of its ponytail, the elastic ripping several strands.

"Okay . . ." Beth pauses, and I watch her try to compose herself. She wants to be the old Beth so badly. To tell me what an idiot I'm being. Instead, she clears her throat and says, "So a part of you wonders. But what about the other parts?"

"Do you *really* think that I should just accept that he was having an affair and leave it at that?"

"You're not answering my question."

"And you're not answering mine." I fold my arms across my chest.

"Fine," she says. "Yes, I really think that. I just worry that going will create even more questions. And then you'll always be wondering what the answers are."

"I hear you. But Nick did make a good point—he said he didn't want to be in denial anymore. That he wants to face it—all of it. And the only way to do that is to be in Maui."

"Wouldn't that be torture? Why would he do that to himself? To you?"

"So we can try to move on." I realize that I've said *we* rather than *he*. I reach into the pocket of the sweatshirt I'm wearing—an old one from James's fraternity days. "He told me to hold on to this." I hand Dylan's driver's license to her. "He said he lived one floor up from her in the same condominium complex. That I could find him there, if I changed my mind."

She studies the ID for a moment, frowning slightly, then flipping it over so we're both staring at the magnetic stripe on the back.

"Okay. So maybe I can understand why he wants to go. But why does he need to take you? And how can you trust him? What if he's not who he says he is?"

"Who else would he be?"

"He might have read James's obituary and be some kind of stalker weirdo looking to prey on you because you're grieving."

29

"You've been watching too much *CSI*."

"Please. You know I'm a *True Detective* girl."

"Whatever. My point is—"

"You think I'm overreacting."

I give her a look.

"Don't you realize it's my job to protect you? Especially now." Her bottom lip quivers, and I put my hand on top of hers.

"Well, if it helps you feel better about him, he's a fireman. He showed me a business card with the station he works at. And he showed me several pictures on his phone, including one of the two of them at a firemen's ball from only a few months ago." I think of the crushed-silk fabric of Dylan's floor-length cobalt dress, her hair swept back from her face, her hand placed across the front of his starched uniform, the sparkling ring on her finger.

"Jacks, I'm sorry; none of that proves she was his fiancée. He could have Photoshopped her in."

"He didn't strike me as a techie—more like a beefcake whose only hacking is done in a jujitsu class," I joke. When Beth doesn't respond, I add, "Listen, I hear you, but he seemed sincere." I think of his hand shaking as he gave me her driver's license. I had resisted my impulse to console him, because what was there to say? How could I convince him there would be a time when his insides didn't feel like they'd been hollowed like a jack-o'-lantern when I didn't believe it myself? I'd wondered how he could stand to look at a photo of her, of them. I had asked Beth to remove all pictures of James from our house for now—it was like a knife slicing into my abdomen every time I looked into his deep-set eyes, always my favorite part of him. Instead of remembering the good times we'd had, all I could see were the years we *wouldn't* have, the dreams we *wouldn't* build, the family we *wouldn't* create.

"You never answered me about the other parts of you, the parts that don't want the details."

"There's a part of me that wants to ball up on the couch. The part that wants to pretend this never happened."

Beth points to her couch. "Go right ahead. I'll get the wine."

I shake my head. "Beth, if I lie down, I'm afraid I'll never get up—that I won't recover from this. If I go to Maui and face whatever it is they were doing there and *why* they were doing it, as awful as it may be, then maybe I'll be able to move forward. To have a normal life again someday."

"Okay, but do you really think you can trust this guy?"

"Yes. I saw his hurt. It was real." And that was what it came down to for me. When I searched Nick's eyes, I saw the grief that mirrored my own.

Beth looks up at me and takes a deep breath before speaking. "Even if he is who he says he is, I don't think it's a good idea, Jacks. Some things are better left alone."

CHAPTER SEVEN

DYLAN—BEFORE

Dylan swiped the credit card receipt off the table, her fingers narrowly missing the puddle of ketchup a four-year-old had squirted there earlier. She had ground her teeth from the service bar while she watched the little boy squeal as the red liquid cascaded from the plastic bottle. She'd exchanged an eye roll with Ted, her favorite bartender, as he whipped up mimosas for the wonderfully childless couple in the booth next to the ketchup terrorist. It was their third round in an hour, and Dylan hoped their impending inebriation would lead to a large tip.

Working Sunday brunch at Splashes Restaurant in Laguna Beach was always a bit of a clusterfuck, but it was also filled with possibilities. You could end up with condiment stains all over your favorite white T-shirt, the one that was so soft you hugged it before throwing it over your head. Or you might meet the love of your life, even though you thought you already had.

Dylan cringed as she calculated the tip from the ketchup terrorist's parents. Ten percent! *What the hell?* Dylan had smiled and said all the right things. She'd been patient as the child had stuttered his way through ordering blueberry pancakes, while his mother played with her expensive blonde extensions and his father pecked away on his iPhone. They were seemingly oblivious that she might have other tables, that she might not find their son's intentionally shaggy surfer haircut as adorable as they did. But she knew that the overpriced brunch came with strings. The patrons pretended it was okay to pay twenty-one dollars for three waffles and a side of fruit, and Dylan pretended she didn't resent them.

"You were a saint to put up with that little devil." A voice wound its way into her ears. She looked to her left and saw that it belonged to the male half of the mimosa couple. He was now alone in the booth— Mrs. Mimosa must be in the bathroom, the champagne finally hitting her. She'd downed the third glass immediately, as Dylan had known she would. It had become an occupational hazard to notice details about the people she served. And she could tell Mrs. Mimosa was looking to get drunk by how fast she'd drunk the first one—even before she'd consumed a single bite of her crab cake Benedict. By how she'd looked expectantly toward Dylan when she'd drained her second flute, as if she'd barely wanted to take a breath before having a third. By the way her plump lips eased out of their frown with each sip. There was something sad in her eyes, and Dylan sensed the alcohol was helping her forget.

Dylan could feel a tense energy between Mr. and Mrs. Mimosa. They'd barely spoken two words to each other since they'd sat down, and whenever Dylan came to the table, it was only Mr. Mimosa's voice she heard, ordering for both of them, asking for more salt, or now, talking to her about that unruly kid. She wondered if they were in the middle of an argument, or worse, if they were just at that point in their marriage where they didn't enjoy each other's company at all.

Dylan smiled at Mr. Mimosa, noticing how his right dimple over-shadowed his left one when he returned her grin. "Thanks. The kid wasn't too bad." Dylan deflected, as she often did. "All part of the job, right?"

"I don't know." He shook his head, glancing at the table where the child and his parents had been sitting. "I get that kids can throw tantrums, but come on. Those parents didn't do a thing to stop it. And I'm not sure how dealing with a child like that should be included in *any* job description. I hope they gave you a huge tip." He smiled again, and Dylan laughed nervously. This wasn't part of the game. Good-looking men with deep-olive skin and fluorescent-green eyes didn't lament with her about the lack of discipline of today's youth. Sure, they smiled suggestively at you when they thought their wife wasn't looking (she usually was), or "accidentally" brushed your boob when you set down their omelet. (She got that too, by the way.) But talk to her like she was a real person? No, they never did that.

"Beautiful ring," he said, nodding toward the two-carat diamond that still felt like a foreign object. She had played with it so much since accepting it the night before that she was already developing a red indentation mark on her finger. It was just slightly too tight, something she was trying not to focus on.

"Thank you," she said, holding it up. "Just happened last night!" Dylan added as Mrs. Mimosa reappeared, stumbling slightly as she slid into the booth. Dylan glanced at the simple gold band on Mrs. Mimosa's finger, something a lot more along the lines of what Dylan would have wanted, and suddenly felt silly about the size of her bauble. She buried her left hand into the pocket of her black apron.

"Congratulations," Mr. Mimosa said, his eyes wandering over to Mrs. Mimosa as if he were silently imploring her to speak.

"When's the big date?" Mrs. Mimosa asked, her words slightly slurred.

"Oh, we don't know yet." Dylan waved her hand in the air. "Don't people usually wait at least a year?"

"Sometimes. But we didn't," she says, pointing at her husband and grimacing so slightly that Dylan almost didn't notice it. Dylan wondered what the woman's pinched face represented. Was she thinking they should have waited longer? Or not gotten married at all?

"Everyone's different, I suppose," Dylan said.

"Well, good luck to you," Mrs. Mimosa said, holding Dylan's gaze for a few beats longer than was comfortable.

"Thank you," Dylan said, thrown off by what felt like more like a warning than a sentiment. She started to clean the neighboring table, taking a napkin and scooping the ketchup onto a barely touched plate of pancakes, the red sauce dripping from the cloth and settling into the accent diamonds in her ring, dulling their sparkle slightly.

Later, Dylan clocked out on the computer and caught her reflection in the small mirror hanging on the wall. She sighed. Her face had that bad kind of shimmer to it—a combination of sweat and grease.

She grabbed her purse, a weathered Kate Spade that was older than the ketchup kid, one her mom had proudly announced she'd found on clearance at the outlet. She still loved the quaintness of the black-and-pink sunglasses print and refused to part with it, despite the frayed edges of the straps.

She fumbled for her keys as she walked up the street to the employee lot. Parking was scarce in Laguna on the weekends, and the best spots were sold for upward of twenty-five dollars on a Sunday. But even after her worst shift, she didn't mind the trek to her car. Laguna Beach had majestic views and a sea breeze that was addictive, and Dylan's spirits would always rise the minute she exited the restaurant and turned right to take in the sweet, salty air and waves breaking below.

"Excuse me," a familiar voice called out, and she knew before looking that it was Mr. Mimosa. She turned and saw him gripping a twenty-dollar bill.

Dylan froze. She'd never had a customer track her down. In her mind, she wasn't the type of girl you went to great lengths for. Nick was the exception. He always found a way to do something extra when he didn't have to, like carrying her trash down to the dumpster when the chute was broken or taking her Volkswagen to the car wash after she'd made a passing remark about how someone had scrawled *wash me* in the dirt on the back window.

"Yes?" Dylan answered, trying to keep her voice neutral. Really good-looking (possibly older?) men like him had gleaming black Range Rovers and gorgeous brunette women like the one he'd been with earlier. They certainly didn't need Dylan.

"I wanted to give you this." He waved the money at her.

"You already tipped me," she reminded him, thinking back to how she'd known Mr. Mimosa would be generous. It was the way he'd slowly given Dylan their order so she'd have time to write it down, how he said please and thank you whenever he asked her for something, how he'd made small talk about her personal life. A customer like that was always a good tipper. He'd given her almost 30 percent.

"So maybe I thought you deserved more. Is that wrong?" He smiled sheepishly, and there were those beautiful eyes again.

"That depends," Dylan said, pressing her lips together in a failed attempt not to grin. But it was impossible, and she felt the corners of her mouth inch upward anyway. There was something about him. Dylan had never known anyone who shined from the inside out before. She found it intriguing, even though she really didn't want to. What she really wanted to do was get home and soak her shirt before the ketchup stain became permanent.

"Depends on what?" He said it like he already knew what her answer was going to be. She liked that too.

"How much more you think I need." She laughed.

He joined her, his laugh low and strong. "Here." He held out the money again.

"I can't," Dylan said, fidgeting with her diamond.

"Is it because you're engaged?"

Dylan absorbed his words, looking at his bare ring finger. "No. Well, yes," she stuttered, flustered at his straightforwardness. "But more because you're married. You are, right? That was your wife?"

"Right," he said simply.

Dylan wanted to ask more questions about her. Why did her face tighten when she talked about her husband? And why had she drunk so much she'd be sure she wouldn't remember the two-hundred-dollar brunch she had with her handsome, seemingly charming spouse? But instead Dylan just said, "I don't even know your name."

"It's James Morales. And it's very nice to meet you." He took her hand in his, slipping a business card and the twenty into it before she could refuse again.

CHAPTER EIGHT

JACKS—AFTER

I'm so tired of condolence cards. First off, they are ugly—like your-grandmother's-curtains kind of unattractive. Second, they never say the right thing. *I'm sorry for your loss. My thoughts are with you. You have my deepest sympathy.* I stopped opening them last week, and they're now stacked on the kitchen counter, where I add three more that have arrived today.

I'm still waiting for the card that says, *I'm sorry your husband careened off a cliff with his mistress in a Jeep he couldn't be bothered to rent for you. I know, because he's dead, that it's bad form to write this, but fuck him!*

That's a card that would speak to me.

I'm clearly in the angry phase now. I'm all kinds of pissed. Like the seeing-red, flaring-nostrils type of mad. I took it out on someone who called the house this morning. I don't even know why I answered the phone. Maybe I was looking for a fight. The unfortunate woman, who sounded like a teenager, was calling from the alumni office of my alma mater, San Diego State University, to update my information. I held it together until she asked if I was still married, and then I unleashed all the pent-up frustration that had been building. I told her off, then threw the cordless receiver across the room.

I know I have misplaced aggression. Clearly it's James I'm raging at. But I can't tell him to go fuck himself and will never get the chance to yell at him for being a lying cheat. To see his gorgeous green eyes shift to the side when I confront him as he decides which way he wants to go—deny it or come clean? To see him hang his head as I cry and ask him, *Why?* To feel the shame deep inside that I might already know the answer to that question.

Naturally the cause of my rage, that little detail, is something that no one in my family besides Beth knows: James was in Maui because he was having an affair—with a girl so young she probably didn't know who Debbie Gibson was. It's obvious my mom suspects there's more I'm not telling her, her eyes searching mine each time she asks why in the world James was in Hawaii without me, not quite accepting my answer that he had a very important client he was courting there. I hate to lie. Especially because it's lies that have brought my world crashing down around me. But I remain tight lipped, knowing she'll just add to the confusion.

And his mother. I can't bring myself to tell her the truth. Even though she's never liked me much—she made that clear years ago—she does not deserve to think about her son that way. To realize you can love a person and not know them at all. To start to question everyone and everything in your life. What else do you not know? Who else is keeping things from you?

Beth, for one. Turns out, she had an admission of her own. After she'd told me not to go to Maui with Nick, her left eye started twitching—the way it has since we were kids. It was her tell—that she'd done something I wasn't going to like. The first time I noticed it, I was seven or eight. I couldn't find my Malibu Barbie convertible. The twitching eye led me to her closet, where I not only located the bubblegum-pink plastic car, but Barbie and Ken in a compromising position in the backseat. So when her left eyelid started blinking uncontrollably in her living room yesterday, I pressed her for what she wasn't saying. At first she denied there was anything. But I wouldn't give up. You see, once you find out there are so many lies sitting right below the surface of your relationships, you want to know them all. Every single one. I used to think that some things were better left unsaid, like when my mom asked me if she was too old to wear that fedora at the pool a few months back. She was. But I told her she worked it because I knew she wanted to wear it. I had reasoned I was helping her feel confident. But now I realize that lies, even small, well-meaning ones, just pile up until they eventually topple over.

Beth finally admitted there was *something* but that my knowing wouldn't change anything. But I was sure whatever had her eyelid in spasms was important. So I kept at it until she told me.

Apparently she'd once seen James and Dylan together.

It was about a month before they'd died. She'd spotted them having lunch at a little sushi place not far from where we lived. Beth had seen them through the window as she'd been getting into her minivan after leaving the boutique next door. She hadn't told me because she figured it was a business lunch.

"Wouldn't that be all the more reason to mention it? Like, 'Hey, I saw James today at Sushi Time'?" I demanded, standing up and looking down at her, my hands pressed into my hips.

"I figured *he'd* tell you." Her eyelid was going full throttle as she said it.

"What does that mean?"

"He saw me see him and nodded his head, then turned back to her. He didn't even raise an eyebrow! And I'd just had dinner with you guys the night before; it's not like I felt compelled to run in there and say hi."

"Did *she* see you?"

"No, at least I don't think so."

"And you really didn't think anything of it? You, who breaks into your husband's email and texts every Sunday morning while he sleeps in?"

She shook her head but wouldn't look at me.

"Bullshit, Beth. I know you. At this point, the salt is already in the wound, okay?"

"Fine. I thought *something*. But it wasn't enough of a something to tell you about it. Because what if I was wrong?"

"Well you weren't, now, were you?"

I'm not proud of what I did next. I lost it. I might have even accused her of indirectly causing his death. Because maybe if she'd mentioned his little luncheon liaison, I would've confronted him and he would've come clean and broken it off with her and never would have gone to Maui. Right?

It was twenty-four hours ago that I stormed out, and we haven't spoken since. It's the longest I can remember not talking to her, someone I usually call or see three or four times a day. Someone I've been accused of having a codependent relationship with by more than one boyfriend or friend.

So obviously I need answers now more than ever. I need every scrap of information, whether it will hurt me or not. I feel like an alcoholic who knows she will feel like hell the next morning but pours herself another drink anyway. Because she can't *not* pour it.

I know now that I have to go find Nick. And then we have to go to Maui.

CHAPTER NINE

Jacks—before

"I like this one, don't you?" James's mother, Isabella, held up a brick-red tablecloth covered in metallic gold leaves, the tasseled corners dangling precariously close to the polished linoleum floor of Crate and Barrel.

The truth was, I hated it. If it were the last tablecloth on the planet, I wouldn't buy it.

But I kept a smile plastered across my face and tried to imagine the gaudy fabric in my mother-in-law's thin hands covering the nicked-up country table I loved so much. It might have seemed odd, but it was always the imperfections that made me like that table more—the gouge in the side of the leg where James had banged it against the doorframe when he'd moved it in; the paint I'd splattered on it when I was changing the wall color in the kitchen from ivory to taupe; and the deep and long scratches—from God only knows what—that covered it. Its wood had always been sensitive; even sliding a plate across the soft pine would make a mark. I worried I'd be betraying my table by covering its blemishes. Like I was agreeing with Isabella that they needed to be hidden. I often wondered if she was somehow trying to cover up my flaws as well.

As she waited for me to sign off, her piercing green eyes identical to James's, I fantasized saying to her, *The table and I are flawed, and that's okay!* But of course, I didn't. Some things are just better left alone.

It was December. Two and a half years before James and his secret girlfriend would career off a cliff together. We were planning to host James's family for Christmas brunch for the first time, and Isabella was helping me prepare. Step one, she'd said, was sprucing up my unsophisticated dining room table. But in true Isabella style, which gave a whole new meaning to the term *passive-aggressive*, she hadn't used the word *unsophisticated*. She'd said *rustic*. But I knew what she meant.

It was a miracle I'd finally been awarded this brunch, a ritual in the Morales family. Isabella usually hosted everyone in the sprawling home she owned with James's father, Carlos, on the coveted Balboa Peninsula. Carlos was the salt-and-pepper version of his son, and could be just as smooth. But for as sweet and accommodating as he always seemed, I'd always felt like he was hard to know. Like there was an invisible barrier between the words he spoke aloud and the ones that danced inside his head.

But I'd seen others given the opportunity to host. Her sister once. James's cousin another time. I'd been asking for my turn to play hostess for several years, wanting to prove that I could fit into their tight Costa Rican clan, and my mother-in-law had finally acquiesced. I'd received an email from her informing me it was finally my turn, but quickly clarifying that she wanted to *stay involved*. I asked James if he had been the one responsible for her decision, and he'd denied it. But there was something in the way his lip curved a little bit higher on the right as he'd said he didn't know anything about it that had made me wonder if he was lying. I'd seen that look before, and would again. I ignored it, as I always did.

James's parents, plus a few of his aunts, uncles, and cousins and their children, were all set to attend with their large broods and had graciously agreed to sit at my unacceptable kitchen table while I attempted to make *gallo pinto*, a traditional Costa Rican breakfast.

I knew by the tone of Isabella's voice when I mentioned I'd be making the customary dish that she was afraid I'd butcher it. But I had plans to practice until I got it right. Determined to win her over by making her family's favorite foods. Something I later realized was naive of me to think. But back then I was blissfully naive. And still hopeful.

So, there we were in Crate and Barrel, my mother-in-law and I, standing in the aisle overflowing with holiday-themed tablecloths, napkins, and placemats. I wanted to please Isabella by being agreeable and letting her buy the tasseled one in her hand. But I also wished we had the kind of relationship where I could tell her that it just wasn't me. That if it were my choice, I'd just put a few candles in the middle of my table and call it a day. Then I realized by her smug expression that she already knew I wasn't going to speak up, that I'd take the easy way out. So I surprised her—and myself—when I did something uncustomary for us. I pushed back.

"I'm thinking maybe no tablecloth."

She glanced at me like she'd smelled something rotten and pinched the red fabric between her fingers, ignoring my statement. "This will be a lovely pop of color in your kitchen, against those beige walls." She said *beige* like just looking at the color was an insult to her sensibilities.

"What if we compromised and got a runner?" I offered, feeling my confidence rise as I pointed one out that was white with a simple gold trim.

She gave me a look then. One I never forgot. One I later realized had nothing to do with the tablecloth or the runner or any of it. Then she'd let out a stilted sound—like a cross between a scoff and a laugh. "So you're suggesting a runner? And that's it?"

"Well—" I started to explain myself, but she cut me off, and I felt my confidence disappear into the air around us.

"And don't tell me that the next thing out of your mouth is that you have no plans to decorate the house. Because I know that's your style when you're *not* hosting Christmas brunch for the Moraleses."

She rolled the *r* extra hard as she pronounced the Morales name. Her accent always grew stronger when she was angry. It was her tell. I waited for her to speak again.

"If the preparation that goes into the brunch is too much, I understand if you want to cancel. I can easily take it over. And no one will say a word."

Bullshit. We both knew she'd speed-dial her sister the minute I left her sight. There would be words. A lot of them. Mostly in Spanish. And I highly doubted they'd be kind.

"I do want to host," I said, but it came out sounding like I was begging for my job back.

Isabella was right that I usually subscribed to a less-is-more school of thought when it came to decorating for the holidays. She'd once come over the day after Thanksgiving, mortified to discover our tree wasn't up yet. Isabella treated holiday decor like it was an Olympic sport. She turned her home into a display every holiday, from Halloween to Thanksgiving to Easter, and even for the Fourth of July. Depending on the festivity, her house would be adorned with ghosts or scarecrows, bunnies or American flags. There would be matching dish towels next to the sink, festive serving dishes on the table, and handmade decorations she copied from Pinterest.

Meanwhile, I'd ask James to drag out our fake tree the weekend before Christmas and would carefully sift through the broken ornaments (How did they break? They were sitting in a box all year!), trying to come up with enough to adequately fill the gaps in our artificial pine.

But no matter how much I tried, there was always more emptiness than I was comfortable with.

This year I had planned to do a little bit more—probably not Isabella Morales more, but more. But I also didn't want to crowd the small space with unnecessary things like frosted pinecones and fake snow.

"I think I should just host. Save you the trouble," she said, ignoring my plea.

"Isabella—" I said her name, then realized I had no idea what to say after it.

"Yes?"

"I appreciate your help. I do," I said, pushing aside her judgments, already mentally ordering the most ornate Santa Claus I could find on Amazon, desperate to bridge the gap that always seemed to exist between us. Last year Beth had surprised me with a *Mind the Gap* T-shirt from her trip to the UK, and it always reminded me of Isabella. I wondered if I spent too much time trying not to slip through the cracks in our relationship. "There's no doubt you know more than me when it comes to decorating." I paused, and she gave me a satisfied smile. "So if you think we should go with that tablecloth, I'll trust you. Because I know how important the holidays are to you," I said, reaching over and squeezing her arm, falling easily back into my typical daughter-in-law role. Agree with Isabella. Repeat.

"Thank you," she said, putting the tablecloth in the cart. "You probably think I'm overreacting about this . . ."

I shook my head. *Deny. Deny. Deny.*

"And maybe I am," she continued. "Because what I'm really struggling with is the realization that I may never have a grandchild to enjoy it."

My hand flew off her arm. "We don't know that for sure, Isabella," I said, my voice faltering slightly. I caught the eye of the woman behind us in the aisle, who quickly focused on a placemat covered in snowmen, trying to pretend she hadn't heard our exchange.

"Oh, but you do know, don't you?" she accused, her eyes steely.

I realized later, looking back, that she had been waiting for that moment. To let me know that *she knew*. Had she held her tongue at Pottery Barn? Bitten her lip at Williams-Sonoma? Was she being patient and calculated, making sure we had the perfect tablecloth picked out before she punched me in the gut?

But the real question was: How long had she known? And why had James told her?

CHAPTER TEN

DYLAN—BEFORE

Dylan rubbed her hands over her bare arms, feeling a chill as soon as she stepped out of the cab.

James noticed her hugging her arms to her chest. "Let's get you inside and on the dance floor. That will warm you up. I can't wait to see you move in that dress." James looked her over, then offered his hand with so much authority that Dylan didn't even question him as he tugged her arm to join the crowd of bodies moving to the music. She'd never been much of a dancer, but she felt her hips obliging with ease and swinging to the beat, as if on autopilot.

James put his arms around Dylan's waist and pulled her into him so she was grinding on his thigh. He closed his eyes and moved his body in time with the song. Dylan couldn't believe the drastic change in him since they'd arrived. He'd been quiet on the ride over, but then he'd inched forward in the backseat of their cab when it pulled into the parking lot. And the second he opened the door of the bar for her and heard the music, every muscle in his neck and face seemed to relax.

He'd brought her to his favorite bar, hidden away in a Hispanic neighborhood in a corner of Santa Ana. She'd never danced to traditional Mexican music or witnessed the enthusiasm, no, the *joy* that it seemed to bring to the people listening to it. Her only exposure to anything like this was an awkward moment with a mariachi band at a bad chain restaurant, their horns blaring as her father tried to swallow the last of his enchilada combo plate that her mother had chastised him for ordering because it was too expensive. Dylan's parents had spent a huge chunk of her childhood discussing the cost of things. *What a rip-off! It's two dollars less at Walmart! Did you use the coupon I gave you?* It always left her feeling embarrassed and a little bit exhausted.

But this wasn't a chain restaurant in Phoenix with stale tortilla chips submerged in bland salsa. This was a hole-in-the-wall in a neighborhood even her roommates, who didn't have super high standards when it came to places to drink, wouldn't be caught dead in. *But they're missing out,* she thought as James spun her around. She was dizzy, but she didn't care. She couldn't understand a word the band was singing, but it was now her favorite song. She had never met the Hispanic couple dancing beside them, but she wanted to be their new best friends. Maybe they'd teach Dylan culture, something she often feared she lacked after growing up in a house that was literally whitewashed—her mother's decorating style bringing new meaning to the word *neutral*.

Dylan had always felt bland—her blonde locks blending into her alabaster skin. A mean girl in middle school had once said Dylan was so plain she faded into the walls. But not when she was with James. He made her feel colorful. And sometimes she could almost pretend that this was their life. That he didn't belong to someone else. That she hadn't become the type of person who danced with another woman's husband in a dark bar so far off the beaten path that no one would ever find her.

Several songs later, James said he wanted a margarita. Dylan wished she liked alcohol, but she couldn't stand the taste, having gotten drunk once and only once in high school, her hangover so terrible the next

49

day she vowed to never drink again. And she hadn't. But she knew the buzz would help blunt the guilt she felt. Because she did feel terrible shame about the affair—she wasn't a monster! Her conscience kept her up more nights than she'd ever admit. Her tossing and turning would often wake her fiancé, Nick, who would reach his large hand to her bare thigh to calm her, falling back asleep with his grip around her leg tight. Then she'd will her thoughts about James to be quiet, lying so still that it was almost like she wasn't there.

She glanced at her phone as the bartender handed a margarita rimmed with salt to James and they said something to each other in Spanish. Dylan thought she caught the words *delicious* and *beautiful*, but she couldn't be sure. She was a long way from the high school Spanish she'd waded through.

Nick was on a seventy-two-hour shift, so she was surprised to see one missed call and a text from him. He worked in a busy fire station in Long Beach and would often take several calls a night, usually coming home exhausted. Sometimes he'd tell her stories that made her heart hurt—a child who had been burned, a mother who had suffered a major heart attack and left her family behind, the homeless man who hadn't bothered to get off the train tracks. He described the situations with such detachment, it was like he was reading the newspaper.

Yet he had no trouble connecting with his buddies at work, who adored him, insisting he use his athletic prowess to be pitcher on their many slow-pitch softball teams, and use the culinary skills he'd gleaned from his mother to win the chili cook-off for their firehouse each year. Nick was a guy who could be counted on. But Dylan wondered where he stored the anger and sadness—the *helplessness* he witnessed each day. Because she knew there was only so much one person could handle, and a small part of her often worried he might be close to bursting. But maybe he was like an earthquake—there would be no way of knowing it was coming until it was already there.

James planted a wet kiss on Dylan's thin lips and smiled. "You really held your own out there, for a white girl."

Perhaps sensing it bothered her, James liked to tease Dylan about her lack of culture. He was Costa Rican and had rich olive skin and green eyes that looked like a beautiful piece of sea glass. Even though he'd grown up in Irvine, California, and had visited Central America only once, when he was twelve years old, he wore his heritage like a medal of honor and talked about it and his mother constantly. She couldn't connect with how James felt about his heritage, feeling no real roots of her own. But now she could see his intense pride in the way he danced, in his body language as he talked to the bartender, in the smile that hadn't left his lips since they'd arrived.

She smiled. "I'm good like that." She leaned in and kissed him, relieved she didn't have to look over her shoulder here. The couple they had been dancing with earlier had assumed they were just like them—out on a date night. "Let's get out of here—we're getting a hotel tonight, right?"

James's eyes flickered, and Dylan's heart sank. She knew that look. "I thought we were spending the night together." She tried to keep the pout out of her voice. He hadn't spent the night with her the last time either. And it wasn't like she saw him very often. It was only one, *maybe* two times a month. They had it down. James would tell his wife he was going to be traveling one night longer than he actually was. Then she'd pick him up at the airport and they'd stay at a hotel James would book—always making sure it coincided with one of Nick's seventy-two-hour shifts at the station. The next morning, James would go home as if he'd just arrived back in town. Dylan marked her mental calendar each time they planned an overnight date and then counted down like a child to Christmas. And now he was going home *again*. To his real life. The one where she didn't belong.

"Babe, I can't. I'm sorry."

Dylan stood up. She didn't know many things for sure, but she knew when a man was becoming bored. So she played the only card she had, the ace she held close. "Good night, James," she said with a tight smile, and started to fight her way through the crowd to the door.

"Dylan! Wait!" She ignored his calls and continued swiftly toward the exit. She'd made it outside and was searching her phone for the Uber app when he grabbed her arm. "Stop being childish. You can't just walk out like that."

"Watch me," she shot back. In general she was a calm person, but James always made her feel out of control.

"What do you want from me? I'm sorry, but I have to go home. I wish things were different, but they're not. I thought we were on the same page about all this."

All this?

"Maybe I don't like that page anymore." Dylan sighed. She hated feeling like an afterthought. They had to mean something. Because if they didn't—then what did that say about her? She wanted, no, she *needed* him to care enough that the risks they were both taking seemed worth it. *All this* was the fabric of their lives, and if it was stripped away, they might both end up with nothing.

"I'm not sure how much longer I can do this." She bit her lip. Losing James would crush her. She wasn't ready to let him go. And she was taking a gamble by threatening it. But she knew there was one thing James could not handle: losing on someone else's terms.

His eyes darkened. "Come on. Don't say that." He looked at his phone and shook his head. "I really can't stay, boo."

A smile crept to Dylan's lips. "It's shameful that a thirty-five-year-old man would use that word."

"Okay, then I'll use my special name for you," he said, pushing the hair away from her eyes. "I promise you, *belleza*, I would stay if I could. What if I took you away somewhere? Just the two of us? We'd have to wait a few months, but I could swing maybe four or five days." James kissed the top of her head softly. And she felt all the anger disappear from her body. She loved when he called her beautiful in Spanish, the one time she truly felt like she was the only woman in his life. And now he was offering to give himself to her for multiple days.

Dylan nodded into his chest. They'd never been together for more than eighteen hours straight. She was desperate to find out what happened in hour nineteen. A small tear escaped from her eye onto his black shirt, which was hot and slightly damp from sweating inside the bar. She wanted to *know more*. About him. About herself. About *all this* that they did together.

Her heart rose and fell as she waited for him to speak.

"I'm going to take you to Maui."

CHAPTER ELEVEN

DYLAN—BEFORE

Dylan pushed her front door open and flipped on the lights as she walked inside.

"Where have you been?"

Dylan jumped at the sound of Nick's voice. "You scared the shit out of me! What are you doing here?" She put her purse on the kitchen counter and poured herself a glass of water. She needed to buy some time, calm down. She'd worried about this moment for so long, him finding out about the affair. That had to be why he was here. He knew.

"I texted you and called. I was worried. Briana let me in and said I could wait." He pointed to her roommate's closed bedroom door.

Thanks a lot, Briana. That girl had never liked her.

Dylan's heart was beating so fast she was sure Nick could see it. He was supposed to be at the station. She had gotten his calls and texts, but she knew if she responded, he'd have questions. He always had so many questions: Where was she? Who was she with? What was she wearing?

"I'm sorry, my battery died." She said the first thing that came to mind, hoping he wouldn't ask her to prove it.

"You look pretty."

She relaxed slightly. Maybe he wasn't suspicious. Maybe he simply got off his shift early and came over to surprise her. She had been listening to a talk radio show a while back—the host had asserted that cheaters often read things into their partner's behavior because *they* felt guilty. Maybe that was all this was.

"Thanks." Dylan walked over and perched on the edge of the couch, hoping the perfume she sprayed in the cab was masking the smell of stale cigarettes from the bar. It had become a habit to carry a tiny bottle of Ralph Lauren Romance and a toothbrush and toothpaste with her so she could clean herself up before she went back to her real life. *Just in case.*

Nick reached out and fingered her dress made from cotton so soft that James couldn't stop touching it earlier. She'd found it on the 75-percent-off rack at Macy's. And when she'd surveyed herself in the dressing room mirror, she'd thought of James, not Nick. She knew his wife could afford much nicer clothes. And she hoped she looked sexy, not cheap. She had turned so she could see the way the fabric grabbed her curves. Would James like it? Would this little black dress be enough to keep him interested?

"Why don't you get all dolled up like that for me?" Nick asked.

So he wasn't going to let it go.

"I do, babe," Dylan said sweetly. "But I thought you liked it better when I didn't have anything on at all." She stroked his arm and smiled. Maybe they could take this to her bedroom and he'd forget. She tugged on his arm to get him to stand up, but he didn't move.

Silently, he gave her a once-over. He started with her face, taking in her minimal makeup, just mascara; her nails (she was in desperate need of a manicure, but couldn't afford one this week); and her slightly scuffed strappy wedges that he'd seen dozens of times before. She knew she looked good, but not too good. She was always careful not to try too hard with James. She didn't want to reek of desperation. She waited for Nick to speak. She wasn't going to say more until he did.

"So where were you?"

Keep it simple, Dylan. Stick to the plan.

"I went out with my old friend Katie." Lie number two. But it was the alibi she'd come up with in case she ever needed to explain herself. For the first few months, she'd been careless. But then she'd heard that radio show. Someone had called in and said cheaters don't get caught if they're smart. And one of the examples was to have a cover story. So Dylan had asked her childhood friend, Katie, who had recently moved from Phoenix to Orange County, if she'd cover for her if it ever came to it. "But it won't," Dylan had said, laughing. "Don't worry."

Even though Katie had said she was fine with it, Dylan had thought she could hear hesitation in her friend's voice. She was married with two young children. Dylan wondered if she was silently judging her or if Dylan was projecting because she constantly judged herself. She hated to put Katie in this position. But she didn't have any other options. Nick knew the few friends she had—most of them from the restaurant—and her other roommates, Grace and Natalie. She knew Nick was resourceful and could follow up with any of them if he were suspicious. But he'd never met Katie and had no way to contact her. Not that he would. She'd given him no reason not to trust her. *That he knew of.*

Her mind was spinning. She needed to calm down. He didn't know anything.

"Come here," he said, pulling her down on his lap. "I missed you."

"I missed you too," Dylan said, using the back of her hand to wipe away any remaining trace of James's lips before nuzzling Nick. Another lie. Tonight, she hadn't missed him. She'd been too intoxicated by James. And once he said he'd take her away for a vacation, she could think of nothing else. That was big. And it had to mean something. The more he risked, the more secure Dylan felt.

"Hey, Dyl?" Nick said, kissing her neck.

"Yeah?" Dylan answered, her skin tingling from his touch. She had wanted James so badly tonight, and there hadn't been anywhere to go. They'd once done it in the back of his car, and she'd felt so cheap afterward that she vowed never to do that again. But now, sitting on Nick's lap as she felt him get aroused, she was getting aroused too. Would it be the worst thing if she had sex with Nick and imagined James?

"Let's invite Katie out to dinner. I'd really love to meet her."

CHAPTER TWELVE

JACKS—AFTER

I have a new appreciation for people who use public transportation.

The city bus lurches forward, and I reach for the pole, trying not to think about the millions of tiny germs that speckle the metal. The people those germs came from. What they may have been into. I draw in a deep breath and push the frantic thoughts from my mind. This happens a lot since James died. Being caught up in my own crazy mind. Part of me hates it. But there's another part that finds comfort in being scared. Like my fear is the only thing that makes sense anymore.

The bus stops again, and several people make their way on and off. The smell of an egg salad sandwich hits me hard as I push my way toward the back to make room for the new passengers and end up face-to-face with a woman bouncing a baby girl on her lap. The scent seems to weave in and out of my nostrils like a snake. Each time I graduate from a short, shallow breath—which reduces the putrid odor—to a deeper one, the smell wades back, making me wonder if I had imagined its absence.

I still can't bring myself to drive. I tried again this morning, feeling overwhelmed after I realized I'd have to take three different buses to get to Irvine. I held my car keys, turning the fob over and over in my palm, trying not to let my anxiety win. But now, as I reach into my purse and squeeze out a large gob of hand sanitizer, rubbing the solution into every crease in my fingers, I understand that for now, the anxiety is victorious.

It takes me a moment to get my bearings when I step off bus number three. I punch in Nick's address on my phone and watch as the map opens up on the screen. I begin to follow the squiggly line, the dot moving as I edge forward. If I stare at that dot, I'll keep moving. Closer to Nick. And Nick will help me find answers.

Beth's face replaces the map a second later, her wry smile staring at me. She's called every hour or so since our fight yesterday. She wants to know if I'm okay. To make sure I'm not going to do anything stupid. I'm not sure of either answer, so I hit "Ignore" and fire off a text telling her that I need some space. I don't mention where I'm going. Or what I'm going to do when I get there. My breath quickens as the blue dot inches closer to the checkered flag.

My phone call to Nick letting him know I was coming had been short and stilted. It was my fault. I was being cryptic because I wanted to be face-to-face when I told him I was ready to go to Maui. I also wanted to look into his eyes and see what was really there. If fear had begun to rule his life too. If we really were in this together.

Two blocks later I find myself staring up at the kind of shiny high-rise condo building that's commonplace in Irvine. I walk through the lobby, passing a dry cleaner and a Peet's Coffee on my way to the elevator. I try not to think about the fact that *she* had lived here too. That she still may have unclaimed clothes wrapped in plastic inside Nice n' Clean.

Nick answers the door quickly, almost as if he's been standing on the other side, waiting.

"Hey," I offer, not sure what the right emotion is for this moment. He smiles, and it puts me at ease. "I'm so glad you came."

The condo is immaculate—did he just clean, or does he always keep his home this orderly? I notice it's decorated in mostly cool grays and whites with a touch of color—a red throw pillow on the couch and yellow pots and pans hanging in the kitchen. I glance back at him as I take in the large space; I didn't expect such modern, minimalist tastes from the buff-looking firefighter whose calloused hand scratched mine when he shook it. I instantly wonder about Dylan—had the design choices been hers?

"Don't tell the guys at the station, but I have a serious love for decor," he jokes, as if reading my mind. "The cheap kind, that is—it's almost all from Ikea." He knocks his knuckles on a white bookshelf. "Looks good now, but what a bitch to put together. I'm not sure the hours of sweat and frustration were worth the money I saved."

"Did Dylan help?" I ask, her name sounding strange when I say it.

"No," he says. "Decorating wasn't her thing."

"What was her *thing*, then?" *Stealing other people's husbands?*

I don't say the last part, but it's clear I'm not really asking what her hobbies were. That I don't really care. I didn't mean for things to start out like this. I planned to have a civilized conversation with Nick. But I didn't think through what being here was going to do to me. How, standing in front of a sleek black couch and a simple coffee table, I can only picture her—here, alive, lying back against the pillows and laughing. Rage swells up inside me.

Nick's eyes are gentle. "Jacqueline."

"Jacks. It's Jacks," I stutter. My mom's steely eyes flash to mind, the sharp shrill of her voice when she'd call me by my full name as a child—only when she was as angry as I felt right now. But I shouldn't take it out on him, even if he is the closest to Dylan I'll ever get.

"Fine. Tell me. Was it knitting? Pilates? Scrapbooking? Is there an album somewhere with pictures of her and James with polka-dot borders and cute stickers that say things like *against all odds* and *more than a feeling*?" My voice cracks.

"Jacks. I get that you're mad and confused and sad. I'm all of those things too." He motions toward the couch, but I shake my head, instead taking a seat on a barstool in the kitchen. Dylan's little pixie ass seems much less likely to have perched up there.

"I hadn't thought about what being here was going to feel like. Stupid, right?"

"No, not at all. I should have suggested Peet's."

"She'd have been there too. She's everywhere."

Nick chews on his lower lip, no doubt having his own memories. And suddenly I feel terrible about my bratty outburst. "I'm sorry for being a jerk," I say, and smile sincerely.

He returns my smile. "It's okay. This is all really hard."

Nick pours me a glass of water and sets it in front of me. "If it helps, remember she didn't live here. She rented a room in the condo downstairs with a couple of roommates."

I can see the deep circles under his eyes. "You aren't sleeping," I say.

"And you are?" He raises his eyebrow.

I shake my head. "No, not well. Even when I take a pill, which most nights I have to."

"Every time I lay my head down on my pillow, I think of the crash. I see horrific car accidents every day in my line of work. To think that Dylan went through that . . ." He trails off.

"I know. Me too." It's the worst part, the movie I've made in my head of what I think the Jeep looked like when it exploded. "I go back and forth between being pissed off at James and worried that he suffered. I hate it."

"That's something I've thought a lot about. That going to Maui could help us not be so damn pissed off anymore. Because there's nothing worse, right, than trying to grieve a death when you are so mad at the person. You know I smashed a picture she bought for me? Flung it against the wall and watched as shards of glass sprayed everywhere. It took me forever to clean up. I'm still cutting myself on the pieces I missed." He looks over to the corner of the living room where it must have happened.

"I got irrationally mad at the creators of sympathy cards," I offer, shaking my head at the memory. "I didn't even tell my sister, Beth, this, but I actually burned some of them on the flame from the gas stove. I set off the smoke detector."

We laugh quietly.

I take a drink of my water, trying to imagine a day when I'm not pissed off at James. For dying. For dying with a woman other than me. For fighting with me before he left. For taking the board shorts from our honeymoon on their clandestine vacation. For not knowing how to drive better on a dangerous road. For driving on a dangerous road in the first place. For marrying me. For cheating on me. So many things. And sure, there's a possibility that if I go to Maui with Nick, I could stand on a beach and close my eyes and meditate and try to let go of that anger. But there's one thing I worry about: that I'll never stop being mad at myself.

"I read a lot about grieving when I'm up in the middle of the night," he says, and I tell him I've done the same thing. That I'm an obsessive Googler—particularly between the hours of one and three in the morning.

"There was an article about a man who lost his wife when she was traveling abroad with her friend. Their hotel had a terrible fire . . ." He shakes his head. "And this guy, he went there. To Spain, I think it was. To the place where the hotel had burned down. And it helped him say good-bye."

"What are you saying? That you want to go to where they crashed?"

Nick walks over to the window, turning his back to me. "No, I'm not sure I could do that—it would be so hard." His voice breaks. "I think I would go to Maui and follow my instincts. See where my heart takes me. Where *she* takes me."

I try to imagine myself standing at the place where the accident happened, looking over the edge. I found Google images of the road to Hana. I saw the winding roads, the sharp edges of the cliffs, the lava rocks jutting out from the ocean. But I could click the little *x* in the upper-right corner of my computer screen whenever I'd seen enough. Could I go there in person? I'm not sure.

Nick continues. "I think that man being able to go to the location of the hotel takes a strength I'm not sure I have. Going to the crash site would be something I'd want to decide once I was there. If it doesn't feel right, I won't go."

"Is this something people actually get over?" I ask.

"I'm not sure. But don't you think we should at least try?"

"I don't know." Forget the accident scene; I'm suddenly not sure I have the strength to step foot on Maui soil.

Nick walks around me, grabbing a stack of papers out of a drawer. "I think these will help." He turns them toward me, and I can make out James's email address at the top.

"Are those the emails they wrote to each other?"

He nods.

"You think reading emails between my husband and his lover is going to help me?"

"No. I think you'll feel worse at first. I think they could crush you all over again. But I think that's a good thing."

I start to interrupt him.

"Please, Jacks, just hear me out."

I close my mouth.

"I think you'll have the same reaction I did. You'll read these, and it will be like opening Pandora's box. Because they're like a teaser. They seem to be from the beginning of whatever it was they were doing. And then they just stop. And you're left wanting more. And also hopeful."

"Hopeful?"

"This is going to sound pathetic. But based on these, it could have just been a fling. They never say love. They never get *deep*. So maybe it wasn't serious at all. And maybe that's what I'll find out if I go. If *we* go."

"But what if the opposite happens—if you find out they were in love?"

"That's exactly why I need you there with me, Jacks. Because I'm not sure I could go through that realization alone." He stops and holds my gaze. "I was hoping that was why you came here today. Because you'd decided to go."

I pick at my fingernail. Because that is why I came here. But now, sitting here on his stark white barstool, drinking out of a beveled glass she might have once pressed to her lips too, I'm not so sure.

"But I'll also understand if you came here to tell me no. I would never want you to do something you're not ready for. If you would rather not know, I'll respect your decision."

But the thing is, despite my fears, I do want to know more. Nick is saying all the things I'd been thinking long before he showed up on my doorstep. I'll take the emails, and I'll read them. I'll probably be up all night going through them. But there's something I'm not sure I can discover unless I go to Hawaii. Had it been the old James, the one I'd fallen in love with, who'd taken her there?

I look out the kitchen window at the Irvine skyline and watch a plane descend, slow and steady, into John Wayne Airport. "Give me twenty-four hours to take care of a few things," I say.

CHAPTER THIRTEEN

DYLAN—BEFORE

Dylan, Dylly, Dyl, D,
What will my secret nickname be for you?
I think it should be belleza, which means
beautiful in Spanish. Because everything
about you is—especially those eyes. God, I
can't stop thinking about those vibrant blue
gems. They belong in a painting, or on a doll;
they're almost ethereal. I know how I must
sound, but there's something about you that
makes me into a guy who would describe a
woman like that. A girl who consumes me,
who makes me throw caution to the wind.
Who makes me not care what happens next
as long as it's happening beside you.

James,
You're the one with the eyes. So green. I'm
not a master of words like you. I could never

describe how they jump out at me when I see them (in a good way), but they are gorgeous. Just like you.

Belleza,
I miss you. It's killing me that I had to cancel on you this week. I'm sorry. I will try again soon. I know it's been a long time. But I promise to make it up to you.

Belleza,
Did you get my texts today? I'm sorry. You don't deserve to be kept waiting. It's just hard to get away after I'm already gone so much. You know?

James,
I did get your texts, but wanted to think. Maybe it's just too much. Too hard. Maybe we should stop.

Belleza,
Don't say that. Let me take you out tomorrow night. I'll figure it out. But I promise you I'll make it happen. It's this Mexican place that's way out of the way and has the best margaritas you've ever had. Please say yes.

James,
God, why is it always so hard to say no to you? Of course I'll go—and I'll wear that dress . . .

Belleza,

I thought about you all night. How much I can't wait for our trip to Maui. I can't believe I hadn't thought of it before—going away on vacation together! I've decided I'll tell her I'm going on a work trip. Kansas or somewhere lame like that. LOL. Not that she cares where I'm going anyway. And don't stress—I'll take care of everything. Just bring your skimpiest suit and those eyes as payment. xo

CHAPTER FOURTEEN

Jacks—after

I glance sideways at Nick as he stares out the window, the Pacific Ocean and coastline disappearing behind the fluffy white clouds as we ascend. When he arrived in a cab to take us to LAX this morning, he looked different—less *I'm a biker dude* and more *I'm a biker dude going on a job interview*. He'd shaved, a small cut on his chin showing where he'd nicked himself. His dark wavy hair was neatly combed and still wet from the shower. Gone was his leather jacket, replaced with a chocolate-brown blazer. Only his worn leather cowboy boots seemed to have made the cut. I shift awkwardly in my pale-green sundress, wishing I'd worn something less *I'm going on a tropical vacation!* and more *I'm a grieving widow looking for answers*.

"You okay?" He turns toward me, opening and closing the safety instruction card while never bothering to look at it.

For a moment, the timing of his question makes me wonder if I've said my thoughts out loud. "Yes, are *you*?" I counter, glancing at the card in his lap, the word *Emergency* in bold red letters, a picture of a woman with a yellow oxygen mask over her face below it.

"Just nervous, I guess," he says, running his hand through his thick hair.

"Hate to fly?"

He gives me a confused look, then realizes I'm looking at the safety instructions he's holding and returns them to the seat pocket in front of him. "No. About the trip."

"You seemed so confident yesterday," I say, then backpedal after I see the hurt look in his eyes. "Sorry. I know this is a roller coaster. And now it's about to get very real."

He turns toward me, his face so close I can smell the coffee on his breath. "I'm just scared."

"I know. Me too."

"She was going to be my future," he says quietly. "I don't know who I am without her." He pauses when the flight attendant stops next to us with a drink cart. We both shake our heads no when she asks if we'd like a beverage. "I bought these matching T-shirts for us once. Mine said *I'm hers* with one of those arrows so if she stood next to me . . ." He doesn't finish his thought, and I say that I've seen them. He finally continues. "And hers said—"

"I'm his," I offer.

"Yeah." He gives me a heartbreaking smile. Like one of those smiles that makes the person look so sad you wish there were another word for that facial expression. "And we wore them to run errands. I think we went to Home Depot and got the car washed. Things like that. And we'd laugh to ourselves when people would raise their eyebrows like, 'Who are those people?' And I just remember thinking that it doesn't get better than this. To be with someone who got me. Who would wear those ridiculous T-shirts."

I smile at him to let him know I understand. I remember that feeling with James. Being so in love that the world felt like it belonged to us and everyone else just happened to be living in it.

"When we were first dating," I said, "we had an entire weekend with nothing planned. So we decided to spend it in bed. We'd just seen some romantic comedy where the couple did that. I think we lasted twelve hours until we finally had to get up because there were crumbs everywhere and we got sick of binge watching whatever show it was." I leave out the part about how we had sex three times and decided we were just too tired to go for a fourth. James had asked, "How do people in porn do it?" and shook his head as he pulled on his boxer briefs.

"Isn't the beginning the best?" Nick asks, and I nod. "And the middle. I just didn't think we'd get to the end part so soon. I thought we'd grow old together. Like blue-hair-and-plastic-hips old."

I notice a pair of newlyweds nuzzling in front of me, her diamond ring and wedding band hard to miss as she wraps her hand around the back of his neck, returning his kisses. I'm jealous. They're celebrating the start of their life together. The same way we did.

James and I also honeymooned in Maui.

This is something I haven't mentioned to Nick, because saying it out loud will cheapen that experience for me. Like it's no longer special to me and James because he also took his mistress there. Which, if I'm being completely honest with myself, is true.

I watch the couple toasting each other with their Bloody Marys. The layers of their onion haven't started to peel back. They aren't to the part where she has to bite her tongue when he leaves his wet towel wadded on the bathroom floor *again*, and he hasn't had to swallow his shitty remarks when she buys yet another pair of two-hundred-dollar shoes they can't afford. The niceties and threshold for understanding haven't slowly morphed into insults and raised voices. They're still in that blessed time before the gloves come off, before they say *fuck it*, roll up their sleeves, and get in the ring.

"I feel bad for pushing you to get on this plane."

"Don't. I made up my own mind—I'm a big girl," I say, pulling my jean jacket tighter across my chest, the recycled cold air blasting me from the overhead fan above us. I reach up to twist it closed but can't quite get it.

"Here, let me." Nick barely raises his long arm and shuts it off. "For what it's worth, I'm glad you decided to come. I don't think I could have done this alone." His voice catches, and he looks away quickly.

"Do you believe in karma?" he asks.

"You mean do I think they died because they were being unfaithful?"

"No, I actually meant do you ever wonder if you did something at some point and the universe is saying, 'Here's your retribution.'"

Before I can answer, he keeps going. "Sometimes I wonder what I did." He looks down. "I've beaten myself up for the times I snapped at her after I'd been on a tough twenty-four-hour shift or when I lost my temper with a driver who cut me off on the 405 freeway. I wasn't even close to perfect. Not to others. And certainly not to Dylan."

"Neither was I," I say, seeing flashes of our argument the last day I saw James. Dresser drawers slamming as he packed his bag. The accusation he slung at me, his words as heavy as a baseball bat. My hot tears after his ride pulled away.

"The last time you saw her—where did she tell you she was going?" I ask.

"To Arizona to visit her parents. That she'd be back in a few days." He shakes his head. "She insisted I didn't need to drop her off at the airport—something I still did, even after almost two years together. Now I know why." He turns and looks out the window, and I follow his gaze, squinting at the sun.

I think of the first time James dropped me off at LAX. We'd only been dating for six weeks, and Beth and I were taking a girls' trip to Vegas.

"You don't have to drive us," I said as I printed out my boarding pass, excited to be in group A on Southwest.

"I want to drop you off. I'm going to miss you," he said, circling his arms around my waist as I watched the paper slide out of the printer. "Three days apart!"

"Are you really this romantic? Or is it because we're still in the honeymoon stage? This is going to wear off, right?" I laughed, leaning my head to the side so he could kiss my neck.

"Never," he said, turning me around to face him.

"Good," I said, putting my hands on his stubbly cheeks and kissing him.

And he was right; it didn't wear off.

It *broke* off.

As abruptly as a plate that falls to the kitchen floor. Seconds before, you'd held the perfect porcelain circle in your hand. And then, as soon as it hits the tile, it breaks in two jagged parts. Which is exactly how I'd describe the shift in James when he stopped loving me the same way. My romantic, big-hearted husband changed shape—into a fragment of who he'd been.

"What was it like between you and Dylan the last time you saw her?" I push aside the sound our front door had made when I'd heaved it closed behind James with all my strength, how it had rattled in the doorjamb so hard I was sure the window next to it was going to shatter, just like we already had.

"That's the worst part for me, I think." He pauses.

"If you don't want to tell me, it's okay. It's personal." I jump in and fill the space, realizing I don't want to answer the same question. Because now he has me thinking about karma and my role in all this. And I don't want to go there.

"I think we're past personal at this point." He smiles, but his eyes don't join in. "I was just remembering her face—she was glowing. She looked so beautiful that day. Her hair was in a ponytail, and she wasn't wearing any makeup. Just pink lipstick, I think. Yeah, that's what it was. Because when I went to kiss her, she told me she didn't want to get it on me and have me get shit from the guys at the station. I was on my way to work."

He stops, and I can picture the scene in my mind. I imagine her wearing a T-shirt and jeans and watch as she playfully brushes off his kiss, standing on her pixie tiptoes and hugging him so she doesn't have to feel his mouth on hers.

"I've replayed our conversation over and over looking for clues. But she seemed totally normal, talking to me about her last shift, and how she'd spilled a glass of red wine all over a woman wearing white linen pants. We'd laughed about how mortifying it had been—Dylan had grabbed a black cloth napkin to blot the wine off the woman and ended up making it worse—the napkin actually shed on the stain." Nick smiled. "I remember watching her as she tried to mimic the woman's Australian accent and thinking, wow, she's in a great mood, she seems happy. *I* make this woman happy." He stops again. "But it wasn't me. I wasn't the one who did that for her." He rubs his palms over his eyes. "Sorry."

"Please don't apologize—especially not to me. I'm riding this emotional seesaw too." I think about being in my bathroom this morning. Grabbing what I thought was my Prozac, prescribed by my gynecologist a couple of years back to help with the mood swings I'd started to experience around my period. I'd put them in the back of the medicine cabinet above our sink with the label turned away. James never said this, but I knew they were a reminder that I wasn't pregnant.

I decided this morning that before I got on the plane, it might help to take one of my happy pills, as my doctor had referred to them after I told her about the anger I'd feel in the days before my cycle started. My recurring nightmare about James losing control of the car and plummeting down the cliff had kept me up most of the night, and I'd almost called Nick three different times to cancel, telling myself I'd made a huge mistake agreeing to go to Hawaii. But instead I'd accidentally grabbed a bottle of muscle relaxers that had been James's—then dropped it like it was a hot skillet, the tiny white pills scattering around the sink. I'd clutched the edge of the counter as I watched the meds roll down the drain, some of them getting stuck and causing a pileup, and remembered why he'd had them in the first place.

He threw out his back helping the deliverymen carry that pine dining room table I purchased while he'd been traveling, the one my mother-in-law can't stand. The one I'm pretty sure James never liked either. It was heavy and awkward, and he raked one of the legs on the doorframe as they were carrying it inside. He caught my eye as I directed the man holding the front toward a nook just off our kitchen, his eyes blazing with annoyance—that I'd made yet another purchase without consulting him. And I shot him an angry look and shrugged, because I made money too. I had a right to spend it. *And don't you dare imply that because I don't make even half what you do on my teacher's salary, I don't have a right to buy this table.* Another reason the damn thing means so much to me. It has always made me feel stronger to have it, even though it was brought into our house during a low point.

He'd traveled fourteen days the month I bought it, and I'd been lonely. And I was tired of him telling me to get a hypoallergenic dog (he was allergic) to keep me company. And I was sick of having dinner with my sister and her husband and my nieces and nephew and feeling sorry for myself as they passed around their perfect bowl of quinoa pasta with basil and fresh tomatoes and perfect sautéed broccoli and garlic and talked about their perfect days. I'd end up drinking half the bottle of red wine I'd contributed to the meal, missing my husband and sad we didn't have a family of our own to sit around the ginormous pine table I'd just purchased.

As James and the deliverymen set it down on the gleaming travertine in our kitchen, James let out a cry and fell to the floor. Let's just say his embarrassment over his back collapsing in front of two twentysomething men—with their proper weight belts and wide eyes, who could've carried it without his help—didn't bode well for the already fragile state of our marriage. We didn't speak for two days. I think about those arguments now—the ones where we'd be in a battle of wills, not talking, daring the other to be the first to give in—and realize we'll never have one again.

I guess you won, James.

"Did you read the emails?" Nick interrupts my thoughts.

I nod, thinking back to the hours I spent poring over them like they were going to explain everything. My husband's words still lingered. *I miss you. Can't wait to see you. Can't stop thinking about you.*

The old James was splayed across the pages. His flirtatious banter. His sexy talk. His persuasiveness. He'd been just like that with me in the early years. He'd write naughty notes and stick them in random pockets of my clothing until I eventually found them—sometimes months later. And Nick was right: there was no indication they'd loved each other. And as dangerous as I knew it was to latch on to hope, it had given me some. Maybe it had just been a casual thing. Just maybe.

"And?"

"You were right. It helped."

He gives me a look, waiting for more.

"It was just flirtation. Early stuff. Maybe their relationship didn't mean anything?"

"Maybe," he agrees. But I know we're thinking the same thing. It probably did.

"It did hurt like hell to read them, though," I add, thinking about how I called Beth and read some excerpts to her—specifically about the eyes. How she listened as I howled into the phone. I don't want to go back to that place right now. I can't. I already feel gutted—he never said anything like that to me about my appearance. He called me pretty and sexy, but never pinpointed a certain body part or characteristic that he obsessed over, the way he had with her. It made me feel plain in comparison.

"I know," Nick says, and we fall into a silence for several minutes—an unspoken agreement to stop talking about them.

Nick is the first to break it. "Here's that list I was telling you about." He hands me his phone, where he's made his notes.

Westin Ka'anapali
Concierge
Maui Jeep Rentals
Restaurants
Sightseeing
Chopper ride
Snorkeling
Whale watching
Surf school
Booze cruise
Horseback riding
Officer Keoloha
Kuau store
The road to Hana?

"James wouldn't ride a horse," I say after scanning the list, thinking of a conversation we had when we were first dating. It was one of those nights where we talked into the early-morning hours about everything, from pet peeves to favorite foods. When we got to the part about things we'd never do, he said *horseback riding* without even a moment's hesitation. I laughed, thinking he was joking because of his matter-of-fact attitude. I'd suddenly had an image of him saddled on the back of a thoroughbred, ambling along a path, and wondered what could be so bad about that. Then a shadow crossed his face, and he told me he was serious, that he simply wasn't a horse person. It was obvious there was more to it than that, but I didn't press. I never wanted to press James. About anything. Only later, after he'd drunk too many whiskeys, did I find out that his brother had loved horses—and that after his brother had died at the age of five, James could barely even look at one without feeling the loss all over again.

"I don't mean this the wrong way." Nick pauses, and I can tell he's trying to be careful about the next words he chooses. "But isn't it fair to say that you might not have known your husband as well as you thought you did?"

I think about the last morning I saw him, before we got into the fight. How I'd been lying in bed when he got out of the shower, and I studied him as he brushed his teeth—marveling as I always did that he actually took the full two minutes to clean them and never skipped flossing afterward. He had one of our taupe towels wrapped around his waist—the one that had hung on the hook in our bathroom until I finally threw it into the wash when I packed for Maui last night. I thought to myself, *He looks good. He looks really damn good. I should get my ass to the gym more often, like he does. Or try running again.* And I was about to suggest that when he got back from Kansas we should sign up for a 5K I'd seen advertised at our Starbucks, when he yelled, "*Goddamn it, Jacks!*" His towel fell to the floor as he stormed into the bedroom and stood at the end of the bed, glaring at me in all his nakedness. And then I saw the pregnancy test in his hand. But instead of saying I was sorry, I fought back. I wish I could've known that none of it was going to matter. But I had no clue. No fucking idea.

"Yes, that's fair," I finally say to Nick. "I obviously did not know my husband at all."

CHAPTER FIFTEEN

DYLAN—BEFORE

"Are you sure you're all right?" Dylan asked, chewing on her lower lip as she watched James. He'd barely spoken since they'd met at the security line at LAX. From the moment he'd removed his belt and put it in the white plastic bin next to his wallet and loose change, she could see it on his face—he'd fought with Jacqueline, *again*. Dylan preferred not to refer to James's wife—even in her mind—by her nickname. It seemed wrong, like more of a betrayal. She knew how ridiculous that sounded. She was already sleeping with the woman's husband; what did it matter if she said her name? But, to her, it was one small thing she could do. She only wished she could ask James to stop using it. Hearing his wife's name slip easily—too easily—from his mouth made Dylan conjure the image of her that day in the restaurant—her full lips, dark eyes, silky hair.

Dylan knew she was a teacher. And she sometimes imagined her standing in front of her classroom while wearing a smart black pencil skirt and slowly trailing the loop of the *z* as she taught her fourth graders cursive. Was she patient? Kind? Strict? Dylan would try to escape these thoughts, because she didn't want to think about Jacqueline as a real person who had feelings. Dylan preferred to live in the bubble that she and James had created. And there was no room inside of it for reality.

"Yes, I'm fine," James finally said through gritted teeth, the muscles in his neck tightening.

"You don't seem fine." Dylan tried again, raising the armrest between them. Wanting him to let go of whatever it was. To climb into the bubble with her.

"Dylan." James's lips formed a thin line as he gave her a look. He wanted her to stop. To let him cool off the way he always did. To go through his separation process. He called it that. His separation process. The time he needed to transition from his marriage to his relationship with his girlfriend. The first time he'd said that to her, she'd wanted to scream that she had to go through the same thing. She had to shift from the way it felt to hug Nick, so tall she had to stand on her tiptoes to reach his shoulders, versus James, who was just a few inches taller than she. To readjust her mind so she remembered it was Nick who hated to wait in lines and it was James who got impatient when he had to repeat himself. She had to transition from Nick's incessant need for her attention to James's tendency to keep her at arm's length. It wasn't easy for her either.

But James never acknowledged that. Because he was the married one. The one who'd stood at the beach, the wind whipping through his hair as he'd said his vows, the one who shared a checking account with someone else, the one who had a mortgage with another person's name on it. He'd never said that to Dylan, exactly, but she could tell he thought his stakes were higher.

Dylan decided to let James have his space and watched as he closed his eyes and nodded off to sleep. She pulled out a magazine and started flipping through the pages. She didn't want to hear about their argument anyway. She wanted to get to Maui and erase the rest of the world. To lie on the beach and daydream about what it would be like if James weren't married, or if she were the most important woman in his life—something she thought about often, but was reluctant to bring up to James in any serious way. Sure, they'd talk in ifs. *If* Dylan ever came to James's workplace, what would she think of his boss? Or the inappropriately short skirts the receptionist wore? Or *if* Dylan's father ever met James, would he accept him? Or would he reject him, like he had with Nick?

(She'd never told Nick, but her dad had used the word *slick* to describe him after they'd met for the first and only time at that dinner. Dylan had shrugged it off, knowing why her dad had felt that way. Nick hadn't been himself at all; usually not one to splurge, always saving his money to buy things he wanted, like a new part for his motorcycle, he had taken over the meal, ordering the most expensive dishes on the menu, including an overpriced bottle of wine. And Dylan had cringed inwardly when the bill came and the waitress handed it to her father— Nick reaching out and grabbing it as her father's cheeks reddened in embarrassment.)

That was the thing—she knew what it was like to be in a relationship with Nick. She knew he'd flinch if she lost her temper but that he'd always offer to rub her feet after she'd had a tough shift, taking great care to stroke the tension out of each toe. But it was the what-ifs that excited her about James—there was still so much to know, so much to explore.

Four hours later, James woke and spiraled a short strand of Dylan's hair around his finger. "I'm sorry," he said, his mouth so close to hers that she could see how much his stubble had already grown.

"It's okay," Dylan said, kissing him, happy not to have to look over her shoulder before doing so. They'd already determined neither of them knew anyone on the flight. When they'd arrived at the gate, they'd played the same game they did when they went to a restaurant or a movie or anywhere—no matter how far out of the way: they acted as if they didn't know each other as they surveyed the crowd, both of them praying they wouldn't see a familiar face.

But still, they had played it cool until they boarded the flight and took their seats in first class. James had bought her ticket and used miles for his, saying he had to be squished back in coach so often with assholes reclining into him that he was going to splurge so they could have big seats, extra leg room, and complimentary cocktails. He'd put them on separate reservations, then schmoozed the gate agent so they could sit next to each other. She had watched from afar as the woman, at first flustered and standoffish, had begun to defrost as James leaned in closely. Dylan couldn't see his face, but she knew exactly what smile he was charming her with. It was the same one he'd had when he waited for her after her shift and opened the door to something more. Like Dylan, the gate agent wasn't able to resist.

"I'm so excited to have four full days with you," James said, nodding at the flight attendant and ordering a mimosa for him and a plain orange juice for Dylan.

"To Maui," James said, after the flight attendant handed them their drinks.

"To Maui," Dylan repeated, just as the captain announced their descent.

CHAPTER SIXTEEN

JACKS—AFTER

Nick pulls the Jeep we rented up to the front of the hotel, and I step out, the air warm against my skin. (Despite the gorgeous drive from the airport, and the second Prozac I'd slipped under my tongue, I'd still clenched the "oh-shit bar" the entire time.)

"Aloha!" A man, wearing a nametag that says *Akoni* and a tan shirt with white flowers and the Westin Ka'anapali logo stitched on the front, welcomes us. He smiles and motions for us to bow our heads. Nick and I pause, glancing at each other awkwardly before we outstretch our necks to accept his offering—a strand of simple white seashells.

Akoni points us in the direction of two glass jugs filled with orange-and-lemon-infused water, and I walk toward it, fill my plastic cup, and take a sip, picturing Dylan pressing one to her own lips. As Nick and I are ushered toward reception, I imagine James and Dylan making these same steps. Had James taken her small hand in his and guided her inside, stopping to marvel at the waterfalls spilling down a wall of rocks into a koi pond occupied by a gaggle of salmon-pink flamingos? Did they try to get Bob, the brilliant blue-and-yellow macaw that lives in the bamboo cage, to mimic them?

The property, at first glance, is stunning: palm trees bending over-head as if trying to talk to each other, the sound of babbling streams and birds filling the air, tables and chairs set up by the ponds to watch the swans swim by, the koi fighting for the scraps of food a group of children are throwing haphazardly their way.

A ripple of jealous anger passes through me as I think of James taking the time to research and book this hotel—something that had always been left to me. I wonder again if *our* trip to Maui—our honeymoon—came to mind as he planned theirs. How did he do that—separate his life with me from the relationship he had with her? Did he talk about me? Confide all my biggest weaknesses and failures? Or did my name never pass his lips—as if he put me in a box in the back of his mind, like the clothes you once loved, but had outgrown and forgotten about? I couldn't decide which option was worse.

"Hey, I checked us in. They put us both in the ocean tower, but we're on different floors. And not that we care, but they upgraded us both to an ocean view!" Nick says as he hands me my driver's license, credit card, and room key, then frowns. "You okay?"

"It's just so strange—to be here." I watch a flamingo dip his beak into the water, wondering how long he can stand on one foot. Hours? Days?

"Surreal," Nick says as we both notice a little boy pointing to an enormous crab sunning himself on a rock.

I ask Nick the question on my mind as I look around. "It doesn't seem like the kind of place you bring someone you're just having a fling with, does it?"

"I don't know. I've never had a fling."

I trail my eyes to the floor and try not to blink, to not let the tears fall. I don't want Nick to see me cry.

"Hey." Nick lightly touches my upper arm. "We don't know any-thing yet. Let's save the tears for when or *if* we need them."

"You're right," I say.

"For what it's worth, I'm completely baffled why James would stray at all—casual or serious. It's still cheating."

I blink at him. "Well, you also don't know me very well."

"Maybe not, but from what I can tell so far, you're an incredibly courageous woman." He motions toward the swimming pool. "To come here and do this. It takes guts."

"I think I may just be crazy," I say as a tear finally works its way out of my eye, and I quickly wipe it away.

Nick shakes his head. "It would be so much easier to give up. To accept all the sympathy and build a shrine to him in your mind, always wondering who he really was but not bothering to find out. Blaming yourself instead."

I do blame myself. But I don't say this to Nick.

When I don't respond, Nick adds, "You know the old saying—the truth will set you free."

"Or will it make things more complicated?" I know these are Beth's words, and hate that she's gotten into my head again. I realize she's only looking out for me, but she could never understand why I need to be here. How even though every single molecule in my body is warning me against it, it doesn't matter. Because he was my husband, and he wasn't the man I thought he was. I won't be able to move forward until I can understand why he did this.

"It might, but at least we'll know, right?"

I nod, thinking about the past few months. About the things I didn't know. That my husband wasn't where he said he was. That he was capable of having an affair. That he could sleep with someone else and then come home and make love to me. That I was being stupid to believe we had a marriage incapable of being broken by an outside party. "Do you have any guesses as to how long they were . . ." I trail off. I think about my sister seeing James and Dylan together a month before the accident, but I knew they'd met long before that.

"A couple?"

"Yes." I move to the side so a woman pushing a stroller can maneuver around us, and I catch a glimpse of a chubby-cheeked baby sleeping soundly.

"I don't know. The emails cut off after a month or so. But there's a span of several months in between the final email and when they came here. So it could have been five, six months?" Nick takes in my face. "But, Jacks, we don't know how often they saw each other during that time. Or if it ended and then started up again shortly before they came here."

But all I hear Nick say is *six months*. And something about that number makes my chest feel cold, like my heart is folding up inside itself because all of the warmth has been sucked out of it. If it had been going on for that long, how did I not see it? I've done a fair amount of reading online about affairs since I found out. One site laid out signs that your spouse may be cheating.

He dresses better.

Definitely not. He was wearing those awful gray pants the last time I saw him.

He guards his cell phone.

Not that I ever noticed. But like I said, I wasn't concerned with his phone or computer the way other wives were. I didn't care to learn his passwords.

He takes new credit cards out in his name.

Obviously he had done this one and I had no idea. How would I?

He has mood swings.

This one is hard. I would have never guessed his emotions were linked to an affair. Because James's moods had always been unpredictable. He wrote it off as being Latin, but I would sometimes wince at how the littlest thing could ignite him. He once punched a hole in the wall in our living room because the Dodgers lost an important playoff game.

James had a temper.

He could also be incredibly thoughtful. But that was mostly before we became broken, back when I'd have days at work that felt two weeks long. Like when my fourth graders refused to listen as my voice ticked up louder and louder, and the time passed so slowly I thought I might explode. Or when a parent-teacher conference went south and ended in confrontation. Back then, James would show up with a salmon-and-avocado roll from Fusion Sushi, driving thirty minutes out of his way to pick it up. Those were the moments that I could recall the man I fell in love with hard and fast—the man who once believed we were a team.

But other times, it was a different story. Boy, could he get pissed off. That last fight we had? That was nothing. Doors rattling, voices raised to yelling? Well, we'd had much worse. In fact, one time, and it was only the once, he grabbed my arm, twisted it, and pushed me up against a wall.

He drops the name of the person he's cheating with into conversation.

This one strikes me as odd, but then again I've never had an affair. I get it. It's supposed to throw you off the trail, because why would he talk about the person he's sleeping with? But this one, I'm quite sure, never happened. She wasn't a colleague, a friend, anyone I knew, and if he'd so much as breathed the name *Dylan*, I would have remembered.

He doesn't want sex.

Our sex life was sporadic, but good. He traveled so much that it's hard to say how often we did it. But when he was home, it would happen. Over those last six months, did I see a difference? Not that I can say.

My lip quivers, and I bite it to make it stop, looking up at Nick, who's watching me.

"I was wondering about something," Nick says.

"What?"

"Is the pill you took to help with this? Is it for anxiety?"

My cheeks get hot. "You saw that?"

"Not much gets past me," he says, then stops short, both of us realizing that nothing could be further from the truth. Dylan had hidden an entire life from him.

"I took it to deal with the car ride. I have trouble since . . ."

"You don't need to say any more." Nick rakes his fingers through his hair. "Why don't we put our bags in our rooms, then grab a drink? I think we could both use a mai tai."

"Agreed," I say, following him to the elevator bank, relieved we've stopped talking about my self-medication. It makes me feel like more of a victim that I have to take pills so I can handle what my life has become.

Nick steps out on the fourth floor of the ocean tower, and I keep going up to nine. As I'm sliding my key card in the slot for 955, my cell phone rings and Beth's face appears on the screen. I could ignore it, but we haven't spoken live since I left her house, and I know she'll keep calling until I answer. She's always been that way—relentless. It's why she's excelled at everything—her SATs, tennis, childbirth. She never gives up. It's something I both love and hate about her, depending on what it is. Right now, I hate it.

"Hello?" I pull back the heavy drapes and open the sliding glass door to reveal a small patio. I see the island of Lanai in the distance and take in a panoramic view of the beach: a deeply tanned, shirtless runner sprinting, the deep-blue ocean dotted with sailboats, and one catamaran with a vibrant-yellow sail that has *Gracie* painted on the side in large gold script. How had Nick pulled this off?

"You're there, aren't you?" Beth launches in.

I lean against the railing and look down at the resort, counting three swimming pools, the largest right below me, the shadows in the water making it look like a tortoiseshell. "Yes," I finally answer as I watch a young couple in matching orange inner tubes holding hands. I can't see their faces, but they seem so happy. Blissful even.

Beth sighs loudly. "I can't believe you actually went. To Maui."

"Well, I did. I'm here. So, go ahead."

"Go ahead and what?"

"Lecture me."

"Come on, Jacks. Give me a break here, okay?"

"So you've called to give me your blessing?"

"I just wish you'd told me."

"And there were things I wish you'd told me too, Beth. So I guess we're even now." I cringe at my testy tone.

"Jacks, I'm so sorry." Her voice catches, and I immediately soften.

"I know," I say, realizing I've already forgiven her. She couldn't have known. Even though I'd love to put this on someone who's still alive so I could unleash the anger coiled inside me, she's not the reason this happened.

"I just—I don't know. Marriage is hard. And I didn't want to make assumptions and create more problems when it could have been a completely innocent business lunch or an old friend. Of course, I feel like shit that it wasn't."

"I know," I say again. She's practically heard it all. Our fights about his travel schedule, about money, about time together. How can I blame her for not wanting to muddy the waters even more, especially when it could have been nothing? Would I have told her if I'd seen Mark out with a woman I didn't know? I would like to say yes, because that's the most convenient answer. But everything is so skewed now that I can't be sure.

"I'm not going to pretend I'm thrilled you jumped on a plane to Hawaii, but I'm here for you if you need me. Do you want me to fly out there? Would that help?"

"No, but I love you for offering. I need to do this without you."

~

An hour later, I'm sitting with Nick at the Relish Burger Bistro bar by the Lanai pool, my hand cupping an almost-empty glass that had been filled with rum and pineapple juice, a bright-pink umbrella piercing a piece of pineapple resting on the rim, and I feel my edges soften.

"Can I get you another round?" the bartender asks, and Nick and I exchange a glance. "It's happy hour!" the bartender declares, and points to his watch. It's four.

Nick looks at my glass and shoots me a questioning look.

"Okay, but I should eat too or I'll be in no condition to . . ."

"Hula dance?" Nick offers, and we both half smile. I wonder if he's thinking what I am—that it feels wrong to laugh. I remember last night I had the TV on while packing, and Jimmy Kimmel was doing his bit about mean tweets, and I laughed when Nicole Kidman read one about herself. I clamped my hand over my mouth to stifle it.

"Maybe—or dance with fire," I say, then tell the bartender we will take that second round. We sip our cocktails, and I listen to the sound the wind makes as it sails through the palm trees, the laughter coming from the kids' pool nearby. Then I feel a wave of guilt. I remember why we're here. I realize James and Dylan may have sat at this very bar.

"We should ask this guy about them," I suggest to Nick. "Maybe he served them?"

"Okay, follow my lead," he says. "Hey, man, can we ask you something?" Nick says when he catches the bartender's eye.

"Sure." He scoops ice into a glass and fills it with rum and Coke for a woman who's waiting.

"We had some friends who stayed at this hotel toward the end of May. You might have read about them in the newspaper. They were in an accident on the back side—"

The bartender cuts him off. "Road to Hana. Man and a woman, right? Jeep?"

Nick and I nod.

"I'm so sorry for your loss," he says sincerely.

"Thank you," Nick says, and takes a drink. "This is a long shot, but did you talk to them at all when they stayed here? Serve them a drink?"

The bartender shakes his head. "No, I didn't. Only saw the write-up in the paper, but that was it. I just hate when I read about accidents over there. It happens more than it should."

"Thanks," I say to him, feeling defeated as he walks away to take a young couple's order. This is going to be harder than we thought. Maui is a large island. What if no one recalls seeing them?

Nick turns to me and surveys my face. "Not everyone will remember them. And that's okay. You never know; it could be just one person who tells us everything we want to know. Let's stay positive."

"I guess it was silly to think we'd get all of our answers on the first try."

I take a long drink, this one not tasting nearly as strong as the first. "What was she like?"

"You're ready to go there? Really this time?"

"No, not at all, but I think it will help," I say, my chest tightening in anticipation as I remember the emails. How he'd missed Dylan. He was thinking of her. What were the qualities in her personality he had been attracted to? I had so many soft spots in my relationship with James. And to find out that Dylan may have filled one or more of them—if she had been strong when I had been weak, I might not be able to handle it.

Nick takes a drink before answering, and I watch him, wondering if he's going through his personal files of memories of her, deciding which ones won't hurt me to hear, which ones won't hurt him to tell.

"Dylan was sweet. Very, very kind," he says as the bartender sets a plate of coconut calamari in front of us.

"Compliments of the house—in case you need your strength for that fire dancing." He winks before walking away again, and Nick rolls his eyes in my direction, clenching his jaw slightly. Just as I'm about to say something to defend the server, Nick breaks into a smile. "I think that guy has a crush on you."

"Please! He just feels bad that he didn't know anything about Dylan and James. Or he wants a big tip. Either way, bartenders flirt." I finish the last of my drink. "James was like that too—flirtatious. Talkative. Outgoing. The salesman in him, you know? He could make anyone feel like they were the only person in the room. Everywhere we went, he'd strike up conversations with perfect strangers, and within five minutes you'd think they'd known each other all their lives."

"Did it ever bother you? Make you jealous?"

"Not really. It was just who he was—like he couldn't help himself. I had always thought it was harmless—" I don't want to finish that thought. Like what if I hadn't thought it was harmless? What if I'd been jealous? Would it have stopped him from crossing the line? "What about you? Did Dylan do anything that made you insecure?"

"I look back now and see certain things in a different light. But in the moment? No. Not at all. I'm a lot of things, Jacks, but jealous isn't one of them." He finishes his first drink and moves on to his second. "But maybe I should've been."

"Me too," I agree, thinking back to when I'd caught Beth snooping on her husband. She'd been scrolling through his iPhone and glanced up at me and said, "The men you never think would stray—they are always the ones with the most to hide." And then we'd laughed—because he was Mark. An accountant she'd been married to for twelve years who, save for tax season, came home every night at six on the dot. Whose biggest self-proclaimed flaw was his penchant for itemization.

I watch the bartender washing out glasses on the other side of the bar, taking in his broad shoulders and coffee-colored skin, the dark rum in the mai tai starting to grab me. I take a bite of the calamari. It's warm and crunchy, and the sweet coconut flavor swims in my mouth.

"So, you said Dylan was kind—what else?" I ask.

Nick watches the bartender blend a daiquiri. "She was a server."

"Where did she work?"

"In Laguna, at Splashes Restaurant."

The last time James and I were there together comes to mind. It was on a whim actually. I'd woken up and craved crab cakes Benedict. And I suggested that restaurant. Bits and pieces of the brunch come back to me. I overdosed on mimosas—the sweetness of the Piper champagne sliding down my throat helped dissolve the residual anger I was feeling from an argument I'd had with James about his mother the night before. He'd defended her yet again when I told him that she'd suggested my oven was dated and I might want to upgrade it. She'd even chip in. He couldn't see why that would get under my skin. How she was constantly putting me down in her passive-aggressive way. He just didn't see it. End of story. It infuriated me.

I try to remember our server from that day. I can't picture her face, but I do recall that she was engaged. James complimented her ring, which struck me as odd because the one he'd picked for me was a simple gold eternity band, and he didn't even wear one.

Ironically, I'd gotten over that fact pretty quickly. It was my mom and sister who'd questioned me when they noticed his ring finger was still bare after our wedding. But I'd waved it off. I'd never been conventional in that way. If it had been up to me, our wedding and reception would have been low key. Just friends and family on the beach catered by our favorite burger place. But it had been the opposite—a large crowd of people, most of whom I didn't know, noshing on caviar. Because that's what his mother had wanted.

"Did she work Sunday brunch?"

Nick nods. "Yes, almost never missed one. Hated it because of all the drunks, but said she made the most tips on that shift over any other."

My heart begins to quicken as I recall something else. We'd just gotten home from the restaurant, and I was kicking off my shoes into our bedroom closet when he said, "I forgot to tip our waitress. I have to go back."

I thought he already had—I'd glanced at the bill, then saw him put down a fair amount of cash, but my mind had been fuzzy from falling asleep in the car on the way home. I told him that and laughed, pushing him down on the bed and nuzzling his neck, my champagne buzz making me horny for makeup sex. But he pulled back. "I have to go. Her shift might be over soon. We'll pick up where we left off as soon as I get home. Promise."

Was that the day he met her? Had my crab-cakes craving been responsible for introducing my husband to his mistress?

I shake my head slightly at the irony. They'd met right under my nose, and I was too drunk to notice it, or maybe too confident. So confident I'd let him travel all over the country dangling his ring-free wedding finger. I don't say this to Nick, not wanting to rehash the memory. Instead, I order a third drink, this time a piña colada, deciding getting drunk right now sounds pretty damn good.

CHAPTER SEVENTEEN

JACKS—AFTER

It's possible I might be the only person living in Orange County who doesn't like the ocean.

Let me rephrase that. I like *looking at* it—there's something beautiful about the way the sun reflects off the whitecaps, making them sparkle. And I've been known to go down to the shoreline and splash my feet, letting the waves brush up against my thighs as they rock me back and forth, licking the salt when the occasional droplet finds my lips. But something always stops me from diving in, from cutting my arms through it like a knife. I like the *idea* of it—of floating on my back and imagining my hair air-drying into loose beach waves that are never actually achievable. But each time, I get only as far as waist deep, eventually inching back onto the dry and safe sand.

Beth thinks it's because our mother taught us how to swim by throwing us into the water. "Sink or swim," Mom had said with a laugh. I realize now that we were in the shallow end of a pool—only three feet deep, and we were never more than an arm's distance away. But still, it was terrifying. Beth paddled her arms and kicked her legs with gusto, propelling her head above the surface the very first time. I froze, sinking quickly, my mother yanking me up before I ever reached the pool floor. The second time, my survival instinct kicked in, and I used my body to fight my way to the surface until I touched the uneven orange tile on the side of the pool. Yes, I learned how to swim quickly. But that didn't mean I had to like it.

From the dock, I eye our boat floating in the ocean and glance at Nick. "Do you think that's safe?"

"I do, but I also run into burning buildings for a living. So I may have a different definition of the word?" he says, sliding his T-shirt off.

When we'd walked up to the check-in point for Blue Water Rafting Adventures, I noticed a woman appraise Nick, and then me, clearly trying to figure out how *we* made sense. *We don't,* I wanted to call out. *He's younger. And hotter. And PS: We aren't even together. We're trying to figure out why our partners didn't want us anymore.*

I tug at my board shorts and reach my hand behind my back to make sure my bikini top is secure before grabbing a life jacket from the shelf, wishing I'd said yes to the coffee that Nick offered me when I'd met him in the lobby at five this morning. But my head had been throbbing from one too many drinks last night as he pressed a brochure into my hand that promised *an exhilarating ride* as we toured grand sea caves and spectacular lava arches. "Lava whats?" I asked, my voice cracking slightly.

"Not a morning person?" He smiled, crunching his empty coffee cup in his hand and shooting it into a nearby trash can like a basketball.

My hangover combined with my unease about our boating adventure had left me feeling off. It didn't help that James had asked me—no, *begged* me—to do this exact trip when we were on our honeymoon, but I'd refused, blaming my fear of the water. He'd said that I was using it as a crutch. I'd called him insensitive. It was our first big fight, and it had happened during a time we were *supposed to be* experiencing wedded bliss. I'd called Beth crying, asking her if it was a sign. Had I married a jerk? She'd laughed and said I needed to take a step back and look at what we were fighting about—a silly sightseeing tour, not something important. I'd hung up feeling better, and hoped our disagreement was just random. And back then, it was. But our problems began to bulge at the seams years later, his insensitivity so frequent that I almost forgot that he hadn't always been wound so tightly. That he used to have more soft spots for me to fall upon.

I tried to talk my way out of this outing as well, but Nick used my desire for information against me, telling me he'd booked us with Adam, the same guide Dylan and James had used. And not only that, but he'd managed to get the concierge to give him a rundown of every activity James and Dylan had done together. "Answers," he said. "Just remember that. We'll get them if we go."

Adam turns out to be a sun-kissed twentysomething with a boy-band haircut and shorts that are dangling dangerously low on his hips. He looks like he's going to use the word *bro* and pump his fist for emphasis. I whisper to Nick, "That's the same guy they had?"

Nick nods, and I try to imagine James taking instruction from a man who looks like a Calvin Klein model. It couldn't have gone well. James had been a natural athlete his entire life, playing soccer and football in high school, even making the lacrosse team his junior year with hardly any experience. He was always in some kind of sports league, and shortly after we got married he took up running—competing in several half marathons. And even though he was still in good shape before he died, he'd definitely been starting to feel older, making several comments about his back feeling tight, his knee giving him trouble. So to take instruction from a younger, very fit guy about anything? That could definitely rock him.

Adam introduces our group to the two other guides, both older versions of him, then gathers us on a corner of the dock and gives us a quick overview of what our boating adventure will entail. He promises it will include secret coves filled with exotic marine life and majestic sea turtles! I suppress an eye roll and half listen as he goes through a few safety instructions, including my personal favorite: not to get out of the boat unless he says so. I size up the other tourists as he yammers on. They include the woman in the yellow bikini and sarong (sarong, really?) and an older gay couple wearing matching Bermuda shorts and zinc strips across their noses. Finally Adam gives us permission to get into the boat, where we are instructed to squat and hold on to a rope.

"Squat?" I glare at Nick, who is clearly amused as he watches me try and fail several times to twist the thick yellow rope around my right hand.

He leans over and wraps his arm around my back, causing me to stiffen even more. "I promise I won't let anything happen to you."

I wriggle out of his grip. "You have no business making promises like that," I say, harsher than I intend.

"Jacks . . ."

"I'm sorry," I say, holding up my rope-free hand. "I thought being here was going to help. But now I'm sitting on a boat I don't want to be on, with, no offense, a guy I barely know, and it just feels wrong. Like this was the stupidest decision I've ever made. Maybe Beth was right." The rope slips from my grip just as the boat jolts from the dock. I slide backward with the motion, my hands searching for traction and finding none.

Nick's reaction is instantaneous. His arm shoots to the left and pulls me upright so swiftly that the members of our group don't even notice. He guides my hand back to the rope, holding it until my grasp is steady.

"Remember, safety rule number one was don't let go."

"Maybe I should've paid more attention," I say loudly over the sound of the engine, hating that I've been so vulnerable in front of him. Hating that I'm showing him the reasons I fear James had wanted Dylan over me: I can be cranky, irrational, and clumsy as hell.

We speed out to the ocean, finally stopping near a cove. I pull my hand from the rope; I've been gripping it so tightly that there is a bright-red burn mark on my palm. I begrudgingly admit to myself that the ride to the caverns was almost pleasant. It wasn't quite exhilarating, but when two silver dolphins sprang from the water, I felt a pinprick of happiness—the first I'd experienced since James's death—but it was so quick I could almost tell myself I'd imagined it.

Adam drives the boat into a cave and ties it up to two steel posts he's clearly used many times before. I swallow my urge to make a sarcastic remark about his use of the word *secret* to describe the things we'll see today as he and the two other guides start handing out snorkel gear. I shake my head when Adam comes to me.

"What? Don't want to get your hair wet?" Nick says so only I can hear as he takes two sets of gear.

I start to tell him I'm scared of the water, but James's cutting words about using my fear as a crutch comes to mind.

"I guess I don't get why we have to snorkel with Adam to get info from him. Can't we just talk to him on the boat while everyone else goes to look at the"—I stop to make air quotes—"exotic fish?"

"Because we have to blend in. We can't just come right out and say what we're really doing here."

"Why not?"

Nick gives me a hard look. "Come on, Jacks. No one is going to tell us anything if we come at them like that. We need to caress the information out of them. Just like last night with the bartender; we need to pretend we're nothing more than James and Dylan's friends who are taking the same sightseeing trip they did. So that means we need to snorkel."

"Is that what you did with the concierge and the front desk girl? Caress upgrades and details out of them?"

Nick smiles. "Something like that."

"You sure we can't caress him in the boat? With our life jackets on?" I try.

"No. Today we are *tourists*, and we came on this tour because we are *really* interested in the *secret* sea life in these caves."

"You caught that too, huh?" I smile, my nerves starting to calm. Well, until I look down at the face masks he's holding; then my heart starts pounding. I have to tell him the truth. "I don't know if I can do this."

"Why not?"

"Never mind," I say, playing with the strap on my life jacket.

"Tell me," Nick says kindly, keeping his eyes focused on me.

"Okay," I say, his gaze settling me. "I have a slight fear of *that*." I motion toward the dark water.

Nick doesn't skip a beat. "I think I can help. Close your eyes."

"What? Why? So you can throw me in there?" I picture my mom standing over me in the pool.

"Why the hell would I do that?" He shakes his head, then places his hands on my shoulders. "Just trust me."

I don't want to shut my eyes, be in total darkness. I want to keep them open—look around, get the answers I need. But trust him? No thanks. Been there, done that. Didn't work out so well.

But.

His eyes.

They are steely gray with a few flecks of gold, and when they fixate on you, they are so comforting. When I look into them, I almost feel like I can see right into his soul.

"Will you just close them?"

"Fine," I finally say, leaning in slightly to let the Bermuda-shorts couple move past, both of them jumping into the water with abandon. Show-offs.

Nick starts to speak, and his voice is calm and steady. He asks me to imagine white light encapsulating me and reminds me to breathe deeply. It feels awkward standing here with my eyes squeezed closed, but my shoulders give way to the tone of his voice, relaxing as he whispers. His breath tickles my ear, telling me a story—one in which I am brave, living in a world where I conquer my fear of the water and finally learn to enjoy what has terrified me for so long. My initial instinct is to laugh—imagining myself in a *Hunger Games*–like competition, clad in a scuba suit with fire painted across it, as I thrash through the water like it's an enemy I'm overtaking—but I don't, because his words are working. I am listening. Until I hear only the sounds of the waves lapping against the rocks and distant voices.

"How do you feel?" he asks when I look at him.

"Much better—how did you do that?"

"In my job I come across a lot of people who are experiencing trauma. Meditation and visualization calms them. A lot of guys on the force who are more old school, they don't do it. But I've noticed a huge difference in how it helps victims—and me."

He says the last part so quietly I almost don't hear him. I think about the terrible things he must see when he's working—nothing compared to my silly fear of water. I say as much to him.

"We all have our demons," he says as he places the mask over my nose, straightening the snorkel until it's just right. I notice Adam watching us.

"You can go ahead and get in, guys," he says, offering me a thumbs-up.

I give him a halfhearted thumbs-up in return and look over the side of the boat into the water, hating that the bottom of the ocean is so far down, the hugeness of it making my heartbeat quicken. But I push the thought away.

"I'm really going to do this? Go in there?"

"Yep." Nick jumps in, making a large splash, then holds his arms outstretched to welcome me.

I lower myself down the ladder slowly, the cold water calling every nerve in my legs to attention as I sit on the side of the boat and awkwardly put on my fins. I widen my eyes at Nick.

"It takes a minute to get used to it, but you will," he says.

"The temperature or putting my entire body in the ocean for the first time—ever?" I say, finally jumping into the water.

Adam drops in behind me and lets out a "Woo!"

He tells us we can join the rest of the tour about a hundred feet away, who he says are watching a pair of sea turtles.

I decide being out in the open water sounds slightly less nerve-racking, so I point toward the group. I arch my arm into the water and hear Adam remind me to use my fins to help propel me forward. It's awkward at first, but finally I'm moving. And I'm not sure if it's the meditation or adrenaline, but I dip my head under the surface, my mask going under but my tube still able to get air. A school of turquoise-and-yellow fish surrounds me, and I feel a surge of panic, yanking my head up and searching for Nick, whom I find just a few feet away, watching me. He points. "The turtles. All you have to do is get to the turtles."

I turn away from my phobia and follow him.

According to Adam, Hawaii has very strict laws about how close you can get to a sea turtle. But you can get near enough to see him blink his eyes, to see his leathery skin, to guess how many decades he's been swimming these waters. As if sensing my curiosity, one of them swims within ten feet of me, letting me take a closer look. He's majestic. Just like Adam described.

I start to swim closer to him, but Nick tugs on my arm, reminding me that Adam is watching us. "So those tiny fish back there freaked you out, but this huge guy is making you smile? In fact"—he motions toward my mouth—"I think that one might actually be real—not that shitty fake one you've been giving me since we met."

He's right. It doesn't make any sense that I was scared of the fish, but not of the *Chelonia mydas*, or green adult sea turtle, which Adam explained is about forty inches long and nearly two hundred pounds. But our fears rarely make sense, right? Isn't that the point? That they're irrational? I reward his insight with my shitty fake smile, and he laughs.

"That's Bob Marley." Adam swims up beside us. "The coolest, most laid-back sea turtle in these parts. And he loves the attention he gets from the people we bring through here. And in case you're wondering, because most people do, he got his name because he always looks like he just smoked a doobie!" Adam laughs. "Check out those glassy eyes!"

Something about Adam's words snaps me back to reality. And I remember why we're here. That James and Dylan probably swam in this same spot, hearing the same story about the Jamaican sea turtle. I look at Nick, who nods. It's time.

"So, Adam, some friends of ours told us about this tour. They said you were the best guide. You might remember them? Just a couple of months ago?" Nick says.

Adam smiles, revealing a row of perfect white teeth. "I take a lot of people out here, so . . ."

Adam must see my face fall because he quickly adds, "But maybe? You never know! What were their names?"

"James and Dylan," I say quickly.

Adam's eyes light up. "James and Dylan! Loved those two. James was my Costa Rican brotha from another motha! Newlyweds, right?"

Nick and I share a look, and I mouth, *What the fuck?* Because this, we were not prepared for.

CHAPTER EIGHTEEN

Jacks—after

Nick and I settle into the back row of the shuttle, and I try to tune out the group's chatter, especially the intermittent high-pitched squeals from Ms. Yellow Bikini as she looks at the *unbelievable* shots on her camera. I just need to think. To figure out why my husband and his mistress said they were married. Because there was no way it was true. James had many questionable qualities—one of them obviously being a cheater with no regard for his marriage vows—but I knew even he would draw the line at polygamy. It would be too messy. Too much work. Too far beneath him. It must have been the thrill—playing the part of husband and wife. Out here on this island, they didn't have to hide. They could be together, in the open.

Or there's another scenario, but one I don't really want to consider: they were planning to leave us and get married.

"What's going on in there?" Nick points to my head after we arrive back at the hotel and step off the shuttle.

"You don't want to know." I fiddle with my wedding band, which I'm still wearing. But that is a whole other *Oprah*. And I'm grateful Nick pretends not to notice me doing it.

"Oh, I have a feeling I already do. It's probably exactly what I was thinking the whole ride back here." Nick rolls his eyes in Ms. Yellow Bikini's direction. "If only her cackling had been just a little louder, then it could've drowned out my thoughts."

"So annoying," I mutter. "How can anyone be *that* excited about sea turtles? I mean, it was cool, but c'mon."

"Well, aren't we surly?" Nick laughs as we walk inside the lobby. "How dare people have fun while on vacation in Maui!"

"I know. I'm being a bitch."

"No, you're not. You're just upset. But for what it's worth, Adam said they weren't wearing rings—that they'd just laughed and nodded when he called them newlyweds. And I think we can both agree that guy's not the sharpest tool in the shed, so his understanding of the situation is probably way off. They probably agreed with what he said so they didn't bring attention to themselves. It doesn't mean he actually wanted to marry her, Jacks," Nick says. Then before I can respond, he adds, "Or that *she* wanted to marry him." His clenched jaw betrays him—the feeling of denial he's obviously trying to bury coming to the surface.

"Maybe," I say, more to appease him than anything else. I imagine James touching Dylan the way you do when it's new. When your hands are like magnets—drawn to each other in a way you can't control. I imagine her flushed cheeks, the glow that must have radiated off Dylan as she basked in his adoration. The way they were acting had made Adam assume they'd just exchanged vows, that there was no way they'd been tainted yet by the real life and problems that eventually wear away the shiny veneer of marriage.

"Want to drink away our sorrows?" Nick finally breaks our silence and looks out to the pool. Happy hour is in full effect, and the buzz from the conversations of the barflies carries over to us as we walk near the pool.

I shake my head. "I'm mentally exhausted. Consuming alcohol would be the worst thing I could do right now. I need to call it a night."

Nick checks his phone. "It's only four o'clock."

I shrug. "It's seven in California. And I think I'm just ready for this day to be over."

Nick looks at me for another beat, no doubt realizing I'm not going to change my mind. "So I'll see you bright and early again tomorrow—six a.m. sharp, right?" he says.

I nod and turn toward the elevator, feeling his eyes on my back as I walk away.

I immediately change into my pajamas when I get inside my room and flop down on the bed. But my mind refuses to let sleep take over—I keep thinking about the way Adam had described James and Dylan. Finally, after tossing and turning for an hour, I call Beth and fill her in.

"That bastard!" The old Beth comes out, guns blazing, and we both laugh. That's Beth's favorite word. Everyone has been called it at some point, including her husband and even her nine-year-old son. Probably me too, when I jumped on a plane and came here. And now James.

"I've missed you," I say as the tears fall.

"I've been here the whole time, hon. And I'd be lying right next to you if you'd just let me come help."

"No, I mean the old you. The one who wasn't afraid to say what she's thinking—even if it's calling her son a bastard."

Beth chuckles. "Remember, we promised never to speak of that again."

"He deserved it." I smile, thinking of how he'd taken her phone and bought a hundred dollars' worth of jewels for some godforsaken app on his iPad.

"He really did, didn't he? Well, I'm glad you like bitchy, inappropriate Beth. The goody-goody one was killing me." She pauses. "Oh, God, I'm so sorry. That word, I shouldn't have used it."

"It's okay. You'd be surprised how often we say *died* or *killed* in our everyday vocabulary. Believe me, I notice every single one now. I've even caught myself doing it."

"Well, I shouldn't have said it, and I'm sorry."

"Seriously, don't be. I love you. And I need you. The one thing I've learned is that no one is doing me any favors by coloring the truth."

"Everyone just wants to protect you from any more pain. You'd do the same thing for me."

"Do you think I deserved this? Like it's some sort of karmic payback for not being a good enough wife?"

"God, Jacks! How can you say that? That because you didn't greet him at the door in a kimono holding a martini, you deserve this? Marriage is fucking hard. We all make mistakes, and a lot of them. But that doesn't mean bad things should happen to us as a result."

"What if I didn't disclose everything to him before we got married? If there were things I held back? Would that change your mind?" I had never told Beth what I withheld from James. I knew she'd insist I tell him, that she'd tell me what I know now—that a secret like that could break a marriage in half.

"Jacks, none of us tell the person we're going to marry *everything*. We all have secrets."

"Even you?" Beth tells her husband everything. She once asked him to take tweezers and pick an ingrown hair out of her ass, and he did it. (Apparently this is a thing?) I cringed when she told me—I had never even peed with the bathroom door open in front of James.

"Yeah, there are things Mark doesn't need to know. But *you* know them all! Because you have to love me no matter what." She laughs.

My stomach rolls. Would she forgive me for not having the same faith in her? Although not telling Beth had nothing to do with not trusting her. I didn't confide in her because I knew I'd made the wrong choice by not telling James. And when you fuck up like that, sometimes it's easier to let the guilt fester in the darkness of your soul, rather than bring it out in the light.

I'd wanted to confess to Beth so many times that I hadn't told James until it was too late. When she'd had her first baby and I'd held his tiny body in my arms. When I watched James—his eyes swimming with melancholy behind his phone as he videotaped Beth's kids tearing into their gifts on Christmas morning. When the clock would strike 2:00 a.m. and I'd still be up, sipping James's whiskey, wishing I could turn back time so he'd love me the way he used to. He never said his love had changed, but I could tell. He looked at me differently. And since I found out about Dylan, I've wondered if my omission was why he'd strayed. Was he trying to hurt me the way I'd hurt him?

I make a decision to tell Beth the truth about why James had come to resent me when I get home from Maui. Clean slate.

After we say good-bye, the knock comes. It's timid, like whoever it is worries I might actually hear it. I sigh, wishing I'd put the "Do Not Disturb" sign on the door. I open it just a crack so I can tell the turn-down service no, thank you, but it's Nick, and he has a pink drink adorned with one of those silly umbrellas in his hand.

He smiles.

I frown. Is he here to talk about what happened earlier? Because I'm not sure I want to discuss it.

"You look upset. Did I wake you?" He studies my face.

"No, not at all. I was awake," I say. "What's that?" I nod toward his glass and wave him inside. As he walks past me, I grab a hoodie and put it on to cover my skimpy pajama top.

"Don't worry, it's a virgin POG," Nick says.

"A what?"

"It's fresh-squeezed passion-fruit juice, orange juice, and guava juice, but *without* the vodka." He bends the straw toward my mouth. "Try."

I take a sip, the flavors of the juices blending together perfectly. It's sweet but not too sugary like so many froufrou drinks I've tried. "It's delicious."

"I brought it for you."

"Thanks," I say, taking the drink from him.

Nick glances around the room, and I cringe as I follow his gaze. My shoes are strewn across the floor; my towel from the shower I took this morning is still draped haphazardly over the back of the desk chair. And then our eyes fall on my lacy black bra and inside-out panties, the crotch staring us both in the face.

We stand there, neither of us knowing what to say about my underwear. I resist the urge to scoop it up and toss it behind the chair, not wanting to draw more attention to it. Before James died, I would have instantly filled this awkward moment with words, any words. That had been my thing—to ease tension out of situations like a masseuse kneading someone's sore muscles. Before, I would have laughed awkwardly, then told Nick stories to distract him—like how I'd walked in on the housekeeper yesterday and she'd screamed. Or how I'd been on the lanai last night and stared down at a couple practically having sex on their balcony. But I don't. Instead, I just stand here in the thick of the embarrassment and absorb it.

Finally, thankfully, Nick speaks. "I hope it's okay that I'm here. I needed to talk."

Here we go.

"Let's go outside." I motion for him to follow me onto the lanai.

We sit side by side in chairs and stare out at the ocean. The sun is low in the sky, a sunset fast approaching.

"Can we talk about things? Is that okay?"

I start to tell him that no, I don't want to rehash the fact that my husband was playing the newlywed game while in Maui. But there's something about the way he's not looking at me, like he's afraid he'll be left alone with it if I don't listen.

"Of course," I say, taking another sip of my drink.

"I was down at the bar for a while, but I had to leave. I was listening to all of the conversations going on around me—about regular things. Someone's house was in escrow, but they worried it might fall out. Another guy's niece had just scored the winning goal in her soccer game, and he was watching a video someone had texted him. I had thought being around all that activity would make me feel better. Give me hope that I could eventually be someone who was talking about things other than my fiancée dying. But right now I worry that won't happen. That I'll never live a normal life. That I'll never be me again."

I know exactly how Nick feels. He's desperate to feel normal. It's all I've wanted since James died. Like when I went to Beth's for taco night and forced myself to engage in the conversation, to laugh when my niece told a story about the new class hamster named Ollie; or when I walked to the coffee shop last week and sat at a table next to a gaggle of preschool moms planning a *Star Wars*–themed birthday party, desperately wanting to do something *regular* like that again. It's as if the world has kept spinning without me, and I'm not quite sure how to get back on the ride. Or if I even want to. "I know exactly what you mean." I lean over my chair and hug him. It's an instinct. To make him feel better. But when he squeezes me back, my body tenses, unsure of how to respond to a man's arms around me that aren't James's. It's foreign, and I feel almost suffocated by them. I try to cover my discomfort by moving over to the railing and making an observation about a luau we can hear down below, but I know Nick felt it. "I'm sorry. It's just strange hugging someone else," I finally say, my back still to him.

"Phew!" he says. "I thought maybe I smelled?"

I turn and face him. "Talk about not feeling normal. Apparently I can't even hug someone anymore without feeling awkward."

We laugh quietly at ourselves. It feels like the only choice.

"I miss her," he says. "It feels like I have a huge hole inside of me— where she used to be. I keep seeing things and think, 'Oh, I need to tell Dylan about this.' And then I realize I can't."

"I miss him too," I say. I miss how he'd wrap one of his legs around mine when he slept. I miss the way he sang off tune to any Eagles song—didn't matter which one; he couldn't control himself if he heard their music. I miss when he'd make me *chilaquiles* with homemade salsa on Sunday mornings. Suddenly it occurs to me that it's been years since he did any of these things. The parts of him I miss the most were gone long before he was.

"Does that make us fools?" he asks. "To miss the people who fucked us over so badly? Especially now that we know they were playing house over here?"

"This might surprise you, but I don't think so. Just because they did a bad thing—several bad things—doesn't mean we can't be sad they're gone."

"Can I ask you something kind of strange?"

"Why not? I'm abnormal. You're abnormal. Maybe it will seem normal when you say it."

"What if you found out he was alive? Like this was all some big mistake? And he knocked on the door right now and asked you to forgive him. Could you?"

"Yes," I say without hesitation, surprising myself slightly, and clearly surprising Nick.

"Really?" he asks after staring at me for a beat.

"Yes," I repeat, realizing that is exactly what I'd do.

"I get that you'd be excited to see him again. I'd feel the same way about Dylan. But what would happen after the initial shock and excitement wore off? You could really get past it? The lying? The cheating? The betrayal?"

"I'd like to think I'd at least try." But I don't tell Nick the next part. Because it sounds pathetic, even as I think it. If James wanted me back—if he chose me, even after *not* choosing me—I'd say yes. I'd planned for us to grow old together—for better or worse. And I now understand how lonely I'm going to be without him. And I'd make it right. I'd delve deep and uncover the old James. The one that had to still be there. The one Dylan probably knew.

Nick whistles. "Not the answer I was expecting."

"Maybe it's because we have a lot more history than you and Dylan do—eight years."

"I would think that would make what he did sting worse."

I look down at a few couples strolling on the path. "Things get complicated after you get past the honeymoon phase, Nick. The layers of your relationship build on top of one another. Good on top of bad on top of good. But you don't tear down the whole thing just because it hasn't turned out the way you thought it would." I think of my own untruth. Yes, it had changed my relationship with James. But he had tried to work through it. Or at least I thought he had. "I'm guessing you wouldn't give Dylan another chance?"

"No." He clenches his jaw as if he's trying to force himself not to say the ugly things that come to mind.

I do the same thing when I think about what James did to me. I push away the mean thoughts. Because calling him nasty names in my mind won't change anything—especially because he's not the only one to blame. Clearly I played a role. A man generally doesn't go out and have an affair for the hell of it, if he's happy with his wife. I should've found a marriage counselor to help us through what I'd done to us.

I've clearly moved into what WebMD calls the bargaining phase. *If only I'd done this. If only I'd tried that.*

"Why not?" I finally ask him. "If she was as wonderful as you've made her sound, why wouldn't you at least try to make it work?"

"The Dylan I knew, the one I was *engaged* to, was as great as I've told you. She was funny and smart and kind. But this Dylan?" He waves his hand toward the hotel grounds. "The one who lied and came here with James? I don't need her."

"Yet you came all the way here to find out more about *that* Dylan? The one you don't need?"

"So I can move on. I never will if I keep remembering the good Dylan—if I continue to romanticize what I realize now wasn't real, at least not to her," Nick says simply, and takes off his sunglasses off his head. "Look at that." He points toward the sky, which has transformed from dark blue to streaks of red, gold, and pink. We watch the sun inch down toward the water until it disappears, and I wonder if I've begun to romanticize James because he's no longer here to prove me wrong.

"Here's to happier sunsets," I say, holding up my now-empty glass.

After Nick leaves, I curl under the fluffy white duvet in my king-size bed feeling slightly better. He reminded me that we were booked on a hiking tour first thing in the morning, and even though the thought of it gave me a stomachache, I smiled at him and told him I'd be ready. Because I was determined to make tomorrow about *me*, about *my* future. About conquering *my* fears. I plan to do the hike like Cheryl fucking Strayed.

But then I dream that James is alive. And that I tell him I forgive him.

It is so real—I run my hands over his cheeks, the stubble tickling the pads of my fingertips; I bury my nose in his chest and inhale his smell—a combination of Old Spice and Irish Spring soap. I feel his chest, his arms, every inch of him, to prove to myself he's really here, because how could I have that kind of detail if he weren't? He tells me that it was all a big mistake. That it hadn't been him in that Jeep, that it had been some other guy. I feel a weight lift. I hadn't been clueless. He hadn't been terrible. We can go back to being the people we thought we were. Thank God.

And when my alarm buzzes, I lie here in my ocean-view suite, the curtains parted so I can see straight out into the still-dark morning, the only light coming from the swimming pools and the stars still blanketing the sky, and realize James is still gone. I am a perfect oxymoron—in absolute paradise but also in utter hell.

CHAPTER NINETEEN

Jacks—after

"How are you feeling today?" I ask Nick as I shake a packet of raw sugar into my coffee cup.

"I'm better." He takes a drink of his coffee. "Thanks for talking to me last night and for the most awkward hug I've ever had."

"You're welcome." I laugh. "It was easy to talk to you. Beth tries, but she has no idea what I'm going through."

Nick gives me a sad smile. "I know what you mean. My best buddy at the station, he means well, but he doesn't have a clue."

"I dreamed about him last night—that he was alive," I blurt. "It was so real, and I woke up feeling like I'd just taken three steps backward. You know what I mean?"

"I do. You'll have a good day where you don't break down in hysterics, where you get through it and maybe even feel a fraction of okay." He leans back in his chair. "And then something will happen; you'll come across a pair of their jeans or something that reminds you of them, and their death crushes you all over again."

"Exactly. You know I only just washed the last bath towel he used?" I shake my head, remembering how it had started to smell like mildew.

"I sobbed as I put it in the laundry because it was one of the last things he'd used at home when he was alive. It felt like I was erasing him."

"I put her toothbrush under my sink, next to a bottle of her moisturizer and a hair tie. I couldn't throw them away—for the same reason. It felt wrong, like I would have been getting rid of her."

I think of all of James's clothes still hanging in the closet, lying in his drawers. I hadn't touched any of it. I couldn't. "Well, I know one thing for sure—it's fucking hard. All of it," I finally say.

"Amen," he says, and laughs.

"Is this helping you at all, being here? Like this hike today—you really think hauling our asses up the side of a mountain is going to make us feel better?"

"Honestly, being here is helping me, but not necessarily for the reason I thought it would."

"What do you mean?"

"I think having *you* here is what's really making the difference. To be with someone who understands what this feels like. Like last night, how you said you'd forgive him. I was up half the night thinking about that."

"And?" I prod.

"Maybe you're right to not be so focused on anger. To not turn them into these monsters just because they screwed us over. I'm tired of being so mad." Nick scratches his head. "How did you learn to let go of it?"

"I haven't." I stop and think for a moment. What did I mean when I said I'd forgive James? Because it would be hard, really hard. Not only to let go of what he'd done to our marriage, but to trust him again. "I guess I meant that *if* he were still alive, I would take him back. And I would attempt to fight through all the ugly feelings that would still be there. I'd want to at least *try* to give him a second chance."

Nick doesn't respond, focused on a small bird that has landed on the table next to us.

"But obviously he's not coming back. And I don't want to spend the rest of my life mad at him. So I'm trying to take control of my anger instead of letting it control me. Does that make sense?" I ask.

Nick nods.

"I've had some really bad moments, as you know. Like setting off the smoke detector when I went all *Firestarter* on the condolence cards." I stop when I see the confused expression on Nick's face.

"You don't know *Firestarter*? Drew Barrymore?"

He shakes his head. "Contrary to popular belief, firemen haven't seen every movie about fires."

I laugh.

"Maybe I wasn't born yet?" he offers.

"And *I* was?" I pull out my phone and do a quick Google search. "Ha—it came out in eighty-four. I was born in eighty-three." I show him the screen. "I'm thirty-three. How old are you?"

"Twenty-eight."

"Baby," I say.

He smiles wanly.

"We're both young. We have our whole lives ahead of us still."

"I wish I could speed up mine. So I can be past this sooner," he says.

"We'll get there," I say, wishing I knew when that aha moment would occur. When I wouldn't feel like the wind had just gotten knocked out of me. I slide the Maui Hiking Tours brochure the concierge had given Nick across the table. "If I'm being completely honest, I'm having a moment right now when I look at this pamphlet. It makes my blood boil that they took this kind of vacation together. That it was all about adventures and fun and bonding." I feel the tears threaten to well up in my eyes.

"I know. It sucks. I once wanted her to do this ropes course with me. Some guys at the station had done it with their spouses and were talking about it. And she said no. And now I have to stomach the fact that she did these things with *him*." He says the word with such disgust, my first impulse is to defend James. But I don't. Because I understand completely.

"Well, I guess we can sit here and continue to feel sorry for ourselves, or we can get up and go." I stand, willing my legs to move.

"If this guide is anything like Adam, hopefully we'll get more good info." He stops, realizing his mistake when he sees my face. "I don't mean 'good' info. Obviously their posing as newlyweds was not a good thing. I just meant *insightful*."

I stare at him. Finding out they were posing as a married couple simply made me sick. It's something I wish I could forget. If I could choose one thing, it would be that.

"And, hey, it says here we're going to see stunning panoramas of the central valley, ocean, and neighbor islands," he offers with mock cheer.

"Woo. Hoo." I match his inflection.

"Fake it till we make it, right?" he says.

"Right!" I pump my fist in the air. "It also says we *get* to hike *ten miles* out and back! You know, someone on TripAdvisor said you need legs of steel to do the whole thing! Can't wait!"

"Well, according to the concierge, James and Dylan only hiked the Maalaea side, which is five miles out and back," Nick says.

We go on like this for a while. Offering up the irritating details to each other in singsongy voices.

We start to walk out to the lobby. "Extremely rocky and steep west Maui mountains, here we come!" Nick laughs.

I stop and grab his arm. "So, hey, how steep we talking?"

Nick laughs again but stops when he sees I don't.

"No seriously. I kind of have an issue with heights."

Nick gives me a look. He juts out his bottom lip slightly and frowns, his eyebrows nearly meeting as he wrinkles his brow. If his expression could be translated into words, it would mean: *Can we just do this, please? Get through this experience like we said we would? Make the best of a horrible situation?*

I know I should stop being so selfish and give him what he wants, but admittedly it's in my nature to wrestle for what *I* want. With James, we each tended to put ourselves first and then fight about it later—the control shifting like a seesaw. I'm not used to someone else thinking of my needs before his. I wonder if Dylan paced her giving with Nick, or did she just take and take, like I'd been doing? I clap my hands. "I can do this. I know you'll help me, right? Work your magic at the top of the trail if I need it?"

Nick nods. "But remind me never to go on *The Amazing Race* with you. You'd be a train wreck."

I wave my finger in the air. "Correction. I'd be a producer's dream. Freaking out on every task? That's ratings gold!"

Nick rolls his eyes.

"I'm going to kick this hike's ass!" I put my hand up for a high-five, smiling wide so he knows that I'm at least trying, even though it was difficult for me.

After locating our guide, Jacob, a fiftyish man with a shaved head, muscular shoulders, and a tiny waist, we take a short drive as he gives the group a brief history of the trail we'll be hiking. He tells us that it's part of the aloloa, or the long road, that once circled Maui and might be as much as four hundred years old. He says that the trail was built in the 1800s and every boulder in every wall and every paving stone was placed there by hand. When we arrive, we gather around a maroon sign with yellow writing. It says: *Lahaina Pali Trail. Please do not scratch or move rocks or break tree branches or leave rubbish on the trail.*

I whisper to Nick, "Scratch the rocks?"

"Well, they were placed there by hand!" Nick smiles.

As Jacob passes out our backpacks, he asks us to go around the group and introduce ourselves. There's a young twentysomething couple that look like Malibu Barbie and Ken, with bright-blond hair and matching skintight T-shirts with *Maui Honeymooners* silkscreened across them. They tell us their names are Trish and Doug, but I can't help but picture them riding down Pacific Coast Highway in a bright-pink convertible Corvette like the one I had when I was little. There's also a man easily twenty years their senior, with dark hair and a thick New York accent, who says his name is George and points out his wife, Nancy, and their teenage son, Parker, who barely looks up from his smartphone to nod at us when he hears his name. When it comes around to me, I stammer. My identity for the past eight years has been intertwined with James's. I'm not sure who I am without him.

Thankfully, Nick jumps in. "We're Nick and Jacqueline—Jacks—and we just got engaged." Nick smiles at me, and I can almost read his mind. *If they can do it, we can too.* And then, as if they won't believe Nick's story otherwise, I grab his hand.

About a mile in, Nick and I are in the back of the pack, and I'm still thinking about the way his hand felt when I'd laced my fingers through his—large and rough, but also like it would protect me from anything. George and Nancy are several yards ahead of us, pumping their arms like nobody's business. And their son is right behind them, taking selfies every few yards, tilting his head until he finds the right angle. When I make a quip to Nick about Parker being obsessed with taking pictures of himself, Nick tells me he's actually Snapchatting. When I give him a blank stare, he explains what that is.

"He's texting a group of his friends while on this hike? Shouldn't he be enjoying the view?"

"Shouldn't I be saying the same thing about you?" Nick stops and puts his hands on my shoulders. It's true. I've been hugging one side of the trail so hard I think it might be getting the wrong idea.

"I'm freaked out," I say, but it comes out like a question.

"And you're going to let that take away the chance for you to look at this breathtaking scenery?"

"No, it's just that I'm concentrating on not falling off the side of the mountain."

"What would you tell your students?"

"What do you mean?"

"What would you tell one of your fourth graders if they were scared of something?"

I realize what he's doing the second I hear the question. Oh, the irony. That I'm a teacher taking care of nine- and ten-year-olds, yet I can't talk myself off the literal ledge of my own life.

"Touché," I say.

"That's not an answer." He stares at me.

"Fine. I would tell them that fear only lives where you let it. That they can do anything they set their minds to."

"Good advice," he says. "Why don't you take it?"

"Fine." As the trail gets steeper, I focus on the back of Nick's legs, how the muscles in his calves flex with each step. From the way he maneuvers around loose rocks and tree roots sticking out of the ground with ease, you'd think he were the guide. I adjust my backpack, which feels like an incubator holding all my body heat under it, and try to match Nick's momentum. But each time I attempt to speed up, I slip slightly and the rocks give way under my feet. I picture each pebble rolling all the way to the bottom, which is well over a thousand feet, according to Jacob, who has an incessant need to remind us at every marker.

When we hit marker number three, Jacob announces that we're going to take a water break and instructs us to check out the spectacular view of the island of Molokini. Barbie and Ken pull out a selfie stick, Barbie giggling as she leans in to kiss him.

I think of James and when we traveled together for the first time. Before our first long weekend away in San Francisco, a city neither of us had been to, I said, "I'll do anything except tours. I don't like being at someone's mercy when I'm sightseeing." His face fell, and he said simply, "Well, I guess we won't be needing this!" And he tossed a brochure about a tour of Alcatraz onto the table. I immediately told him I was sorry and offered to go, but he refused. I could tell he felt stupid, and after several attempts to apologize, I gave up. And now, as I listen to Jacob ramble about Maui, I have to live with the fact that he'd taken another woman to do the things I wouldn't.

"You know you're facing the wrong direction?" Jacob says, sticking out his pointer finger. "The view is thataway."

I laugh awkwardly. "I know. I'm just a little freaked out about how high up we are."

Jacob raises a bushy eyebrow, which seems comical against his bald head. "Interesting choice for a sightseeing trip."

"I know."

"Then why are you all the way up here when you could be down there? I'm sure you read about the many fine things Maui has to offer at sea level—or below, if that's your bag."

I catch Nick's eye and nod so he knows I need him. Because obviously I can't tell Jacob the truth: that my husband died on the road to Hana when I thought he was in Kansas and we were still in a pretty decent marriage. And I'm here with his mistress's fiancé, retracing their footsteps up this west Maui mountain range to try to figure out why they wanted each other instead of us.

Nick drops his backpack in front of us. "Great tour, Jacob," he says, shaking his hand. "Our friends did this hike in May and raved about you. Said you are an amazing five-star tour guide and we absolutely couldn't let Jacks's fear keep us from taking your tour." Nick puts his arm around my shoulder. "Right, honey?"

"Right." I lean my head against him, the earlier awkwardness gone. My torso fits perfectly into the groove of his side, and I try to brush off the flash of guilt that passes through me.

Jacob laughs. "Wow. With praise like that, I hope your pals gave me a Yelp review! Who were they?"

"Dylan and James," Nick says; then when Jacob doesn't recognize them based on just their names like the others had, he describes them. As I listen, I'm struck by how he speaks about James—as if he knew him his entire life. And I wonder, would James and Nick have been friends under other circumstances? Would Dylan and I have been friends if I'd bumped into her at Target?

"Yes, I remember them now." Jacob frowns, and I wonder if he read about their accident in the newspaper. So far, only our first bartender has connected the dots. "But if they're the couple I'm thinking of, I don't think *they'll* be giving me a five-star review."

Obviously he doesn't know. He's still speaking about them in the present tense.

"Really?" Nick and I say in unison.

"I probably shouldn't say anything."

"It's okay, James confided that they were having some problems." Nick jumps in and twirls the lie without skipping a beat.

"Ya, it sure seemed like that. I overheard them bickering before we even started the trail." He pauses as if he knows what we're wondering. "I have no idea what about—but you know, that didn't seem that unusual to me—I've seen it all. Honeymooners duking it out, newly engaged folks just like you two, battling. Even in a place like this, it happens."

Nick and I nod. I'm not sure if Nick really knows what Jacob means, but I do.

"Then once we started hiking—we weren't even to marker one—she sat down. Said she was a bit dizzy. That she didn't eat breakfast. But she didn't want to stop. We both kept checking in, asking her if she was okay. And she said she was, but it was clear she was having a hard time. Finally, James told me they had to quit—that she wasn't up to it."

Nick bites his lower lip and balls his hands into fists at his sides. "Did they say what was wrong with her?"

"No, just that she was tired. I offered to stop the tour and escort them back to the bottom of the trail, but James refused, arguing that they weren't that far up anyway. And Dylan agreed with him. So I let them go back on their own, just hoping the boss didn't find out.

Because it's really against policy. But I could tell James wasn't going to take no for an answer."

Jacob stops talking, and a palpable silence descends until he starts again. "So was she okay? Was she just overheating or maybe even a little out of shape? Because this hike isn't easy, especially on a hot day like that. Maybe she'd had too much champagne the night before? We see it all here." He stops again and looks at Nick. Before Nick can respond, Jacob waves his hands. "Ah, I'm being rude. It's none of my business anyway; we'd better get on with this hike!"

An hour and a half later, we reach the top. Jacob explains that we're at the Kealaloloa Ridge and tells us we're looking at the Kaheawa Wind Farm and there are thirty-five wind turbines stretched out before us that are visible from all over Maui. I take a deep breath as Jacob rambles about the history of the wind farm and decide that this time I don't need Nick's guided meditation to help me through. If I learned anything yesterday, it's that I'm stronger than I've ever given myself credit for. I made it up this ass-blasting, thigh-burning, steep and rocky hike without a single anxiety attack. And I also accomplished it when *she* couldn't. And I know how that sounds—that she got sick and I'm happy about it. And maybe that's true. But I can't help but feel competitive. She was sleeping with my husband, after all.

"You did it." Nick walks up behind me, placing his hand on mine.

"I did," I say as I look over the cliff's edge toward the ocean below, letting the wind slice through my hair. I'm shaking, and my heart feels like it might burst through my chest. But you know what? I feel alive.

CHAPTER TWENTY

Jacks — before

I sipped my piña colada, the cool mix of rum, pineapple, and coconut tasting exactly like I imagined paradise would. My head still buzzed slightly from all the wedding festivities. I was no longer Jacks Conner. Now I'd answer to Mrs. James Morales. And rather than merely drooling over pictures of the cabanas at the Four Seasons hotel in Wailea, I was relaxing in one, the attentive pool boy popping by every few minutes to see if I needed a refill, a cool towel, or *anything at all*.

I'd never had anyone wait on me, and it felt surreal to be lying under the giant white cabana facing the pristine pool with the grand fountain in the middle, the deep cobalt ocean waters just in the distance. I hadn't planned to be *here*. James and I were supposed to be in a Victorian room at a quaint B and B in Santa Barbara. The limited savings we had between us would have barely covered airfare anywhere, so we'd decided to go somewhere local and take a honeymoon later, when we could afford it.

But James's mom had surprised us with this trip during her toast at the wedding reception, wryly joking that there was no way her son and his new wife were missing out on a *proper* honeymoon. The bed-and-breakfast we'd booked in Santa Barbara just wouldn't do. The crowd had tittered and laughed, and I'd noticed James tense at the slight dig his mother had made, but it hadn't bothered me. I agreed that we deserved a real vacation and would have charged it on a credit card if James had let me. We needed to bond as husband and wife. And if we didn't go away now, I suspected we'd be one of those couples who never did.

At the reception, I'd been giddy and flushed from the champagne I'd been drinking, and I'd run over and hugged Isabella tightly, feeling thankful I'd inherited such a generous mother-in-law. Isabella flinched slightly when I squeezed her, but I wasn't surprised. I'd quickly noticed that giving material gifts came easy for my mother-in-law—it was offering the emotional ones she seemed to struggle with. Hopefully, in time, that would change. I was used to an affectionate family—you could never enter my parents' house without giving them each a tight hug. Once my mom embraced Isabella so tightly at Thanksgiving that I thought she might break her, the pinched look on my mother-in-law's face something Beth and I had laughed about later.

I had started to pull away from Isabella, but she held on to my shoulders, then leaned in closer, and I'd involuntarily inhaled a strong whiff of her Chanel No. 5 perfume as she whispered, "You can use this romantic getaway to start trying! James told me he's ready."

I'd stepped back so I could see her face. I studied Isabella's hazel eyes. She was serious. James had talked to her about this? I shook off the uneasy feeling that washed over me. I thought about the check that Isabella had given us last month. The money she'd insisted was a gift for the nice *big* house she wanted us to buy. Which I now clearly understood was payment for the pack of grandkids I was to provide for her. I stood in the center of the ballroom at the Pelican Hill Golf Club and wondered: Would Isabella's generosity always come with strings?

Now at the hotel, I adjusted my white straw hat to shield my face from the hot sun that was beginning to peer into the cabana. I knew we couldn't wait long. James and I had talked about kids; I knew he wanted them. My stomach tightened as I thought of my last gynecologist appointment when I'd gone in for my annual exam. I swished the memory away. We were still so young, just twenty-five and twenty-seven, respectively—I still had plenty of time to figure things out.

"What have you been thinking about? You've been staring off into space for ten minutes." James stood over me, his olive skin already a deep brown from the sun, drops of water falling from his red swim trunks to the concrete, creating a speckled pattern by his feet.

I swatted him playfully with my magazine. "Were you stalking me?"

"What if I was?"

"Then I'd say that's pretty damn creepy!" I laughed.

"If you want to call me names, then fine. I'll take it. But I blame you!" He pointed at me.

"Me?"

"Yeah. *You.* It's not my fault if I couldn't keep my eyes off of you. You're the most beautiful woman here."

I smiled. "You said that to me the first time we met."

"I did?" James sat on the edge of my chair and put his hand on my ankle, sending an electric current up my leg.

I cocked my head. "Yes! How can you not remember that? Or were there so many pretty girls at the store that day that you went from aisle to aisle until one of us took the bait?"

~

I had been chewing on my thumbnail, debating between a cabernet and a pinot, when I saw an arm reach past me and grab a bottle. "This one," he'd said as he set the Wild Horse pinot noir in my cart.

I had whipped around, ready to be annoyed. Because, really, who did that? Until I saw his face. The way his eyes sparkled. The slight five-o'clock shadow. And his smile. It shone like a beacon.

"Why should I listen to you?" I'd teased, and pointed at the six-pack of Corona Light in his hand. "You look like a beer drinker to me. And also a fan of kid's cereal, it seems." I nodded at the Lucky Charms under his other arm.

"I'm multidimensional. When I'm with the guys, I drink this," he said, and held up the Corona. "When I'm with the most beautiful woman in the room, I drink this," he said, grabbing the pinot out of my cart. "And when I'm alone, I eat this." He held up the red box with the rainbow and leprechaun on the front.

"So what will you be doing tonight?" I blurted before I could stop myself. He was cheesy and had obviously done this before—his charm was effortless, like a skill he'd been honing for years. Yet. There was something about him. In just one minute he'd made me feel more special than my last boyfriend had the entire three months we'd been together—he'd always made me work so damn hard for it. But this guy? He was making it so easy. I was ready for easy.

James had smiled and tucked the bottle under his arm. "Drinking the wine with you, of course."

I knew Beth would roll her eyes so hard later when I told her the story. But I hadn't cared. "Tell me when and where."

That was the beginning of it all. We were married nine months later. And now we were in Maui.

~

James laughed and stroked my leg. "I may not remember what I *said* to you at the store that day, but I do know what I *thought*."

"Let me guess. You were thinking, 'She'd better have good taste in wine or this is never going to go anywhere.'"

"No way! I was hoping you'd have some milk for me Lucky Charms," he said with a poor attempt at an Irish accent.

I pushed him in his tight abs. "You know, surprisingly, your cheesiness was one of the things I loved from the moment I met you." I ran my fingers through his thick, wet hair. "You wear cheesy well."

James smiled. "Thanks. I think? You should have seen the look on your face when I grabbed that wine bottle off the shelf!"

"I was about to reach for my Mace until I saw how cute you were!"

"Hey. Cute guys can be psychopaths too."

I kissed him deeply. "I decided I'd take my chances."

"Good thing." He reached up and caressed my breast over my triangle top, and my body caved into his. "Maybe we should go up to the room," James said. "That cabana boy is going to be here any second. And if I didn't know better, I'd think he was coming up with excuses to check on you. He's been over here every five minutes!"

"Whatever," I breathed, running my finger inside the waistband of his swim trunks.

"I'm not going to be able to stand up for a couple minutes!" He nodded toward his erection, and we laughed.

I hoped our sex life would never change, that a simple touch could always send sparks flying—that we'd never stop wanting each other with such hot passion. But if I listened to Beth, apparently the odds were stacked against us. My sister had gotten married only four years before and recently confided that their sex life had become *routine* and she'd found herself fantasizing about George Clooney.

I'd been incredulous; Beth was only a few years in—practically a newlywed! "That's the pregnancy hormones talking. Look at you! You're about to burst—almost eight months along." I'd leaned over and rubbed Beth's swollen belly and said a silent prayer I'd also have one someday. "After you have the baby, you'll get the passion back."

Beth had only rolled her eyes at me as she waddled into the laundry room to wash some baby clothes she'd just purchased.

I traced James's chest with my finger. "Can I ask you something?"

"If I can get up yet? Nope! I keep looking at your boobs in that bathing suit, and well, unless I want to scare some children, we should probably wait." He pulled my hands away. "And you should probably stop doing that, or we're never going to get out of here."

I flung a towel at him. "Gross! Seriously, I want to ask you something."

"You have my undivided attention." James smirked.

"Do you believe in monogamy? Like long-term, forever, never-seeing-another-vagina monogamy?"

"Isn't it a little late to be bringing this up?" James laughed and pointed to my ring. I noticed his bare finger, remembering his declaration that he didn't see himself wearing a wedding band. He'd said he'd just lose it, claiming his mom had once bought him an expensive watch and he'd misplaced it the next day. At first I'd been upset, arguing that it would look like he didn't want to appear married. But he swore that wasn't it at all. That he loved me, and why did it matter if *other* people thought he was someone's husband? All that mattered was that we knew it.

I hadn't been able to argue with that.

"I'm being serious. Do you really think it's possible to keep the spark alive with the same person you've been having sex with for fifty years? Beth is already preparing to fantasize about whatever hot actor *People* chooses as the sexiest man alive. And she and Mark have only been married *four years*!"

"Do people even have sex when they're seventy? That's how old my grandmother is!"

"Will you stop? I'm trying to talk to you here. Forget fifty years. What about five?"

"Five? God I hope we're still into each other like this when we're only five years in. But, Jacks, marriage is about a lot more than sex." James said the last part with an air of authority that slightly bothered me. Like he was an expert on the subject.

"I know that." I sat up and crossed my legs. "I'm not just talking about the physical part. I mean *all* of it—the same person day in and day out. You don't think that's going to be hard?"

"Of course it will. We're both going to find ourselves attracted to other people along the way. That's normal. What's *not* normal is acting on it."

"True," I said, and thought about the story Beth had told me last week about her neighbors. The wife had just found out her husband had been cheating on her for a year and a half. She'd sobbed to Beth that she'd had no clue. I had shaken my head, not understanding how betrayal could be undetected in a marriage for so long.

"Have you ever cheated on anyone?" The question flew out of my mouth. I'd never asked him before. But that story about Beth's neighbors had gotten under my skin. Made me think that maybe I should have.

"No! But is this some secret plan to make my erection go away?" He looked down. "Because it worked."

I laughed. "No. I heard this horrible story about Beth's neighbor the other day, and it made me think," I said, and gave James the details. That a text had come in on her husband's phone, and she'd grabbed it thinking it was their son in college who always checked in on Sunday mornings. But it wasn't him. It was a picture of a naked woman lying in bed. And when she asked her husband who it was, he told her everything. And the hardest part, she told Beth, was how relieved he seemed that she finally knew the truth. That he didn't have to hide any longer.

James kissed me lightly when I finished. "That won't be you and me. I promise. We just need to make sure to be completely open with each other. And we need to be the kind of people who don't look at each other's phones."

"What's that supposed to mean?" I balked.

"I'm kidding, Jacks!" He reached over and handed his phone to me. "Here you go. I've got nothing to hide."

"Aren't you going to ask me if I've ever cheated?"

James stroked my hair. "I don't have to. You're the most honest and loyal person I've ever met. It's one of the many reasons I fell in love with you," he whispered.

Now was the time to tell him. Especially after what Isabella had implied at the reception. The house. The honeymoon. It was only a matter of time before she'd start putting more pressure on him. That'd she want to be paid back in the form of a grandchild.

But I couldn't find the words. I wanted to savor every minute of our honeymoon, not taint it with bad news. That could wait until we got back. "You're right," I whispered as I stood up and guided him away from the cabana and toward the hotel room.

CHAPTER TWENTY-ONE

JACKS—AFTER

My mom likes to check boxes. Dry cleaning, *check*. Pick up prescriptions, *check*. Jacks is okay, *check*.

She's called me twice today—trying her best to tick that box next to my name. I'm not sure if it's because Beth told her where I am (even though I asked her not to) or if her mother's intuition is kicking in and she knows I'm somewhere she wouldn't approve of. Doing something she might classify as crazy. But either way, it's just another thing I'm going to have to deal with if I answer her call. Manage *her* needs. She *needs* me to tell her I'm fine. That I'm getting through it. She wants me to say something I may never say again: that I'm "back to normal."

Because the thing is, my mom doesn't do well when things don't go as expected. She's always needed Beth and me to dot our i's and cross our t's, to pay our bills, to be good daughters and wives. If she knew I have a therapist, she'd flip her lid. *Why on God's green earth would you do that?* Just like how she reacted when I told her I was engaged to James after just three months.

"Hmm." My mom pinched the fabric of her canary-yellow cardigan sweater just below her neck. Someone looking on would think she had a chill, but I knew better. She was pissed.

"Not exactly the reaction I was hoping for." I poured a glass of iced tea and sat on one of the barstools by the kitchen counter, waiting.

"What did you think I was going to say?" Her voice was light, but her eyes told the real story: I'd rocked the boat. And *that* she didn't like. "I've never even met this man." She started to pace the room.

"I know. And you will. Tonight." My voice came out sounding needy, desperate. James and I had planned for him to come over, to bring her roses and my dad a bottle of his favorite whiskey. I knew once they met him, he'd charm the shit out of them. Because that's what he did.

My mom started to lap the kitchen island. I knew what she was thinking. How could I go off script? This wasn't how we did things in the Conner family.

"I need to process this." She stopped and pressed her palms into the counter.

"I know it's fast. We've only been dating a few months, but he's—" I had planned to list my favorite things about him. He was smart, he was a gentleman, he was close with his own mom. But she cut me off.

"Are you pregnant?"

"What? No!" Our eyes locked. "Don't you think I would have led with that?" I finally said, then started to pick at a hangnail on my thumb. My mom began walking again. I could be five, fifteen, or my current age, twenty-five. It didn't matter. This was how conflict between us looked. I presented my case weakly. My mom wouldn't listen, her disappointment dripping from her, so palpable I could almost reach out and touch it. I'd usually start to backpedal, my mom's approval suddenly meaning more to me than what I'd wanted her to approve of. But something had shifted in me this time. I wanted James more than my mom's blessing.

"How can you know someone well enough to agree to marry them after just three months?"

She was right, of course. It was probably intellectually impossible to know someone that well in ninety days. But I didn't care. Because I knew how James made me feel. Like the most beautiful woman in the room. Like he loved me more than anything. He made me feel desired.

I recounted to my mother the story of how I met James in the wine aisle at the supermarket, and she wasn't nearly as charmed by it. What I didn't tell her was what had happened next.

He'd taken me out for sushi at a little hole-in-the-wall that didn't even have a menu—the chef just whipped up whatever was fresh. The salmon sashimi had melted in my mouth, and the wine had slid smoothly down my throat. James had this way of putting me at ease—unlike on other first dates, I didn't feel awkward or grapple with words.

That's probably why I'd let him take me to back to his apartment and fuck me in a very ungentlemanlike way on the floor as soon as his front door closed. I'd woken the next morning as the sun streamed in through the brown-and-orange plaid sheets he was using as curtains in his bedroom. I'd propped myself up on one elbow on his futon. (Yes, futon.)

"What is that thing men say to each other?" I'd laughed as I pulled the blanket over my chest for warmth, not discretion. James had allowed me an instant comfort about my body I'd never felt before. Not with words, but with his eyes, the way they drank me in. Suddenly the small-ish breasts I'd always despised were perfect. The ass I constantly tried to cover up was juicy. And my face, the same one I'd dissected from every angle, was beautiful. That was James's superpower—he could make you addicted to the way *he saw* you. Probably because it was so much more flattering than how you viewed yourself.

"Don't they say that there are the girls you fuck on the first night and there are girls you marry?" I hadn't waited for him to answer. "I guess I'm in the former category, so the pressure's off!"

Despite the fact I'd given myself to him so easily that first night, we'd fallen fast and hard for each other. I'd finish up in my classroom, then count the hours until he was off work. I blew off my other friends. I forgot to call my mom back. Every breath began and ended with him. Every thought was laced with his scent. The real world became distant. The only thing that mattered was the time I spent with James. Beth thought I was obsessed. I was scared she might be right.

I hadn't planned on hoarding our relationship forever. But before I could introduce him to my family, he'd proposed. He'd taken me back to that sushi place and knelt down on the dusty floor and asked if I'd take a leap of faith with him. Would I be his wife? There was no question in my mind. There was no way I could ever be without him.

I said yes.

I realize this may have not have been the best decision—marrying someone whose middle name I'd learned the day before he proposed. (It's Julian.) That it may have led me here, chasing his cheating ghost along the Maui coast. But if he'd asked me a million more times, the answer would always have been yes for me.

~

A picture of my mom holding her fourteen-year-old cocker spaniel pops up on my phone. Her third call. But I don't answer. Because I'm nowhere near normal. She'll hear it in my voice. She'll question me. And the thing is, I'm so tired of lies. But the truth is just too much work. I send her to voice mail, kick off my sandals, and dip my toes into the sand. It's soft and warm, and I let it soothe me. Nick shoots me a questioning look.

"I'm not ready to talk to her yet," I say, and look around for our server.

"Want to start with the coconut calamari and the crab-and-macadamia-nut wontons?" Nick asks, looking up from the Hula Grill menu.

"Yes, and can we get some fries too?"

"Anything else, hungry girl?" Nick laughs.

"What can I say? I'm eating my feelings." I smile.

I watch the band getting ready to perform on a small stage. Our table is literally sitting on a floor of sand, and in front of us is an amazing view of the beach that's so picturesque it makes you say touristy things you never thought you'd say, like, *We're in paradise.* Or, *This looks like a movie set.* (I'll admit, I said that one to Nick a few minutes ago.)

"I'm so happy we didn't have to go on another *tour* today." I roll my eyes at Nick. But I don't say the next part: that it was nice to hang out with him and not think about *them.* To not have them infiltrate every thought.

"Oh, please! You know you were bummed we didn't go rock climbing or skydiving."

"Actually, I was hoping for some deep-sea fishing." I laugh and snort, covering my nose with my hand. "Whoops."

"A snort, huh?" Nick says, and leans back. "I guess you're finally getting comfortable with me."

I feel my cheeks heat up. "I hate when I do that. It's so embarrassing."

"I think it's cute."

"Really?"

"Sure. I've always thought it's the quirks that make a person interesting."

I take a drink of my water, thinking of how my snort bugged James. Not at first. When we'd met, he thought it was cute too. Even used to playfully mimic me when he heard it. But later, when things changed, it began to irritate him. I remember being at a party once, and he glanced my way when he heard it. He knew how to work a room and expected me to do the same. Snorting was not an option.

"You know it's not something I can control!" I said on the way home that night, trying to hide how stupid I felt, how sad I was that we'd ended up here—in a place that made it okay for my husband to chastise me for simply being *myself.*

"Oh, come on, Jacks." He kept his eyes on the road as he spoke, and I was thankful because he couldn't see how much his criticism hurt. Then he delivered the blow. "Sure you can."

And after that I did learn to control it. Except for when I drink. When I drink, I forget. My smooth edges become rough again.

I look up from my thoughts and notice Nick watching me.

"What were you just thinking about?" he says. "Your face got all dark."

"Nothing," I say. "It doesn't matter anymore." I shake off the memory of James and force a smile. "What about you? What are the quirks that make *you* interesting?"

"Oh, I'm wildly boring. Supremely uninteresting." Nick laughs.

"Is that your way of saying you don't have any idiosyncrasies?"

"Saved by the bell." Nick points to my phone, which is ringing again. "Is that your mom again?"

"And Poochie Poo."

Nick presses his lips together to stifle a laugh. "Poochie Poo?"

"Yep!"

"She keeps calling. Aren't you concerned something might be wrong?"

"No, she's just worried about me."

"So then why not answer? 'Unworry' her?"

I give him a look.

"She doesn't know you're here, does she?"

"Nope. At least I don't think so."

"Does she know about James and Dylan?"

I shake my head and chew the inside of my lower lip. She eventually got over the shock of my whirlwind romance, and as predicted, James eventually charmed her and grudgingly earned her acceptance. But she never let me forget that I hadn't properly *vetted* him. She actually used that term. Like he was running for Congress, not becoming a member of her family.

"Are you serious, Mom?" I was holding a card he'd given me for our one-year wedding anniversary. A ridiculously sappy one that he'd bought me as a joke. The idea that someone else had to explain your *deep romantic emotions* had made us laugh. "You're really going to use that word?"

"Your father could have run a background check!"

"Mom, he doesn't have a criminal record, okay? And I've known him for two years—don't you think he would've murdered me by now if that were his goal?"

My mom took a deep breath.

"People don't always do things by the book, Mom. You need to get over your obsession with coloring inside the lines."

"What's that supposed to mean?"

"That you always need everything and *everyone* so orderly. Sometimes life is unpredictable. Messy even. Sometimes you just have to trust your gut. If you spend your whole life scared to make the wrong choice, how is that really living?'

"You can be so naive, Jacks," my mom said, like she felt sorry for me.

Back then, her skepticism made me angry. It even drove an invisible wedge between us that we never acknowledged. But when the police told me James had been in Maui, the first person I thought of was my mom. And how she was right. I had been naive. But not anymore. Now I finally know the man I married. Or I'm getting to know him, anyway.

"It's complicated why I don't want to talk to my mom," I finally say to Nick. "Have you ever had a Blue Hawaiian drink?" I ask, and point to one on the table next to us, trying to change the subject.

"Why don't you tell me about it?" he says.

"The Blue Hawaiian?" I ask, and smile. Then I snort. Again. The floodgates have been opened.

"No, silly." He laughs, and his eyes soften. "Tell me about your mom."

I start to explain that I'd rather not, but there's something about how he's looking at me. Those eyes again. He wants to know. Not just to pass time. He wants to understand more about me. About what makes me tick. And he doesn't mind if I snort while telling him. I blurt out everything—our quick engagement, my mom's obsession with normalcy, my fear that she was right. That I'm not sure I can ever trust my gut again. How much that scares me. "I can't believe I just told you all that," I say when I finish.

"I'm glad you did."

"Me too. I feel better." I think about how easy it is to talk to Nick, how I never feel judged by him. James had an arrogance about him. It was subtle. But I picked up on it a lot. Like how he sounded so condescending when he'd say something like, *Oh, is that what you decided to do,* like he was thinking he would have made a better choice—the *right* choice. During one of our particularly bad fights, I told him he had a superiority complex. He laughed and told me I was delusional.

Nick and I listen to the band, eat our food, and sip our cocktails, a comfortable silence between us. "Let's get a drink at the bar," Nick suggests when we've finished our dinner.

"I'm going to buy their CD first." I start for the stage.

"That's those Blue Hawaiians talking," he calls after me. "You'll never listen to it."

"Maybe not." I think of the CD James and Dylan purchased for their road to Hana drive as I hand the singer a ten-dollar bill. Then again, maybe I will listen to it.

Nick orders two POGs, this time *with* vodka, and I think about our day. We drove to Lahaina and had giant cinnamon rolls at Longhi's. We shopped for silly souvenirs, and we got ice cream cones while walking around Whalers Village. We mused at the number of pay phones we'd spotted around the island. We even took a selfie with one, laughing about how we were old enough to remember them. For several hours, I pretended to be a real tourist on vacation, forcing any thoughts of why I was actually here from my mind.

"Hello? You're awfully quiet over there."

"I think I'm drunk."

"That means we're doing our job right," the bartender says as he sets our drinks down, the skin around his green eyes crinkling, his stubble-covered chin reminding me of James's. I look away, and Nick clinks his glass against mine.

"To finding out more about Dylan and James."

"Did you just say Dylan and James?"

"Yes," we say in unison.

"That's weird. Because I met a Dylan and James a couple months ago. I'm sure they aren't the same people, but *Dylan* is just one of those names that stands out to me because I'm a huge Bob Dylan fan."

"Was she in her twenties? Blonde? Big blue eyes?"

The bartender nods. "And he was a good-looking guy. Dark hair, in sales?"

We nod.

"How is she?" the bartender asks with what seems to be a genuine concern.

I keep quiet because obviously I can't say *dead*. And I realize the news of their accident must not have caught the attention of many people. That saddens me for a moment. I wonder what the first bartender we talked to saw in the paper. A paragraph? A couple of sentences? A few words? Was that all they got? All they deserved?

"Why do you ask?" Nick says.

Nick told me that we should always deflect when asked a question we can't answer, but I'm not quick enough on my feet to do that.

"She was feeling pretty sick when she was here. Did she find out yet?" Our matching blank stares must trigger something with the bartender. "Oh, shit. You didn't know?"

My head gets heavy, and I instinctively grip the edge of my stool for support, hoping that I've misunderstood him.

I watch a waitress deliver a hamburger with bright-orange melted cheese slipping out of the bun to a man sitting across the bar; I feel the vibration of a buzzer, then see its lights shining bright red as a young couple giddily jumps up to claim their table. Then two women laugh and proclaim their luck as they slide into the stools that were just abandoned.

"What are you saying? Did she tell you she was—" Nick stops, and out of the corner of my eye, I see his shoulders slump.

Please, God, don't let the bartender say the word.

I can't look at Nick. I'm afraid he'll confirm my fears.

The bartender leans in, oblivious. "Pregnant," he says easily, oblivious to the impact of his words.

Nick's head moves slowly up and down, and my insides are twisting so tight I can barely breathe.

"You didn't hear this from me, okay? But when her husband got up to use the bathroom, she told me the smell of the shrimp he ordered was making her sick. So of course, I asked what was up with that. Like were they bad? Because we make an amazing shrimp cocktail here!" He waves his arm covered in hemp bracelets behind him, where the kitchen presumably is.

I nod to encourage him to keep going, because I have to hear every word of what he has to say. If I don't, I know I'll talk myself out of believing it. And as much as it hurts—as in, feels like someone is punching me in the stomach over and over again—these are things I need to hear. I came here for the truth, no matter how much it might tear me apart.

"She tells me she'd been feeling sick to her stomach and had already made up enough excuses for why she'd been so nauseated. I remember thinking that was weird. That she couldn't tell her husband what was up, but I didn't say that. You know, a bartender's job is to listen. So

I quickly pulled the shrimp cocktail away, offering to replace it with something else. Her big eyes filled with tears when I did that, which totally tripped me out. I was like, what is *going on* with this chick? Then she asked me where the nearest drugstore was, and I was like, whoa, now I know."

"You think she wanted to get some Tums?" I ask, although I'm quite sure that's not what Dylan wanted.

"Nah, dude. You can buy those next door at the gift shop. Which is what I told her. That's when she told me she was worried she might be pregnant. But then her dude came back, and she acted like nothing had happened. It was a trip."

"My God," Nick says.

I watch the man across the bar eat a bite of his cheeseburger, lick his fingertips, and take a long drink of his beer. I hear the bleached-blonde woman with the worn face snarkily remark from the stool beside me that there are cuter men at Duke's. I look up, and our bartender has moved on to take someone's order. As if he hasn't just wrecked me.

But really, how could he know that I couldn't give my husband a child, so he found someone who could? That the wound inside of me has never had a chance to heal because it has been ripped open again and again with each negative pregnancy test, with every fight between James and me, and now with the words, *she might be pregnant?* On the outside, I give nothing away. But inside I scream and I cry and I pound my fists. Like the baby I could never give him.

The bartender walks back over to us and picks up right where he left off. "So crazy, right? But we hear it all, man," he says, then turns to make a drink, still having no idea of the bomb he's just dropped on us.

CHAPTER TWENTY-TWO

"Jacks! Wait!"

I sprint away from the sound of Nick's voice, my feet cutting through the sand, my sandals dangling precariously from my hand. The thing is, I can't wait. I need to get as far away as possible from the news I've just heard. Maybe, if I keep moving, I can outrun the truth. Dylan had been pregnant. I can't deny the possibility that James might have been the father. And my biggest fear has been confirmed: my own omission may have been the glue that bound their relationship.

I trip over a pile of flip-flops that lie in the sand awaiting their owners—the sunset booze cruises just docked on shore. My right knee slides into the sand, and I quickly manage to heave myself back up.

It's amazing how agile desperation can make you.

I glance back to see Nick jogging behind me. There's no doubt his pace is deliberately slow, that his strong legs barely feel the burn that mine already do. But, wisely, he keeps his distance as I barrel toward the black rocks on the north end of Ka'anapali Beach. We both know I'm running myself into a corner. That he will catch up to me.

It's hard to let go of who you thought you were. Take me, for instance. I've always considered myself a decent person. I teach the youth of America. I like animals and babies. I cheered when the Supreme Court legalized gay marriage. But I now realize that those were the easy choices. That just because you aren't a complete asshole that hates kids and kittens, it doesn't mean that you're *good*. It simply means that you aren't *bad*. And it's that in-between area that gets tricky. I'd never thought James and I had a *bad* marriage. He didn't verbally abuse me; I didn't nag him. He'd only gotten physical once. But had it been good? Not really. We existed somewhere in between. In the middle of the screaming and the love.

I begin to slow down as I approach the black rocky peninsula that marks my dead end, unless I want to attempt to scale the wet, slippery, sharp rocks—which will definitely not end well. The sun has just set, and darkness begins to sweep the ocean. I take a left turn and walk into it, the waves lapping my calves. A few steps farther, and the water teases the hem of my yellow sundress, the one that James told me made my skin sparkle. If you really think about it, his compliment didn't make sense. Eyes could sparkle, but skin? But James had a way of romancing his words, of making the false seem true.

I feel Nick's hand grab mine when the water reaches my torso.

"Jacks." He tugs me gently. I'm taking a postsunset swim in my perky dress after I discover my husband got his mistress pregnant, and Nick doesn't know what to do. I don't blame him. I don't know what to do either. Do I keep moving into the deeper water, hoping the searing pain I'm feeling dissipates as my head goes under? That the silence under the sea will quiet my demons?

"Jacks! Come on!"

I shake my head as the first tears hit my chin. "I'm not ready." And it's true. I'm not. In my mind, the shore is where reality lives. Here, in the sea, I still have the choice to float away, to leave all this bullshit behind. I shake my hand free from his and take two steps toward the skyline—the lingering orange and red hues from the sunset muted. The sky will be completely black soon. I'm ready for the darkness to consume me.

Nick curls his arms tightly under my legs and pushes forcefully through the water toward the beach. I struggle, but I have no chance of breaking free; I'm no match for his strong grip.

Nick puts his mouth to my ear as he carries me. "Shh," he whispers over and over, the same chant I used to calm my nephew when he was an infant. I'd pace the living room as my sister slept, her exhaustion finally forcing her to call and ask for my help. I'd rocked him back and forth until he calmed. In Nick's hold, I'm much like my nephew, succumbing to the calming sounds, losing my will to struggle and becoming limp as he sets me gently on the sand.

I wrap my hands around my knees, licking my salty tears, and Nick and I sit side by side on the sand for quite a while, listening to the soft waves lapping onto the shore. Finally I work up the courage to ask Nick the one question I need an answer to. "How can you be so sure the baby wasn't yours?" After the bartender told us Dylan had been pregnant, Nick assured me he wasn't the father.

Nick takes a long pause, running his wet hand through his hair, leaving a trail of sand at his hairline. "We hadn't had sex in at least two months."

"Oh," I say, thinking about my sex life with James. We used to have sex every few days, but it had slowed in the past two years. Still, we never went more than a few weeks, no matter how bad things were. It was that addiction we had to each other. That need to be physically intertwined even when we were emotionally fragmented. "I had no idea."

"It's not something you brag about." Nick looked away.

"Does it make it any easier?" I ask gently, feeling terrible that I wish it had been his and not James's. Because it would make things better for me.

"Because the baby wasn't mine?"

I nod.

"I don't know. I think I'm just numb at this point. And I've got to keep my shit together right now—especially when you're out there pulling a Virginia Woolf."

I laugh softly. "Don't take this the wrong way, but I didn't think you were a literary type."

"There's a lot you don't know about me yet." He offers me a sad smile, and I reach over and grab his hand, sand rubbing between our palms.

"So, tell me then."

He thinks for a minute. "I make a mean Italian wedding soup. I broke my leg skiing when I was nineteen. And I *do* love to read—everything from Stephen King to Hemingway."

"Well, for the record, I wasn't trying to drown myself out there." I stare out at the dark water. "I didn't have a plan. I just wanted to get away from this." I wave my hand in the air, not sure what I'm pointing at. Him. Me. The hotel. Maui. All of it.

"I know," Nick says, somehow understanding what I mean even when I'm not sure I do. "And I'm sorry."

"For what?"

"I convinced you to come. If you hadn't, you wouldn't know these things. You wouldn't have to go through this."

"It's not your fault. Maybe this is how it had to be. Maybe we needed to know."

I let go of his hand and lie back on the sand, letting the cool granules overtake my wet skin. The stars are beginning to emerge, and I trace my finger around the Big Dipper, remembering when James and I lay on this beach on our honeymoon and did the same thing. "It's right there," he said, grabbing my hand and guiding it. "How can you not see it?"

"I do! I do!" I laughed and pointed up. But I hadn't seen the stars connect the same way he had. I just didn't want to disappoint him. I hated to do that. Disappoint people.

I close my eyes to turn the stars off. They know too much.

"Hey," I hear Nick say.

I open my eyes and stare up at him.

"You look cold. Your arms are covered in goose bumps."

Suddenly I realize how cold I am. I sit up and wrap my arms around my knees.

I feel Nick's arm around my shoulder. "This okay? Or does it feel like that terrible hug?" he asks, and I want to laugh, to go back in time to when we were sitting on the deck of my hotel room with no clue about Dylan's baby. But my sobs. They're sitting so high up in my throat that it burns to push them down. So instead we sit in silence.

"It's not our fault, you know," he finally says. "This. Them. The pregnancy. These were choices they made, for whatever reason. This isn't about you—or me."

I could nod and pretend I agree. I could let Nick believe his own words. But I can't. I have to tell someone.

"You're right. It isn't about you. But it is about me," I say.

Nick shakes his head vehemently. "You can't blame yourself."

"Actually I can," I say, and begin to tell him why.

~

I'd kept a critical piece of information from James while we were dating. Something he had a right to know, but that I didn't tell him because he might not have married me if I had.

When I was twenty-one, I was diagnosed with severe endometriosis. I'd been bleeding abnormally and finally went to see my ob-gyn, who, after an ultrasound, grimly delivered the news: scar tissue had developed around my ovaries and could keep eggs from being released. Pregnancy would be difficult. Unlikely.

"How unlikely?" I'd asked. I was so young. At an age when *not* getting pregnant was the priority. I wasn't that concerned. My only experience with babies had been when I'd babysat. And all I remembered was drool, poop, and crying.

Dr. Reynolds narrowed her green eyes. I'll never forget their color—like moss on the back of a wet rock. "You might have a twenty percent chance of conceiving."

"So I have a twenty percent chance?" I was naive. Twenty percent seemed doable. Plus, my reproductive prospects at that time were limited to a guy I'd met at a dive bar in Redondo Beach who used the word *legit* to answer almost any question. Back then, a family seemed so far away. So surreal.

James brought up having kids on our first date. I'd smiled and thought how different he was from the other men I'd dated recently—whose noses scrunched up if the word *baby* was mentioned, even in passing. He brought it up more seriously the night after he proposed. We were lying in bed, me wrapped around him. At that time I was like a sponge, desperate to soak up every drop he gave me. I'd sleep with my body pressed up against his each night, our legs twisted like a pretzel.

"So, when do you think we should start?"

"Start what?" I asked. Things I thought he'd respond with: training for the 5K he'd mentioned, getting our real estate licenses to flip houses because that was all the rage back then, or saving for a trip to Italy we'd talked about.

What he actually responded with: "A baby." Then before I could respond, he continued on. "How many kids do you want? I'd like three, maybe four."

The conversation with my doctor came rushing back. The way she'd looked at me like I didn't understand the seriousness of what she was saying—that there was an 80 percent chance I *couldn't* have a baby. The way I'd looked at her like she didn't understand how young I was, how that wasn't something I was even thinking about.

I was so devastatingly ignorant.

But now my future husband wanted to know *when* I could make him a father. Not *if*. He kept going, telling me about how he wanted to give his mom a bunch of grandkids.

And I wanted nothing more than to do just that—I was dying to see if our brood would inherit his brilliant-green eyes, the deep dimple on his right cheek, the shallow one on his left. Or would they possess my dark hair and quiet intensity? I felt desperate to know.

"Oh!" I responded in surprise.

James's eyes narrowed. "I know that's a lot of kids. But you'd be a great mom, and I'm going to be a dad who's totally invested. I want to coach their sports, teach them to swim, everything."

My silence must have concerned him, because he grabbed my hands and gave me the most serious look I'd seen from him at that point. "I should have told you something sooner. I had a younger brother who died when I was six. He had leukemia. My mom was going to have more children, but after he passed away she just couldn't do it. She was so afraid of losing another child. And my dad, he was so upset. We're Costa Rican. We have big families. My dad has five brothers. I have so many cousins, I forget their names." He laughed gently. "I just feel compelled to continue our bloodline for him."

I was beginning to see the downside of a whirlwind romance. In the few months we'd been together, we'd been busy falling in love and having fun, not discussing important details like this.

And now, after he'd told me his heart-wrenching story, how could I share mine? Because that would have been the time to do it. If I'd been honest, if I'd just repeated the three words my doctor had said to me—*20 percent chance*—would he have scooped me up in his arms and told me those odds were good enough for him?

I'll never know.

I guess I was afraid he wouldn't say that. That he'd leave me. And I loved him. God, how I loved him. And I wanted to be his wife. And I wanted to be a mom. And there was a chance. Maybe not for multiple kids, but at least for one. Because I could be that one in five.

And if I wasn't, I thought the longer we were together, the more it upped *my* chances—not necessarily of having a baby, but of keeping him. Because I loved him in a way I'd never loved anyone. He got under my skin in the best and worst ways. So instead of telling him what I'd heard as I sat on my ob-gyn's table in my paper robe, I said, "Four kids sounds wonderful."

Because it was true; it would be.

But we didn't have four kids. The only *four* we experienced was the number of years that went by without children.

It was New Year's Eve when I finally told him. We'd been married for a little over three years at that point. Lots of unprotected sex had been had. There was no baby. James wanted answers. And for some reason, at 11:58 p.m. as one year was about to turn into the next, I decided to give them to him. I couldn't start off another year with lies.

Let's just say we didn't kiss at midnight. Or for a while after that.

James was so angry. I'd never seen him that mad before. He called me a liar. He said I'd trapped him. That he'd have never married me if he'd known. I cried. And when I screamed at him that he'd only wanted me for my offspring, he told me I was the biggest mistake he'd ever made, and if it wouldn't cost him half his 401k, he'd have divorced me. He shattered the mirror hanging on the wall next to me with his fist, and I retreated into a stunned silence. And suddenly our argument shifted into what he'd done instead of what I'd done. And I let it. He finally apologized profusely, literally down on his knees, and swore to me he was sorry if he'd scared me. That he wasn't violent. That he didn't mean what he said. I chose to believe him.

Our marriage was never the same again. We were a broken version of what we'd once been. I'd betrayed him. He'd told me I was a mistake while shards of glass splintered in the air around me. Neither of us could undo the terrible thing we'd done. And he changed. The man I'd said my vows to was replaced by some other guy, a guy I didn't like very much.

But I tolerated him. Because I'd made him like that. The temper. I had given it a reason to take up residence in our relationship. The holes he made in the wall with his fist? The broken objects he smashed in a rage? The angry words he couldn't take back? Those things represented the children he'd never have.

We went to specialists—reproductive endocrinologists, holistic healers, psychics. We tried acupuncture, hypnotherapy, in vitro fertilization.

And with each negative pregnancy test, the space between us grew wider. He was adamant about not wanting to adopt. The children needed to be *his*. One of the times we fought about it was when I printed a bunch of information about international adoption off the Internet. He ripped it to shreds. I fell to the floor, picking up the pieces of paper, shutting my eyes and trying to conjure the man I'd fallen in love with. The one who used to bring me two pints of my favorite ice cream on his way home from work every Friday night because he knew one wouldn't be enough. The man who'd written me a poem and recited it to me on our second anniversary. The husband who'd once told me when we were playing one of those what-if games that he'd still love me even if I lost all my hair in a freak accident.

On the last morning I saw him, our recurring argument happened again. It came up every 28 days or 280 days, depending on when he chose to wield it like a weapon in his arsenal. And that particular morning he'd found the test in the trash can. I thought I'd buried it deep enough down under tissues. But I'd been in a daze when I tossed it. Because I'd been so sure that I *finally* might be pregnant. I'd been in this fertility yoga class for a few months. And I felt different, so different that I actually bought a test instead of waiting for my period to show up as it always did. But then, after I'd peed, there it was, that single pink line.

And I'd been so mad at myself for telling him. For letting him hope with me. I'd shared the changes I'd felt in my body—the tender breasts, the cramps in my lower abdomen. And I had felt all those things. But they'd been phantom pregnancy symptoms. A surprisingly common occurrence in women who are waiting to take a test, I'd learned when I looked it up. After I'd stared at the white plastic in my hand, my hopes crushed when that single pink line appeared. I couldn't bring myself to tell him. To confess that my body had failed us once more. But I'd planned to—when the time was right.

He came flying into the bedroom with his white knuckles around that stick.

"Goddamn it, Jacks! I thought you were sure this time! When were you going to tell me it was negative?"

I sat up tall in the bed and tried to collect the right words. That I hadn't told him because I couldn't bear to disappoint him again. That when that lonely pink line appeared, I had lain on the bathroom floor and given up. On myself. On the notion that we could create a baby together. On us. And I was terrified that he would see it all on my face. So I had said nothing.

"James, I was going to tell you . . ."

"Enough with the fucking lies!"

Like an allergic reaction to his roaring voice, tears spilled from my eyes.

"How could you do this to me? You were so sure. I even told my mom there might be a chance."

I flung the sheets back from my body and got up on my knees on the mattress, absorbing his words. His pain.

Looking back, I wish that I'd thrown my arms around his neck and told him I was just as disappointed. That I had felt a swishing in my abdomen when my period hadn't shown on the twenty-eighth day, and that I told myself that flutter could be the child that would bring us salvation—from my deceit, from his anger. But instead of comforting him with my own intense sadness, I attacked.

"To *you?*" I waved my arms across my abdomen. "I'm in this too, in case you've forgotten. You will never understand how much I suffer every single time it doesn't happen. And I'm sorry. So very sorry I didn't tell you before we got married that there is so much scar tissue around my ovaries that this whole area is most likely shot." I pointed at my stomach again, my cheeks burning from a mix of anger and embarrassment.

"No. I told you. I got over the initial lie. I'm still pissed at you because you fucking sold it. You sold me that twenty percent like you were a goddamn used-car salesman. You made me think it was a real, actual possibility."

His words sliced through me. Every syllable, another sharp cut.

I wanted to believe it was a possibility.

"The doctor didn't say it was *impossible.*"

"But she also didn't say it was very likely."

"Twenty . . . percent—it's still something." I was crying so hard, I could barely get the words out.

"Enough with statistics, Jacks. Enough! If someone told you that you had an eighty percent chance of dying, would you feel good about those odds?"

I glared at him. Searched his dark pupils for the man I'd thought I'd married. But his eyes were cold, his jaw set, his stance like that of a bear about to pounce. And in that moment, I was convinced he might actually hate me.

"Are we ever going to get past this?" I asked him, my voice soft and measured. This argument had become an endless circle, a wicked carousel that neither of us knew how to escape. It was true—I'd let my emotions cloud my judgment when I met James. His love for me had made me feel invincible. And that 20 percent had felt conquerable. But I had been so wrong. About myself. About him. About us. And I was so, so sorry about that. But I didn't know how to explain that to him. How to say it without sounding hollow. "You're going to have to choose to stop resenting me if we're ever going to make it. Because we can't go on like this."

James looked at me, his eyes flickering, and I held his gaze—I had to see what was really behind those beautiful eyes, the ones that had instantly engaged me so long ago. We stared at each other without saying anything until, finally, he broke away and looked down.

"It's very possible that I may never get over it." He forced on a pair of pants, then a shirt, not bothering to tuck it in, then grabbed his roller bag and flew down the hallway as I tried to holler after him, his words having cut me so close that I could barely breathe.

I've played back that morning so many times, wishing I could change things—that I could wrap my arms around him instead of hurling insults, that I could have chosen differently so he didn't walk out the door that day with resentment burning in his heart.

But learning about Dylan has made me face the reality that I'd lost James long before that argument. He had slipped away from me once and for all on that New Year's Eve. He may not have cheated on me until several years later, but the fuse had been sitting there, waiting to be lit.

Nick doesn't speak right away when I finish my story. He may not understand why Dylan would stray, but now he knows why James did.

"It's still not your fault," he says after several beats.

"How can you say that?"

"He could have left, Jacks. If he was that upset about your lie—which, by the way, I think is a pretty understandable one to tell—he could have divorced you. He didn't need to have an affair, to get another woman pregnant."

"Maybe it was his *fuck you* to me," I say.

"From what you've told me, he wasn't an evil genius. He was a guy who didn't appreciate what he had but was also too much of a coward to let you go. If he really loved you, you guys could have adopted children."

I thought of his family's zealous pride in their Costa Rican heritage. How whenever we were with his mother, grandchildren—or the lack of them—was always a topic of conversation. She'd mention how many kids James's uncles had between them. Eighteen! How out of place she felt at family gatherings as she listened to all the other grandmothers brag about their star soccer player grandsons or their granddaughters who were learning to cook paella. James would simply glare at me as his mom rambled on. I once overheard her asking James if he planned to divorce me if I couldn't conceive. "It's not too late for you. You're still young; you could meet a nice young *childbearing* woman," she said, and I walked away before I could hear his answer.

I shake my head. "That's not how they do it in his family."

Nick sighs. "Then that was on him. You guys had options. James was just too much of a prick to consider them."

"And now he's dead."

Nick pauses before responding. "I'm sorry that he hurt you. But if we leave this island with one thing, it's that I want you to know that Dylan and James were adults who made their own choices. We could beat ourselves up about the things we did that may have pushed them away, but they chose to betray us. That's on *them*, not us."

Intellectually I know he's right. But my heart will always believe my lie pushed James away.

"Fuck them," Nick whispers. He's huddled close, his face almost touching mine.

His proximity feels right. After all, I just shared my deepest regret. It seems fitting he's as close to my heart as he can be.

CHAPTER TWENTY-THREE

DYLAN—BEFORE

Dylan sat on the toilet in the ABC drugstore bathroom and held her hand to her mouth. She'd been pretty sure the two pink lines would appear, announcing that her life was about to change. But she was still surprised by how intensely the realization that she had a baby growing inside of her took her breath away. By how torn she felt—both deliriously happy that she would share a part of James that his wife didn't, and scared shitless that he might not be as thrilled about the news as she was.

She knew James wanted children. Once, when they were drunk, she'd worked up the courage to ask him. She played mind games like that sometimes. Extracting the kind of information from him she would if they were in a real relationship and the answers would actually impact her. But when he'd told her that he did want kids, her heart sank sharply. What if his wife got pregnant? Would he stay married to her? He didn't elaborate, and Dylan had fallen silent, shocked at how much his words had hurt. That had been an opportunity for him to say, *Yes! With you!*

And she feared, for the billionth time, that she'd never be more than the girl he hid behind closed doors.

But at least she knew he wanted to be a father. She just didn't know if he'd want to be a dad to *this* baby.

Dylan put her hand on her abdomen and wondered when she'd first feel the little life move inside of her. When she'd first hear the heartbeat. She was embarrassed to admit she didn't know much about being pregnant—her only friend with kids was Katie, and they'd reconnected after she'd had her babies. But as soon as Dylan got home, she'd buy that book about what to expect and go see her doctor. She'd get all of her questions answered. Although there was one she knew only James could give her—would he be with her at that appointment?

If he weren't there, Dylan was convinced it would be because of his wife. They had a strange marriage, in Dylan's opinion. Sometimes when he spoke of Jacqueline, his mouth would twist in a weird way, his voice would take on an edge, and his body would tense. But other times he seemed almost melancholy, hinting at the better times they'd once shared, or recounting a positive anecdote about her. It was almost like he saw his wife as two different people. And Dylan wondered if she was replacing the one James didn't like, and if somehow she and Jacqueline made up the *one* woman he wanted. But separately, would Dylan be enough? Would this child swing the pendulum in her favor? Dylan only knew one thing for sure: this baby was going to speak the words she never could and make James decide between her and his wife. That was the only way this relationship could continue. That meant there was no hiding anymore.

She'd first thought she might be pregnant on the morning before they left for Maui. She'd been feeling run-down and squeamish for the past week—her lower back aching at the end of her shift, her belly swirling when she served the huevos rancheros. She'd thought it was the flu and had been panicked—she was counting down the days to her vacation with James, and because Dylan believed in signs, she was terrified that getting sick and missing the trip would be the universe's way of telling her that they weren't meant to be. But then, as she was packing for Maui, she'd thrown up, and as she'd knelt by her toilet, she'd noticed a box of tampons on the counter and couldn't remember the last time she'd had her period. But she'd been irregular before. Plus, she felt nauseated and had a terrible headache and was exhausted—all symptoms of the flu. At that moment, she was more concerned she might miss the trip entirely. She worried about that a lot—the price she'd have to pay for her actions down the road.

And now she wondered if her baby would too.

She'd asked James about karma once. They'd been having breakfast in bed after she'd met him in downtown LA the night before. That was Dylan's favorite time with James—the mornings. She loved the feel of his arm wrapped tightly around her waist as he slept. She always woke before him so she could listen to him breathing, wanting to cherish every moment before he went off to live the part of his life that she didn't belong in.

James had been telling her a story about getting a flat tire and waiting two hours for help. Then the spare had popped on the way to the mechanic. "It felt like the universe was conspiring against me!" he'd said, a smile creeping across his lips.

"Do you think it was? Because of us?" Dylan asked. She had begun to read significance into each poor tip she received, long line she had to sit in, anything—big or small—that didn't go her way. She worried she was being punished.

"What? No way!" James had laughed before pausing when he saw the look on her face. "Do you really think that?"

"Sometimes," Dylan said. But what she was thinking was, *All the time.* "What we're doing is wrong. Don't you think at some point this will catch up with us?" Dylan motioned toward the bedsheets.

James sighed. "Dyl, people make questionable choices all the time, but it doesn't mean bad things happen to them as a result."

Dylan had thought about those words a lot after he said them. Was that how he saw her? As a questionable choice? But, like so many times before, she was too timid to push him to elaborate. So scared of saying the wrong thing and causing him to leave her. Wanting to be his refuge, not more of what he had at home.

James had continued. "Look at all the greedy politicians and executives. They do terrible things every day and only get richer and more powerful." He pulled her in for a kiss, and Dylan tasted his coffee on her lips before he said, "You worry too much."

"I guess the universe makes exceptions for true love." Dylan laughed but studied James's face intently. It had been four months, and he hadn't told her that he loved her yet. There were days she was sure that he did, like when he sent her soup when she was sick or when she told him that she was cutting costs and had to stop buying her favorite soy milk latte at Starbucks, and he'd loaded one hundred dollars into the account on her phone while she was in the bathroom. Those things meant love, didn't they?

But James's eyes betrayed nothing. "Maybe it does," he'd said, and pushed their breakfast tray aside, pulling her body toward his.

∼

Dylan got up from the toilet and splashed water on her face. She knew she'd been in the bathroom too long, that James would come looking for her if she didn't hurry up. She struggled to remember when she'd had her last period, finally recalling Easter brunch—how the new hostess had slammed her with too many tables, and Dylan had bitten her head off, then run to the restroom shortly after and realized why she was being such a bitch. That was over two months ago. But she was always careful when she had sex.

Except.

That night she'd met James in Ventura. It had taken her hours to get there in traffic, the cars on the 405 and 101 freeways an endless parade of lights. Dylan had pulled down the rearview mirror every few minutes to check her makeup. To brush her hair. The minutes before she saw James were always the best and the worst. The anticipation. The anxiety. It melded together until she laid eyes on him—then it fell away.

They'd found a little Spanish tapas bar near the beach and sat outside. It was spring, but the weather hadn't quite caught up with the season, and it was chilly even with the heater. They'd feasted on small plates of stuffed olives, *croquetas*, and prawns in olive oil. Dylan had never tasted food so good and loved how he took the time to explain each dish to her. They'd walked next door where an eighties cover band was playing, James making a joke that she hadn't even been born when those songs were on the radio. They'd danced until they could hardly stand, then stumbled back to James's hotel room, him sliding his hand up her skirt in the elevator, kissing her so deeply they missed their floor. Once they got to the room, he'd thrown her down on the bed and hiked her skirt over her hips. She turned to face him, but he twirled her back around hard and pulled her panties aside. Dylan had been shocked— James had never been this dominant with her before. It felt dangerous and selfish, but also exhilarating. She found herself wanting him to tell her what to do, who to be—wanting him to own her. And in his rush, James hadn't put on a condom.

After, as they lay in bed, James was back to the James she knew, sweetly cuddling her, blanketing her bare shoulder with soft kisses. "Sorry, I got a little carried away there."

Dylan laughed. "You think?"

"Did it scare you?"

"No," Dylan said quietly. "I was surprised, but I liked it."

"I was just watching you dancing in the bar, your skirt swinging up and giving little hints as to what might be under there, seeing the way the other guys were looking at you. It was so hot, I couldn't control myself when I got you alone. I wanted you to know you belonged to me."

Dylan took a deep breath. "I do."

～

Dylan startled at the sound of the knock at the door. "Dylan, are you in there?"

"Yes, sorry, I'll be out in a minute!" she said as she frantically wrapped the test in toilet paper and stuffed it in the bottom of her straw purse.

"Sorry," she said as she swung the door open.

"Still having stomach problems?" James asked.

"Yes, but not too bad."

"You sure?" he said, and took her hand. "You gonna be okay?"

Dylan searched James's face. "I'm going to be just fine."

CHAPTER TWENTY-FOUR

DYLAN—BEFORE

"You got us a Jeep?" Dylan leaned against the cherry-red door and raised an eyebrow at James.

"I did. You like it?" James twirled the key around his finger proudly.

Dylan tried to smile, but all she could think about was how bumpy the ride was going to be. How the sharp twists and turns of the road to Hana were going to make her more nauseated than she already was. She'd hauled herself out of bed this morning, running the water and quietly gagging over the toilet so James wouldn't hear. All she'd wanted to do was sleep all day. But she also understood that this time with James was precious, and she wanted to savor every minute.

"Oh, shit. I should've asked you first. I just assumed." He turned away, obviously disappointed. He'd been talking about this Hana adventure for weeks. The Jeep was part of the fantasy for him.

"No, it's going to be great," Dylan said quickly. "I'm just going to need this." She grabbed the Dodgers hat off his head and put it on hers. She took a drink of the overpriced bottle of water she'd purchased at the coffee kiosk by the front desk, trying to distract herself from the acid swirling in her stomach.

"You sure this is okay, that *you're* okay?" James squinted at her. "We don't have to do this."

"Totally fine!" Dylan sealed her lie with a grin. Earlier, after James had left to get the rental car, Dylan had run back to the bathroom and vomited twice—unable to keep down the orange juice or the oatmeal with dried fruit that had seemed like such a good idea when she'd ordered it.

James put his arms around her neck. "Good. I thought it would feel great on a day like this," he said, looking up at the cloudless sky. "Besides, now you'll be the hot girl in the Jeep. And I'll be the lucky guy who gets to sit next to you."

Dylan blushed at his compliment, forgetting her sick stomach for a moment.

"This dress, by the way. It makes your skin sparkle."

Dylan poked her finger between James's ribs. "Okay, now you've gone too far—you can't be serious with that line! So. Cheesy. Has that actually worked on someone before?" Dylan laughed. She had a voracious appetite for James's compliments, but sometimes he walked a fine line between making her feel special and sounding like a bad *Saturday Night Live* skit. She always told herself it was part of his charm and pushed away the inauthentic nature of his words.

James laughed and pulled her into him.

"What's so funny?" Dylan tilted her head back and let him kiss her deeply.

He tucked a strand of her hair behind her ear. "I love that you just said that to me. Where's that sassy Dylan been hiding? I'd love to see more of her." His hand moved down to her hem, and he teased her by putting one of his fingers under the white fabric and stroking her thigh.

"You would, huh?" Dylan pressed herself into him and felt him get hard. She loved how she could turn him on so easily. Nick was so much more intense and dramatic about what making love meant. He'd never have done it here, in the parking lot of the hotel. He would have needed them to be home, in the bedroom, where couples having "sexual intercourse" belonged. For James, having sex was like an animal instinct. She knew he'd fuck her right there on the side of the Jeep if she'd let him. She wondered if that desire would change after she told him about the baby.

"What's wrong?"

Dylan hadn't realized she'd stopped kissing him. "Nothing."

"Dyl. Come on. I know something's been on your mind. You seemed upset last night. Tell me what's *really* going on in there." James touched her head lightly.

Even though it had only been less than a day since she found out she was pregnant for sure, the secret she was literally carrying inside of her felt too big to contain for much longer. She studied the dark-green flecks in his eyes, the way the skin between them knotted as he watched her, and contemplated telling him. Would he be happy? Disappointed? She put her arms around his waist. "James—"

"Get a room!" A few teenage boys with a tanned faces and sunbleached hair leaned out the window of a passing pickup truck, the back piled high with surfboards.

Dylan jerked back.

"Dyl—"

The moment was lost. What had she been thinking anyway—about to give him life-changing news right here? She needed to think, to plan the right time to tell him. "I'm fine. I told you. I caught some sort of bug, and I think it's still lingering, but I'm okay."

James frowned. "Promise me?"

Dylan crossed her fingers behind her back. "Promise."

"Okay, good." James opened the door and motioned her in. "It's getting late, so we might end up driving some of the road at night. But it will all be part of the adventure. You ready?"

Dylan swallowed hard at the thought of maneuvering the narrow roads in the dark. But she didn't say that to James. Instead she said, "Always," and climbed in, pulling her seat belt across her chest.

As James drove them toward the town of Paia, where they planned to stop at the Kuau general store and stock up for their drive, Dylan found herself thankful they had the top down, grateful for the wind that made it nearly impossible to talk. Plus, the fresh air was helping with the nausea, so she closed her eyes and breathed in as much as her nostrils would allow and let it lull her to sleep.

$\sim$

"Dylan?"

Dylan opened her eyes.

"We just got to Paia. You fell asleep." James leaned over and kissed her forehead. "I think you needed it. You tossed and turned all night."

"I feel better," Dylan said, thankful it was the truth. "I'm starving."

"This place makes the best paninis on this side of the island, according to our concierge. But first, I wanted to show you this." He motioned behind her.

"What is it?" she said as she turned.

"You're looking at the longest surfboard fence in the world!"

"It's incredible." Dylan got out of the Jeep. "I'm going to take a selfie!" she called over her shoulder.

Dylan leaned back and positioned her phone above her head, smiling brightly. "Hey, get over here—my arm's not long enough to get the boards in," she yelled, just as she lost her balance and fell backward, causing several of the boards to shake slightly under her weight while an angry brown-and-white Akita barked behind the fence.

"Come on now. All we need is for you to knock all these over like dominoes!" James laughed, grabbing the phone from her. "And what's with wanting a selfie anyway?" James said as he took the picture. "You're not even on Facebook!"

They walked into the small general store, and Dylan's mouth watered at the fresh quinoa salad in the deli case. She remembered the oatmeal, hoping she could get it right this time. "Maybe I'll join someday," she said as she grabbed a bottle of coconut water and a loaf of banana bread.

James wrinkled his nose at the black- and-blueberry chia-seed pudding and grabbed a log of goat cheese and a stick of salami instead. "Oh, really? I thought you said social media was lame." He pulled a *Road to Hana* CD guide from a rack, then turned toward the pretty cashier with long black hair flowing down her back in even waves and piercing dark eyes. "Where do you keep the wine?" he asked. She pointed to the back of the store, and he headed that way, motioning Dylan to follow.

"*Nick* thought social media was lame," Dylan said as James debated between a cabernet and a pinot. "I had an account when I met him, but he asked me to deactivate it." Dylan rolled her eyes.

"Well, I hate to side with the guy, but I really don't get it—why I'm supposed to care about what some person I went to high school with thinks about the presidential election."

Dylan shook her head. "That's not the problem he had with it."

"What was it then? The cat videos?" James laughed.

"Can we change the subject, please?" Dylan frowned, recalling Nick's words. *I don't like other men looking at pictures of you. It's creepy.*

James threw his arms up. "You brought him up!"

"I know. Sorry." Dylan stared at their surfboard selfie on the screen of her phone. She liked how she and James looked together. His olive complexion and dark hair complemented her lighter skin tone and blonde locks. She wondered which of his physical traits their baby would inherit. "It's just that Nick didn't get why *I* wanted to be on it. I really liked being able to share my life with the people I care about." Dylan pointed to their selfie. She knew she was testing James—that she wanted to know what he'd think of Dylan sharing *their* life. If there was ever going to be a time when she could.

Dylan felt herself getting hopeful as she waited for James to respond and tried to force it down. The thing was, she'd convinced herself this trip to Hawaii didn't need to mean anything. Even as they'd let people believe they were newlyweds. And maybe she'd been lying to herself all along anyway, but that was *before*. *Before* the pink lines had appeared. Now it wasn't up to her how to feel. This child inside of her made everything different, whether she liked it or not. But she didn't want the baby to influence James. She wanted him to choose her before he knew she was pregnant with his child.

"Hey, belleza," James said lightly as they walked out of the store. But even before he uttered the next words, she sensed what he was about to say. "Even if you do join Facebook again, you know you couldn't post about *us*, right?"

Dylan felt a sharp sting in her chest and looked away from him quickly so he wouldn't see her disappointment. She wasn't moving out of mistress status anytime soon.

"I'm sorry. You know I wish you could, but obviously it's just not possible. You get that, right?" James tilted her face back toward his. "We want to stay in control of things. Not get sloppy."

Dylan sucked in a long breath and made a decision to push her sadness away. She leaned against the Jeep and curved her lips into a wide smile. "I totally get it." Then she glanced around before pressing herself into James, unsnapping his jeans and sticking her hand inside his waistband. She thought of the most seductive and sassy thing she could say. "You're my dirty little secret—just the way I like you."

CHAPTER TWENTY-FIVE

"Stop the car!" I scream over the wind blowing hard through the Jeep, gripping the door handle with all of my strength. When Nick doesn't hear me, I jerk on his T-shirt and repeat myself.

He turns the steering wheel left and stops abruptly in a turnout overlooking a deep, tree-lined canyon that backs up to a rocky beach. It looks so far away that it feels like another island.

I fling the door open and rush out, sucking in short breaths, pressing my hands against my thighs. I open my mouth to speak, but I can barely get words out. "I think . . . I'm . . . hyperventilating."

Nick gets out and comes around quickly, taking my arm to swiftly guide me to a concrete table and bench that back up to a short stone wall. "Here, sit down. Hold your breath for as long as you can."

I widen my eyes at him, panting like a dog, feeling light-headed.

"Trust me. This is what I do, okay?"

I comply, holding my breath for several seconds and finally releasing it.

"Better?" Nick asks, crouching in front of me and putting two fingers on my wrist. I nod.

"Your heart rate is slowing. But now I want you to breathe in and out through your nose, slowly."

After a few minutes, my breathing steadies, and he sits beside me. A lone tear runs down my cheek, and I let my body go limp into his side.

"Have you ever had a panic attack before?" Nick asks as he strokes my hair.

I think back to Beth finding me in my garage, keys dangling from my fingers while I leaned up against the bag of fertilizer, and nod.

"I'm sorry. This is my fault. I should have known this drive would be too much. That renting a Jeep was a bad idea."

"This isn't on you. I told you I could handle it. And I really thought I could. I'm just tired of being so weak." I start to stand, but my knees buckle beneath me. "Fuck," I mutter as Nick grabs my arm.

"Easy there," Nick says. "You've got nothing to prove to me."

"Why did this have to happen?" I whisper. "I'm just an elementary school teacher who used to think an exciting night was binge watching Netflix while eating chili-powder-seasoned popcorn. I know it sounds gross, but it's really good." I laugh slightly, and Nick frowns, then half smiles, clearly not sure how to react. "And now all these secrets. So much drama. My life has become a complete shit show!"

I breathe in again, slowly exhaling to please Nick. "I just don't get how life as you know it can change in an instant. Like, you think it's one thing, that you're a certain person. Did you know I'm the teacher who gets oddly excited when her end-of-the-year textbook count comes out right the first time? Who tears up when I have enough extra school supplies to donate to another country? Who is meticulous about separating the sad crayons, as I call them, from the ones I can feel good about giving to the art teacher?" I sigh. "I always took pride in my work, in my life. And now I feel like it's all been for nothing."

Nick shakes his head. "I wish I had an answer for you, for *us*. I see unfair things happen to good people every single day at work. And no matter how often it happens, I still can't figure out the reasoning behind the madness."

"You know what I've been thinking about? If I could go back to the last day I saw him. This time, when we fight, I'd give him a divorce and let him have his life. I'd let him live. Even if it was with her."

"Really?" Nick asks.

"Don't you ever wonder if they'd still be alive if we hadn't been so naive?"

Nick shakes his head. "I don't understand."

"If I'd bothered to question one damn thing, I'd have probably figured out he wasn't being honest. If I had confronted him, he could have confessed to me that he was in love with someone else. He could have left. I would have earned the right to hate him, to be fueled with anger and jealously and ugliness."

"And that's what you want? To be filled with all that negativity?"

"No, of course not," I say. "But then maybe they wouldn't have snuck off together. Maybe they wouldn't be dead. Even if I hated them both, they'd still be here to feel it." I waved my hand toward the tree-filled canyon below. "Not somewhere out there."

Nick stared at me intently, an unreadable look on his face. "Even if you had found out, and confronted him, there's no way of knowing if that would have saved their lives. I'm not sure there's anything you could have done to change what happened."

"How can you say that? I could have done a *million* things differently. I could have been honest with him about my endometriosis. I could have refused to fight with him the last time I saw him." I pause, my words catching in my throat. "I could have been a better wife," I whisper.

"Jacks, we could all be better. Better husbands, better wives, better sons and daughters. But the people who love us, the ones who truly care, they accept us, even if we aren't perfect. James could have forgiven you. Or he could have left you. He did neither. That is on him."

"But *she* was able to give him the one thing I couldn't. That baby didn't deserve to die that day. None of them did."

Nick tightens his grip around me, and I look up at him, my lip quivering so hard I have to bite it.

He puts his hand under my chin and tilts it up, using his thumb to wipe away my tears. It starts to rain lightly, the sky crying with me.

I close my eyes. This moment feels so raw, so real. And when you realize your life has been filled with more lies than you probably even know, you cling to any shred of honesty you can. So I allow Nick to close his mouth over mine, his lips soft and tentative.

The kiss feels different and unexpected. It's been years since I've kissed another man. I haven't memorized the curve of his jaw, the feel of his tongue. I lean in closer, our hearts beating hard against each other. I tell myself that I need Nick, and that he needs me, in a way no one would ever understand. Not my mom, who has never spent more than three nights away from my father. Or Beth. Even though she and Mark bicker constantly, they would walk across hot coals for each other. They wouldn't understand the way Nick's words feel like a life jacket that's been thrown to me right before I slip under the heavy current.

Nick wraps his hand around the back of my neck and presses his mouth harder against mine. I moan softly, the sound seemingly breaking the spell we're under.

Nick pulls away so fast it startles me. "We shouldn't be doing this," he says, moving a few inches away as if creating a physical distance will stop whatever it is we've become. "I'm sorry. I don't know what happened there."

"It's okay," I say, trying to separate the conflux of emotions I'm experiencing. Grief. Passion. Confusion.

"No—I shouldn't have done that. And here—of all places—my God." He cradles his face in his hands. "I just . . . I don't know what came over me."

The sky opens up, and the light drizzle that's been falling turns into a full downpour, but neither of us moves, the ground below us becoming slick.

"Nick—" I start to say more but stop because I don't have any words ready. As the water soaks me, I wait for my own moment of shock to wash over me. For rational thinking to override my irrational emotions. But it doesn't. That kiss was the most genuine feeling I've experienced since the police showed up at my door. As if it had finally righted the slant I'd been leaning into since James's death.

Nick looks up, his face tightening. "I'm so sorry, Jacks. I promise I won't ever take advantage of you like that again."

I bob my head up and down several times in agreement and hope he's lying to me.

CHAPTER TWENTY-SIX

JACKS—AFTER

"I don't think I can do this." Nick shifts away from me. It's subtle. The distance between us is barely noticeable, but it feels as vast as the canyon below. A moment ago we were pressed together into one; now we're two again.

The rain is pounding so hard that every drop is pricking the bare skin of my arms and legs. I wonder what he means. That he doesn't think he can continue the drive to Hana? Or can't continue with *me*? Or both? I say nothing and turn my head to shield my face from the downpour and hide the tears that are flowing again as I glance at the topless Jeep. The heavy rain is falling into it in thick sheets, and I'm not sure which would offer us more of a reprieve from the storm: the concrete bench we're sitting on or the Jeep. A lightning bolt cracks, making the decision for us.

"It's close," Nick yells as the thunder roars a moment later. He jumps up and grabs my hand, pulling me toward the car. "I need your help with this!" he shouts, the rain whipping his face as he jerks his arm toward the soft top that's retracted in the back. "It's too slippery to pull by myself."

I open the back door, climbing onto the seat so I can get a better grip on the wet fabric. "See there?" Nick points to the hook on the roll bar. "We need to latch it first." Nick heaves as he pushes the roof cover into place and then motions for me to do the same on my side. I thrust and get within an inch, but the hook can't quite connect. My foot slips on my third attempt, sending me spiraling onto the gravelly ground, and I scrape my elbow, a sharp sting slicing up my arm. I hear another lightning bolt crack. Nick was right—it's damn close. I lay my head back down, my arm throbbing, and close my eyes—the fight in me almost gone. I wonder if the only thing keeping me going is Nick. And now I've somehow ruined that too. Let the bolt come closer, let it hit me right in the chest—it can't make me hurt any worse than I already do.

Nick stands over me. "You've picked a hell of a time to take a nap." He smirks. "Your elbow okay?"

I examine it, see blood mixed with gravel, and nod. It's the least painful thing I feel right now. He pulls me up, and I slide into the Jeep, a pool of water already on the seat. But at least the roof is now secure, providing a welcome barrier against the pelting rain.

"We don't have time to attach the back windows, so this will have to do," he says as he turns the key and makes a U-turn.

So he's heading back the way we came. I have at least half my answer. That he can't continue the drive to Hana.

Part of me is relieved. I'm not clueless—I realize what this trip is doing to me. But leaving now makes me feel like I'm quitting on James, because somewhere along the way, this mission has morphed from an investigation into a good-bye.

"Aren't we going the wrong way?" I ask, testing him.

"No. We're finally going the *right* way," he says, keeping his eyes on the road that's barely visible in front of us. "This was a mistake."

"Is this because of the kiss?" I ask, even though I already know it is.

Nick shakes his head. "I don't know. I thought coming here, driving this road, following Dylan's path, that it would help. Not just me, but you too. I wanted to help you—"

I cut him off. "I know that."

"But I never expected that I'd—"

"Have feelings for me?" I offer in a burst of confidence.

Nick doesn't respond for a moment, his eyes still trained on the highway, the wipers thrashing back and forth, barely clearing the water away from the windshield before we're completely blinded by the rain again. My heart pounds, both for his response and for our safety.

Finally he speaks again. "I never expected I'd turn into the kind of guy who's mourning his fiancée but kisses another woman." He clenches the steering wheel harder. "God, this rain; I can barely see. I should pull over. But I'm afraid another car won't see us and will hit us."

I grip the door handle, fear suddenly taking over. If Nick is scared, then I should be too. The rain belts down harder, and I will the windshield wipers to catch up. The road to Hana is dangerous on its best day, and in this weather it's formidable. Will this be it? Will we die on the same road they did?

I stay silent, letting him navigate the Jeep, and finally, after several miles, the storm begins to let up. One of the craziest things about the Hawaiian Islands is how rainstorms can come out of nowhere and disappear almost as quickly as they appear. Kind of like my confidence. I felt stronger after swimming in open water and hiking, but since I discovered Dylan had been pregnant, I've felt outside myself. Like I've had a white-knuckle grip on my own life all over again.

"It was wrong to kiss you."

Hadn't we kissed each other?

"I'm sorry," he adds.

"Me too," I say, but I'm thinking about how I was sleepwalking before Nick showed up at my doorstep. Yes, I'm hurting like hell right now. But at least I'm feeling *something*.

"Can we just agree our emotions were running high and move forward?" he says, and I nod. Because how can I tell him I'm not sure it had been a mistake after he just told me it had been?

"I'm going to stop here," Nick says, and he squeezes my hand and pulls into the Halfway to Hana market that we'd passed earlier at mile marker seventeen. Before the rain, when we could see the lush rain forest, the trees bending over the road. The calm before the storm. The calm before the kiss. "I need something—coffee, probably stronger than that, but I'm guessing they don't sell booze." He reads a sign boasting that it's the home of the original banana bread. "Or some of that. Want to come?"

It's interesting how, in such a short time, I've learned so many of his tells. Like now, it's subtle, but he's tugging on the corner of his T-shirt, which means he's holding back. Not saying *everything*. That he needs some time alone.

My phone buzzes. We must have cell service. Finally. It's been spotty at best the entire trip today. Going from three bars to none in a single bend of the road. "You go ahead," I say when I realize it's Beth.

~

When I returned to my room last night, I called my sister and told her about Dylan's pregnancy, and she cried with me as I lay in bed, grasping my pillow—and her voice—for comfort. "I don't know if I can get over this part of it," I whispered. It was one of my biggest fears since I found out he'd been in Maui with another woman. That instead of just being a widow the rest of my life, I'd be a victim. People say that's a choice, and they're right. But the thing is, when it's your shit hitting the fan, it's ridiculously easy to lean into the sadness.

"You can," Beth said, and sniffled.

"I lost it tonight."

"That's understandable."

"No, I mean, I really lost it," I said, and confessed that I'd waded into the ocean and had thought about floating away.

"Jacks, you need to come home."

"I don't think I can. I have to see this through."

"You're freaking me out."

"I'll be okay. I have Nick."

"I don't even know who the hell this guy is, and now I'm trusting him to make sure you don't drown yourself? I'm not comfortable with this."

"I'm not coming home."

"Then I'm calling Mom."

That got my attention. The last thing I needed was our mother knowing where I was. What was happening. "You wouldn't! Or have you already? Is that why she's been calling me?" I thought about how I hadn't answered her and had finally shot her a cryptic text that I wasn't in the mood to talk. I knew I was going to have to face her soon enough. But now? Forget it. There was no way I could add her into this. It was already too complicated.

"I haven't, but I will if I have to," Beth said. "You're not giving me much of a choice. Do you realize how hard this is for me? To be so far away and not able to help?"

I sat up in bed. "Okay, here's the thing. I know how my story sounded—about wading out into the water. I don't know how to find the right words to explain that I need to be here. I feel so empty. And right now, I need to fill that space with something."

"Or *someone*? Like Nick?" Beth scoffed.

"What? No!" I lied, but my heart was pounding. I hated how my sister could always see right through me.

"Well, if that's true, then why not just leave, come home, let *us* fill that hole? Your *family*?" She dragged out the last word, and our most recent Christmas card photo came to mind, the one we all took together: me, James, Beth, Mark, their kids, and Mom and Dad. I could see us, all wearing the same kelly green Mom had insisted on.

"I will, soon—promise."

"Jacks—will you please be careful?"

"Yes," I said, propping myself up against the pillows. "I just can't come back yet. But I hear you. And you don't have to worry about me. I'm going to be okay."

I wasn't so sure about that last part. But I knew Beth. She wasn't going to stop until I convinced her.

"Okay," she said slowly.

"Thank you for talking to me. I needed to hear your voice."

I told her I'd call her the next day—today—but I haven't been able to reach her the few times I got a couple bars of reception. I pick up her call as Nick walks into the market.

"Where have you been?" I ask in greeting. "So much for all that concern you had about me," I tease as I hear rain in the background. "It's raining in the OC? It's June!" Rain this time of year is a rare occurrence in Orange County and usually the lead story on every newscast when and *if* it happens.

"Actually, funny story about that rain you hear . . . ," Beth begins. "I just landed at the Hana Airport. Can you come pick me up?"

CHAPTER
TWENTY-SEVEN

Dylan—before

"I finally got reception!" Dylan said, staring at her phone, waiting for the website to open. "It says here that there aren't any guardrails!" She finished reading, arching an eyebrow at James. After they'd driven away from the general store, James had sprung on her that he didn't want to stop when they reached Hana. He wanted to keep going. Around the back side.

James grabbed her cell and tossed it in the backseat next to her purse. "There was a reason I didn't want you Googling this. What is it with women and their obsession with Google? Is this a phenomenon of some kind? Is the world going to end if you don't know every single fact about everything?" James laughed, but there was something about its hollow sound that told Dylan he didn't think it was funny at all.

"What are you talking about?" She studied his face. He seemed different. She couldn't put a finger on it, but he hadn't woken up acting like himself. And for that matter, neither had she. She couldn't get rid of the bad feeling that had been following her around since she tiptoed to the bathroom this morning, turned the water on, and vomited. She knew it wasn't the baby. That, she was happy about. Frightened, yes. But also content. It was something else. And that scared her more than the life that was growing inside her.

"Nothing," James said, squeezing her knee, working his lips into a smile. One of his thin, fake ones, but still. He was slowly looking more like *him*. "Anyway, yes, it's true that there aren't guardrails *in some places*, but driving the back side will be so much cooler—I read that the views are incredible, and if you drive slow it won't matter that the road isn't as finished as the one through Hana is."

"What do you mean, *not as finished*?" Dylan bit her lip. What had gotten into him? He wasn't this man. A risk-taker. As far as she knew, this affair was the biggest and only major risk he'd ever taken. And while he didn't discuss it with her, she could see the toll their secret relationship was taking on him. The fights were getting worse with Jacqueline—probably because his wife sensed something wasn't right. And Dylan had noticed his fuse had been just a little bit shorter on this trip. It was subtle, like how he'd sighed when she'd forgotten her cell phone and had to run back up to the room. Or when she was telling him a story about her roommates or some catastrophe at work—there was something distant about his expression, and he'd snapped to attention only when she asked him if he was listening.

This slight disconnect made Dylan try harder—to be less forgetful, to be a better storyteller. Her time with James was slipping through her fingers, and she didn't want to think about what would happen when they returned to reality. Obviously things were going to change once James found out about the baby. The world she'd imagined for just the two of them would now include three. But Dylan couldn't be sure which way the ax would swing when she told him—or which way she wanted it to. Either direction would bring chaos, burst their bubble, and alter their lives forever.

James had actually described himself as boring when he'd first met Dylan. He was something of a workaholic, working nights and weekends—whatever it took to get the deal closed. When he'd flown, it was always United Airlines, always the aisle seat, always direct. Unless a layover absolutely couldn't be avoided, like when he was flying to Amarillo, Texas. He followed routines. He was predictable. His words, not hers. Dylan had reasoned that their clandestine relationship had brought something to his life he'd been missing. She just worried now that it was the risks he was taking with her that were addictive, not Dylan herself.

"There are a few miles that aren't completely paved. But really, it just means the road isn't as commercialized—it's what the locals would drive. And I want that. The real experience. We've come all the way here; why not go for it?" James smiled at her. That smile that twisted her up inside, that made her giddy and scared and flustered all at once.

Dylan considered his pitch. He had already taken her on some amazing excursions, ones she would have never gone on otherwise. If it had been up to her, they would have lain at the pool all day, her reading fashion magazines and him massaging oil into her shoulders. She remembered Nick asking her to do a ropes course once. She'd scoffed and told him no, that she didn't want to navigate balance beams hundreds of feet off the ground suspended between trees. What if she fell? She'd said she had zero interest in being a trapeze artist. "I'll make sure you don't fall," he'd said slowly. "I'll take care of you."

And she'd had no doubt that he would. It had begun to feel like Nick was obsessed with taking care of her. As if she weren't capable of it herself. But still, she didn't back down. The idea of being up that high scared her.

But when James told her he'd planned all of these excursions, she heard herself saying okay. Even though she wasn't okay with any of it at all.

But she wanted to be with him, wherever that was, even if it meant driving on a road with no guardrails.

The thought sent a shiver through her. It wasn't just them anymore. There was a baby to consider. She needed to tell him. She needed him to know. But something was stopping her. That bad feeling was back again. Overpowering her. Consuming her. She sucked in a deep breath.

"And . . . ," James said, and Dylan looked over at him. "The views of the Pacific—they're some of the best on the island."

Dylan frowned.

"And right before we get to the back side, we'll see the ʻOheʻo Gulch, also known as the Seven Sacred Pools. I think we should stop there. They're supposed to be to die for."

"I'm not sure anything about the drive to Hana would be worth dying for!" Dylan pushed James in the shoulder.

"Yeah, sorry, probably not the best phrase to use." James shook his head.

Dylan smiled. "Why do they call them the Seven Sacred Pools?"

"As the story goes, if you swim up all seven tiered pools, you'll be welcome in heaven," James said, watching her face.

Dylan thought about James's words. And the way she'd been feeling all day—as if a black cloud were following them. She wanted to tell him that they should just go back to the hotel and relax—spend time together the way *she* wanted to.

"Look, if you don't want to take the back road, I get it. I don't want to push you. But there's just something about being here with you that makes me say, 'Fuck it, let's live!'"

That familiar and dangerous feeling swelled inside of her. *Hope.* And she couldn't control herself; she reached out and grabbed it and held it tight as she listened to James.

"This is considered one of the most spectacular drives in the world, and I think we should make the most of our last full day together." He paused and locked his eyes on hers, reminding her that they had to go back. To reality. She just wished she knew what that was going to look like. "We can hike in—it's not far at all—and swim in the pools.

Or just dip a toe in, whatever you want, and then have a picnic; I was thinking it would be a good place for us to talk," he said, and Dylan felt a weight in the pit of her stomach. Was this why he was acting so strangely? Because he had something to tell her? Was he going to break up with her? Or could he be leaving his wife?

"What? You don't agree?"

Dylan hadn't realized she'd been moving her head back and forth. She looked into James's eyes, so full of life, the life *she'd* breathed into him. She decided to push the bad feeling away and trust him. To see where this road would take them. Hoping that at the end of it there would be a future—for all three of them. And she decided right then that she was going to confess that to him, no matter what his response was—good or bad.

"Let's do it," Dylan said, and kissed him. "I'm ready."

CHAPTER
TWENTY-EIGHT

JACKS—AFTER

When I was sixteen and Beth was seventeen, she kicked a boy's ass for me.

Okay, so she didn't exactly kick his ass, but a slap was involved. And it left a mark.

I'd just found out that Alex Henderson had asked another girl to Homecoming, which was a problem because Alex was my boyfriend and he'd already asked me.

"He what?" Beth adjusted her backpack on her shoulder and fiddled with the knot on her denim shirt.

I leaned my head against my locker and told Beth I'd heard from my friend Janet, who'd heard from her lab partner, Carrie, that he'd asked Heidi O'Reilly to the dance.

"But he's *your* fucking boyfriend."

"Apparently he's not anymore," I said, a tear rolling down my cheek that I quickly wiped away with the sleeve of my sweatshirt. "He told Heidi we were broken up."

"What the hell is wrong with him? What a jerk. I never liked him."

My eyes pooled with tears, but I held them back. "You don't like anyone I date."

Beth gave me her *well, can you blame me?* look. "I'm going to find him."

"No, don't," I pleaded. The last thing I needed was a scene. I already felt stupid enough that he'd dumped me and hadn't even bothered to let me know.

"Too late," she said, heading toward the quad where he and the other basketball players would sit during lunchtime.

I trailed behind her, trying to convince her to stop, but she marched forward, her backpack bobbing up and down behind her.

"There he is. Alex!" she yelled as she approached him.

Alex whipped his head around at the sound of his name, shrugging at the two guys he was talking to as Beth approached. I couldn't see her face, but I knew the expression that was fixed upon it. It was her scowl. And that combination of knotted eyebrows and pursed lips could scare the shit out of anyone. She dropped her backpack and barreled toward him, calling him an asshole. I stopped short as a small crowd gathered, wishing I could disappear into the grass when she asked him how he could do this to me. Then Alex's eyes found mine, and for a moment I thought he was going to come to me, explain it had all been a misunderstanding.

But he smirked and looked away. "I was done with her." He laughed and high-fived his buddies.

And that's when Beth slapped him across the face. He winced, drawing his hand to his cheek. His entire face turned bright red. "What the hell?" he yelled. "You're crazy!"

He wasn't laughing anymore.

Beth strode back to where I was standing. "Come on. We're going to Carl's Jr. for fried zucchini and a huge Dr Pepper. My treat," she said.

And I couldn't help but smile at the thought of my favorite meal, that my sister was so badass, that someone cared about me that much.

I think I've taken for granted how often she's done that for me over the years, protecting me, even when I didn't think I needed it.

I know that's why she's come to Maui.

~

"Are you okay that she's here?" Nick asks as we see a sign for Hana Airport. "That she just showed up?"

"Of course," I say. "Why?"

"Well, she got on a flight and came six hours without even asking you. What if you hadn't wanted her to come?"

"I would always want my sister with me." I frown at him, deciding not to admit that I had, in fact, told her not to come. Wondering if he's the one who's put off by her arrival. "Are *you* not okay that she's here?"

"I'm fine with it! I mean, the timing is just a little crazy. After everything that just happened." He looks at me, and I know what he's not saying. The kiss. "And we're still wet." He pulls at his T-shirt, which is clinging to his chest. "But if you're all right, so am I."

"We'll dry. We'll be fine," I say, even though I feel certain about only the first statement. "And anyway, if there's one thing you need to know about Beth, it's that she does what she wants, when she wants. That's just who she is. And you know what? Most of the time, she knows what I need more than I do."

"She sounds like a good sister."

"She is."

"Well, I'm intrigued. Tell me more about her," Nick says, and I realize he was just looking out for me when he was asking about Beth. We'd been living in our little bubble for days, without seeing anyone from our real lives, so I'm sure it was a shock for him that she's here.

As we weave our way down the wet Hana Highway, both of us looking away as we pass the stone bench where we'd kissed earlier, I share my favorite Beth stories. He laughs when I tell him about her twitchy-eye tell, and he nods in approval when I mention the slap heard round the world, as we'd come to call it.

We fall into a comfortable silence as he slowly drives the narrow road. A car whips around a corner and blares its horn at us, and I think of James and Dylan's accident—the last seconds before their worlds went dark. Had James been trying to avoid an oncoming car and swerved too hard, losing control?

I don't know the exact location of where they crashed. Nick does, but I asked him not to share it with me. Not until I'm ready. And after my panic this morning, I'm not sure I'll ever be ready. I know from Officer Keoloha that they had been driving on the back side of the road to Hana, considered much more dangerous than the front part—in places, it's as high as one thousand feet above sea level. It's deemed so perilous that rental car companies advise against driving it.

It struck me as so odd when I heard that—James had never been a risk-taker. So I was shocked he'd chosen to venture into such uncharted territory. But then again, I was surprised to hear he'd had an affair. I'd wondered if Dylan had brought out a different side of him that had lain dormant while he lived his predictable life with me. Or maybe Nick was right. Maybe I hadn't known my husband at all.

As we turn down the long road toward Hana Airport a few minutes later, I'm not sure what the plan is after we pick up Beth. The subject of returning to the hotel hasn't come up again. We're dancing around it like a bear we don't want to poke. I glance at Nick's profile and wonder if he still wants to leave the road to Hana before we make it to the back side. Because now that my sister is here, now that we're pulling into the parking lot and I can see her standing in front of the tiny terminal that looks like a house, wearing a white blouse and tan capris, her hair pulled back into a messy knot, I realize I'm not ready to go home.

Just the sight of her is giving me strength, and I feel a pull toward James. I want to know where he took his last breath. To say good-bye.

Maybe it's Beth I've needed by my side all along. To hold my hand, to make sure I don't get too close to the edge. To be there for me after I let James go once and for all. To protect me. I hope Nick will decide to stay longer, to say his own good-byes. To get the closure I know he needs as well.

Beth waves at me excitedly, and I unlock my seat belt and slide toward the door, the car not yet stopped. I can feel happy tears in the back of my eyes.

I grip the door handle and turn toward Nick, who's laughing at me. "What? We're basically twins. We're *very, very* close!"

Nick stops the Jeep, and I jump out, running to avoid the light rain, and hurl myself into my sister's arms.

"That was quite a scene back there," Beth says a few minutes later as we sit at the bar of the Hana Ranch Restaurant, a few miles from the airport. "The three other people who were on my flight were staring at us like we were reuniting after years! It's been, what? Five days?" She laughs.

"I know. I bawled. But I think I needed to," I say, and look over at Nick, who's sipping from a mug of coffee. He seems unusually quiet, but then again, when Beth and I are together, it's hard to get a word in. "Thanks for loaning me one of your shirts, by the way." I say, pulling at the cotton fabric. "I was soaked to the bone," I add.

Beth smiles. "That's Hawaii weather for you."

I glance at Nick, who's wearing a T-shirt with a guy flashing a shaka sign that he got from a shop across the street from the restaurant.

"So how are *you* doing?" Beth looks across me toward Nick.

He takes a breath before responding. "Well, I'm finally dry. So there's that." He smiles and takes a sip of his coffee.

Beth doesn't respond, waiting for his real answer.

"It's been hard, harder than I thought it would be."

"Nick's being modest—he's been the strong one. My rock. I've been the hot mess."

"Did Jacks tell you I didn't want her to come here to Maui?" Beth asks. Apparently ready to jump right in.

Nick looks at me again. "She didn't," he says slowly. "But I get it. Getting on a plane to Hawaii with a complete stranger after her husband had just died. Seemed crazy, I'm sure."

"To put it mildly." Beth offers a tight smile.

"Is that why you're here? To make sure I'm not a serial killer?" Nick laughs.

"Maybe." She smirks and takes a sip of her beer, eyeing him.

"I don't blame you! You've got to look out for your sister. But for what it's worth, I'm not."

"Did I mention Nick's a firefighter? If anything, he's been making sure I *don't* get hurt."

"Except for your little escapade in the ocean. I think maybe you fell asleep on the job that night, Nick," Beth says, not unkindly. Beth's words never spill menace. It may not be what you want to hear, but she always speaks the truth.

But she's off the mark this time. A very small part of me had wanted to keep going into that ocean. To let the water envelop all my pain. And he had pulled me back to reality—literally and figuratively. "Hey," I interject before Nick can answer. "That's not fair. He saved me."

"No, she's right," Nick says evenly. "I should have done a better job of keeping you safe—stopped you when you were running down the beach, before you went into the ocean. Especially after what you'd just discovered."

"You're not my bodyguard. And you are going through the exact same thing I am. You'd just heard the same terrible news," I say, and look pointedly at Beth. "He's not here on vacation, you know; he lost someone important to him too." I'm surprised by my forcefulness. By how protective I feel toward Nick. But this thing we're doing out here—it's ours, and no one from the outside could possibly understand it.

Beth's face relaxes slightly. "I don't mean to be insensitive. And I'm truly sorry for your loss. I can't imagine. It's just that—"

"You want to protect your sister." Nick finishes her sentence.

"Always," she says.

"I get it. I do," Nick says, and I can tell he's sincere. "But for the record, I want to protect her too." I notice his shoulders stiffen.

Beth nods, but I'm not sure she believes him. "It just seems like this trip has created more problems than it's solved."

"Maybe," Nick says, but doesn't elaborate.

"I feel like every time Jacks calls me, she's in tears about some new piece of horrible information you guys have found out. Information that serves no purpose but to hurt her."

"I never said it was going to be easy," Nick says, a slight edge to his voice.

I jump in. "Beth, this decision was mine and only mine. And it's been hard, but I was prepared for that."

I can read Beth's mind. But if Nick had never showed up on my doorstep, I wouldn't be here dealing with all of this hard stuff. She blames him.

"I just don't want you to get hurt any more," she says to me, giving Nick a look.

"And neither do I," he says.

I look at Nick. "Is that why you want to turn back? To protect me?"

"What do you mean?" Beth asks before he can answer.

"Well, Nick—*we* weren't sure we should keep driving the road to Hana."

"Really? What happened?"

"I had a freak-out while we were driving. After that storm came out of nowhere . . ." I think about his lips on mine, his hot breath, his hands in my hair. Obviously, I can't tell her this part. Not right now, anyway.

"What?" Beth gives me a look.

"Nick suggested we go home."

He hadn't actually said those words, but I want to find out if that's what he meant.

"It sounds like Nick and I finally agree on something," Beth says, and looks at him for a reaction.

"I just didn't want to push Jacks any more than I already had," he says, and I feel my heart sink. I guess he's ready to give up on the whole thing. "I'm worried about her." He runs his finger around the rim of his mug. "When I convinced her to come here, it sounded like such a good idea. Like we could finally get the closure we're both desperate for. But now," he says, locking eyes with me for a split second, "now I think it will send us tumbling backward to see where they—"

"I understand." Beth holds her hand up before he can finish. "So then it's settled? We're all going back home?" Beth looks at us.

And suddenly I realize this is exactly why she came here. Not just to protect me, but to talk me into leaving—and now she thinks Nick has done her job for her. I can tell she doesn't like Nick. She probably made up her mind about him the day I first told her he'd come to my house. And once Beth has something in her head, it's hard to change it. Her dislike is subtle. But I can tell by the way she chews on her lower lip when he talks, not really listening but observing, by how she's holding her shoulders as if on guard, by the way she's held her gaze firmly on him. She's definitely not a fan.

Nick nods. "Yes, I think it's the right thing to do."

I suck in a deep breath just as Beth lets out a sigh of relief. Her shoulders relax. At least they can agree on this, she's thinking. Maybe he's not so bad, she concedes.

It blows my mind that Nick would give up now. I know he told me back in California that he'd decide once we were here, that he'd let his heart guide him. That he'd let Dylan show the way. But we're *so close* to seeing everything. To discovering the secrets this highway holds about the people we loved. He pushed me to come here, pushed me to face both James's demons and my own. It has to be the kiss. It's changed everything.

"Okay then," Beth says, standing up. "Mine could be the shortest trip anyone has ever taken to Maui." Her eyes light up as she watches me. She thinks she's getting exactly what she wants. She believes I'm going home.

"No. Wait," I say. "I want to stay. I'll call Officer Keoloha and tell him I'm ready to see where it happened. I emailed him when I arrived, so he already knows I'm here and that this is a possibility. He offered to escort me if I decided to go through with it." Even if I had decided not to go to the crash site, I'd planned to say thank you in person for all he'd done for me. "The police station is just down that way." I point toward the road we'd driven to the restaurant. "I've come this far. And I can't turn back now. And I hope you *both* will go with me."

I wait, hoping Nick will change his mind. Hoping Beth will support me. But even if they both say no, I'm going. I can do this. I can stand on the edge of the cliff where my husband died, and I can say good-bye. I owe that much to him, and to myself.

"Oh, Jacks, you don't have to put yourself through that. Nick is right: it could set you both back," Beth says gently.

"Look, Beth, I love you. I don't expect you to understand this. But, Nick, I have to say, I'm really surprised. It was your idea to come all the way here."

Nick looks down.

"Can I talk to you for a minute—in private?" It's a question, but Beth's not really asking.

I nod and she grabs my hand, then looks at Nick. "Sorry, I just need to have a sister-to-sister chat for a second." And he nods, but locks eyes with me, giving me an apologetic smile.

"I don't like him," she says as soon as we get out front.

"I know, Beth, but you never like anyone. It took you almost a year to warm up to James."

"True," she says.

"You don't know him, Beth."

"Neither do you."

"Yes, I do," I say, looking toward the restaurant. "We've talked a lot on this trip. He's shared things with me and I with him. Just give him a chance."

"Fine. I'll give him a chance, but I'll do it back in California. I'll invite him over for dinner. I'll make risotto. Sound good?" She folds her arms across her chest.

I roll my eyes at her. "I'm not leaving. Not yet. I need to say good-bye to James."

Beth is quiet for several seconds. "Okay. If this is really what you need to do, I'll go with you. But I think you should let Nick off the hook. If he doesn't want to go, then he doesn't want to go."

"You just don't want him to go."

"Maybe." She smirks.

I hug her. "Thank you."

We walk back inside. "I'm going to stay," I say, and look at him, wondering if he is too.

He simply shakes his head.

"What about Dylan?"

"I'm sorry," Nick says softly. "I can't."

"Well, I'm sorry too. But now isn't the time to be weak," I say as I walk back out the door, Beth following like always, watching my back.

CHAPTER TWENTY-NINE

DYLAN—BEFORE

"There is no way I'm jumping off here." Dylan inched toward the side of the bridge, feeling woozy just staring at the freshwater pool at least fifty feet below.

"If you guys aren't going to jump, do you mind?" A young man, maybe eighteen, with deep-brown skin and a shark tooth necklace, motioned toward the edge, giving them a look that said, *What are you doing up here anyway? Aren't you too old to be jumping off this bridge?*

Yes, we are, or at least he is, Dylan thought, looking at James, taking in the occasional silver thread that wove its way through his light brown hair.

"You live here?" James asked the boy.

"Born and raised."

"How deep is it?"

"That one, it's maybe twenty feet, but you have to hit it just right because it's shallower on the sides. You really thinking about doing it?" He widened his big brown eyes at James. "We get a lot of people who chicken out once they stand up on the edge."

"Not me. I'm doing it. I want to jump and then swim in the seven pools. Like they say you should."

"Hey, brah, this 'they' you're talking about is some dude who made it up to help with tourism. There are way more than seven pools, and I'm not sure how much closer to heaven you'll be if you get your skin wet in all of them."

James looked over the edge. "Doesn't matter to me—the jump is what I really want anyway. That feeling. That rush!"

"It's like nothing else. But you'd better be quick. The park rangers will get pissed if they see you. You guys aren't even supposed to have parked your Jeep over there." The boy looked up the road to a curve where they'd stopped. "That's yours, right?"

Dylan and James nodded.

"After you," James said, and he and Dylan silently stepped aside and watched as the boy got up on the edge and jumped, grabbing his knees to his chest and letting out a high-pitched scream all the way down. He plunged under the water, and when he came up, a group of his friends whistled and clapped. And Dylan released the breath she'd been holding. She didn't even know the boy and she'd been worried about him.

"I'm going for it," James said, taking his shirt off. "Will you hold this? Just take the Jeep after I jump and enter the park, which should be another quarter-mile or so down the road. I'll meet you down at the water."

"James—" Dylan thought of what the boy had said. That he had to hit it just right. What if he wasn't as lucky as the boy they'd just watched? She looked over the bridge again, five of the pools separated by small waterfalls stretched out before her. In the distance, she could see people on the rocks surrounding the pools or swimming in them. But they'd probably arrived there the right way. Through the park. Not by jumping off this bridge.

James tossed the black T-shirt he'd purchased yesterday—with *Maui Locos* printed on the front in big white block letters—onto the ground when Dylan wouldn't take it. "What?" he said as he stood up on the bridge and put his arms out to the sides like Leonardo DiCaprio in *Titanic*.

Two days ago, she'd been swimming with a two-hundred-pound sea turtle named Bob Marley in open water, and now that her pregnancy suspicions had been confirmed, she was frightened to put one foot in front of the other. When James had first brought up jumping off the bridge after he'd convinced her to consider driving the back side of the mountain, she hadn't said anything to him, but just the thought of him doing it scared the shit out of her. He kept piling on the risks, and she wondered why. She'd tried to push away the idea of him getting hurt—or worse—but it kept chipping away at her insides. And now it was pounding inside her head.

"Don't do it." She grabbed James's hand and pulled him back down to the ground. "Let's go have that picnic you talked about. A little salami, a little cheese. I'll even take a sip of that wine." She nuzzled against his bare chest, surprised by how fast his heart was beating.

James pulled back. "You know I can't wait to feed you banana bread and drink that pinot noir. But first I jump. It's perfectly safe. If he can do it, so can I." He pointed to the boy sitting with his friends on the rocks below. They were all yelling for James to jump.

Dylan was reminded of when she was a teenager, begging to do the same things her friends were. *Their parents let them stay out past midnight. Their parents give them money for the movies. Their parents don't rag on them.* Her mom would fixate her deep-blue eyes on Dylan and say what she always did: *If so-and-so jumped off a bridge, would you do it too?*

Apparently James would.

Dylan felt her arms prick with goose bumps even though it was at least eighty degrees. "I just don't want anything to happen to you."

"You're being ridiculous. *Nothing* is going to happen to me. I promise." He punched his arms in the air. "I'm invincible, baby!"

Dylan studied his eyes—wide and dancing with impulse. She wondered what was going on inside his head. He rarely opened up about anything serious. She knew he had a brother who died young, but that was only because he'd slipped and said something while he was drinking. When she'd asked more about it, he wouldn't get into the details. Did he want to try to defy death because his brother couldn't?

"Are you okay? Is this about your—"

James shot her a look, and she thought better of finishing her sentence.

"Come on, Dyl, this isn't really going to be a problem for you, is it? Because I can't have, you know, another person nagging me. Being all wifelike."

"Wifelike?" Dylan pressed her hands firmly into her sides. "You cannot be serious." James *looked* like himself. His bare torso showing the hard work he put in at the gym, his stubble-lined jaw showing the hours that had passed since he shaved this morning. But he still didn't *seem* like himself—at all. Once, he'd told her that he wasn't a very good husband. That he could be a real ass. At the time she'd giggled. There was no way James could *ever* be an ass. Now she saw glimpses that his words had probably been a confession, not a joke.

"I'm as serious as a heart attack," James said, refusing to break eye contact with her. She flashed back to the Huelo lookout point, where they'd stopped a couple of hours ago. It was a romantic spot, and they'd walked down steep concrete steps to gaze at the ocean through a sea of lush palms. James had grabbed Dylan by the waist, pointing at a string of hand-painted coconut bras that were hanging on a line. Dylan hadn't wanted James to buy her one, but he had insisted. Finally she relented, knowing full well she would never wear it. But it was so hard to say no to James.

Even in an affair, there's a honeymoon period, Dylan thought. *And then it expires, just like in a regular relationship.* Just like it had with Nick. She knew she was being tested in this moment. If she kept pressing him not to jump, she could tell they would probably end up in a fight. She'd looked forward to having all this uninterrupted time with him—to know what it felt like to share both the sunrise *and* sunset on the same day. To not feel like their precious moments were slipping away like sand through her fingertips. To believe that the life they had together was real. And she *had* done those things and enjoyed them. But she'd also seen behind the sheen of his eyes, where the other side of his personality lived. Dylan understood, of course, that James wasn't perfect. But now that she knew about the baby, she was questioning everything.

"Dylan, come on," she heard him saying. "Where's my belleza?"

"I'm right here," she said, and stood stiffly.

He scoffed. And even after he closed his mouth, she could see his jaw tighten, his teeth grinding. "No, she's not. I'm looking for the woman who doesn't take my shit, but who also doesn't *give me* any either."

This was giving him shit? Caring if he lived or died?

"I need to do this, Dyl."

First he'd wanted to drive the unpaved back roads without guardrails, and now he needed to jump fifty feet into a pool of water that was maybe twenty feet deep? What was next? Skydiving without a parachute? Two young couples, probably in their twenties, were walking toward them, and she didn't want them to overhear her trying to convince him this was a bad idea. It was already too embarrassing to admit that her feelings weren't going to weigh into his decision. That he simply didn't care what she thought. She knew he was jumping whether she wanted him to or not.

"Fine. But if you end up paralyzed, I'm not going to wipe your ass and spoon-feed you applesauce. That will be your *wifey's* job."

"Harsh," James said, and hurled his body over the edge before she could respond. She watched him fall into the water below, his body a rigid, straight line. He plunged below the surface, feet first, and finally reappeared, letting out a *wooooh!* and pumping his fist above the water. The two couples behind her oohed and aahed over James's jump, thankfully not noticing the tension on Dylan's face long after he'd sailed over the edge. They might have been impressed, but Dylan wasn't.

James had been right: nothing had happened to him. But in the last two minutes, something had happened to her. She'd seen a side of James she hadn't known was there, or hadn't wanted to believe existed. She couldn't be sure. She was forced to accept the truth. Their little bubble could be penetrated by reality after all. She liked existing in it not just because it shielded them from the rest of the world, but because it hid their flaws. If they spent all their time drinking and dancing at bars or rolling around between the sheets, they didn't have to deal with tense situations like these, where their true personalities would shine through. But on this vacation, where they were spending so much time together, the flaws were coming out without permission.

And now Dylan realized one very important thing about James that was not going to change: he was going to do what he wanted, when he wanted, whether she agreed with him or not. She pressed her hand to her stomach and sighed. What did that mean for their future?

CHAPTER THIRTY

JACKS—AFTER

"What was that all about?" Beth and I are standing next to the Jeep, and I glance back toward the restaurant wondering if Nick is going to follow us out. Wanting him to appear almost as much as not. "You storming out like that?"

"Nothing." I say. A huge lie. Obviously.

"It definitely wasn't *nothing*," Beth says slowly, pursing her lips to accentuate her point. "It just seemed like a real fight, you know, like one between—"

"Between whom?" I dare her with my eyes. *Say it. Accuse me.*

"I don't know. Never mind," she says, wringing her hands.

I release a long steady stream of air through my lips. Thank God. I'm not ready to discuss Nick. Or our relationship. Or whatever it is. I'm not even sure I could put it into words if I tried. All I know is I'm pissed at him for not wanting to finish what he started in Maui. Or maybe I'm pissed at him for not wanting to finish what he started *with me.*

"So now what?" Beth asks.

I wait a beat, watching my sister. Imagining if it had been her husband who'd been in Maui with his mistress when he was supposed to be on a business trip in Kansas. She would collapse into herself. Thinking first about their three kids—how would they move forward? Then eventually about herself. But in between, she'd be like a lab rat in a maze, desperately trying to find her way out, but only hitting dead end after dead end. Because Mark is her center. Her gravitational pull. His yin to her yang. Sure, she's buttoned up, and I guarantee she printed an Excel spreadsheet of her kids' activities and prepped a slow-cooker pork roast before she left for her flight here this morning, but that's part of her routine.

But *this*. This would paralyze her.

I'm not saying the same hasn't happened to me, that I'm not half of who I was. But it's different. James and I were a mess more than we weren't. Always one terse word away from someone sleeping on that damn red chenille couch. Even though I had no idea he was cheating on me, that he was lying to me, it wasn't an unusual occurrence for us to be shocking each other, pushing the edges of our relationship, testing our endurance. But I'd naively thought we kept the betrayals inside the walls of our own house. That our messy relationship was the canvas of our life together.

"I'm calling Officer Keoloha," I say, and press his name in my phone.

And he answers. Just like he always has. Thank God this man hasn't stopped taking my calls, hasn't given up on me. Beth watches as I tell him I'm at the Hana Ranch Restaurant with my sister. And that I'm ready to see where the accident happened. He tells me to stay put. That he'll come right over. And I think about this man whom I've never met in person, but who has listened to me cry, babble, question, you name it—without so much as a complaint—and I wonder how he's able to be so unflappable, how he can do his job without getting emotionally attached.

I think of Nick again. And the pressure he's constantly under as a firefighter, the pain and anguish he sees. And I wonder if it simply takes a certain type of man—who is calm, who knows his limits. Nick must really know himself, how much he can take. And that what he will see and feel if he goes to the accident scene, he won't be able to detach from.

"He's coming," I say to Beth after I end the call.

"And then what?" she asks, wringing her hands. The planner in her needing to know what comes next.

"And then we go," I say, looking down at my feet, noticing the polish on my big toe is chipped.

"What do you think Nick's going to do?" She glances at the restaurant.

"I have no idea," I say, following her gaze to the front patio where we can see a couple with matching vests and white hair perusing a guidebook and sipping fruity drinks. I feel my eyes well with tears thinking of what Nick said about wanting to grow plastic-hip old with Dylan. And it really hits me that I'll never know James with gray hair. That he'll never see the lines that will eventually crease my face. "Am I crazy?"

Beth puts her arm around me, and I lean into her. "No. Not at all. You're brave."

"Me? Brave?" I scoff. She might as well be telling me I'm a supermodel.

"Yeah, you." She gives me a long look. "You're stronger than you think, you know. I could never have made it through something like this."

"I haven't yet."

"But you will." She grabs my shoulders and looks me directly in the eye. "You will."

"I want to believe that."

"You know, Jacks, I loved James. I did. There were things about him that made him a great husband. Especially for the first few years. But there was something about him—"

"That you didn't like. I know. I know. *I know.*" I drag the last one out for dramatic effect.

"I suppose I deserve that," Beth says. "But that's not it. I did like him. Because you loved him and he was your husband. What I was going to say was that something about him sucked something out of you. Over time with *him*, your confidence slowly seeped out of you. Do you see that?"

"I do," I say, tears starting to fall.

"Oh, honey, I'm sorry, I didn't mean to make you cry. I shouldn't criticize him. Not now."

"It's okay, it's not you," I say, thinking about how everything changed after I told him about the 20 percent chance.

"Then what is it?"

And that's when I tell her. Everything.

CHAPTER THIRTY-ONE

JACKS—AFTER

Beth hugs me for several minutes and doesn't say anything. She strokes my hair, and I squeeze her, letting my tears fall thanks to the silent permission only a sister can give. It's hard to put into words how it feels to have finally told Beth the truth about why James and I had unraveled. Why he'd changed. Maybe even why he'd had the affair.

It feels like I'm me again.

For so long I've been so ashamed and embarrassed. And there was a part of me that had always been scared to admit to her that I hadn't told my own husband the truth.

"You and Mark tell each other everything," I say to her. "And maybe this is stupid, but because you have kids, I worried you might side with him." I shake my head slightly.

"Oh, Jacks," Beth says. "I might be a mom, but you're still my sister. I'm sorry you didn't feel like you could come to me."

"I should have."

"You did the best you knew how to do at the time and hoped it would work out. That's all any of us can do, you know?"

"Clearly this did not work out the way I had hoped," I say, and give her a sad smile.

"I'm sorry," Beth says, and hugs me again.

"Will you make a deal with me?" I ask.

Beth nods.

"Let's not be sorry for me anymore. Okay?"

"Okay," Beth says simply, and I'm more grateful for her in this moment than I can ever tell her.

~

Nick still hasn't come outside when Officer Keoloha pulls up next to us a few minutes later. I've made my choice, and Nick has clearly made his. I only wonder which of us has made the right one.

When Officer Keoloha steps out of his white SUV, he pushes his sunglasses on top of his head and smiles. I feel a pull toward him. My anchor to this place. My lifeline all these weeks. Because of that bond, I walk over and hug him like an old friend. He seems momentarily surprised, but he pats my back quickly, then releases himself from my arms.

"It's nice to meet you in person," he says.

"You too." I smile. "Officer Keoloha, this is Beth," I say as they shake hands and exchange greetings. I recall my first words to him about her—that she's like a part of me, my other arm. And I know he understands why she's here with me now, because she can't *not* be.

"You sure about this?" he asks as he looks from me to Beth, locking eyes with my sister.

"She is. She's ready," Beth answers for me.

He nods, but the look in his eyes, the way his jaw is set, gives nothing away as to what he might be thinking about my choice. He's just going to guide me to James. Beth grips my hand, and I squeeze back without looking at her. We're silent, but I know from the feel of her touch that she finally understands why I'm going. That, despite what James did, he was still my husband. And I still loved him.

Officer Keoloha opens the passenger door for me and the back door for Beth, then starts the car. "So we've never talked specifically about the stretch of road where the accident happened. Do you have any questions?" he begins as he pulls the car onto Highway 360, and soon we're surrounded by the lush greenery of the rain forest. Save for the regular signs warning of one-lane roads or reminding a driver to yield to oncoming traffic, it would be possible to forget this is a highway full of just as much danger as hope.

I want to tell Officer Keoloha that even after he takes me to where James had his last moments, I will still have so many questions. Questions that may never be answered, that I will have to live with for the rest of my life. Questions that I can only pray will eventually settle in the back of my mind next to my memories. But today, what did I want to know? What could he tell me that would really answer the one question that was eating away at me day after day: Why did my husband have to die?

"I just wish I knew why James would drive on the back side if it's so dangerous," I say to Officer Keoloha. I can only imagine the level of tragedy he's seen on these roads. I wonder where my husband's crash ranks.

"The back side of the road to Hana is intriguing to certain travelers because it's not considered touristy," Officer Keoloha says, then stops so a compact car can pass from the other direction.

"I just never knew James as risk-taker."

Officer Keoloha doesn't respond, and we're all silent for several minutes, none of us knowing what to say. Finally, he speaks. "Once we see the Seven Sacred Pools, it's about another four miles or so until we will be officially driving on the unauthorized section of the road. The accident didn't happen far from there."

Beth squeezes my shoulder from the backseat, and I reach over and put my hand on top of hers.

We ride in silence as Officer Keoloha maneuvers the SUV through the roads, bending and winding sharply. I think of a pregnant Dylan, how nauseated she must have been. About thirty minutes later Officer Keoloha points to his right. "That's Wailua Falls there."

We see a group of people standing on the side of the road taking pictures. My insides are clenching. Because I know we're getting closer. Soon after, we cross over a bridge and Officer Keoloha points down to where the pools are. I can't help but wonder where James and Dylan might have stopped along the way. Did they eat barbecue at that place right before the main turn into Hana? Did they stop at one of the many unmanned fruit stands along the road and grab a fresh papaya to share, leaving a dollar in the jar? Had Dylan made James slow down so she could take a picture of the waterfall we passed a few miles back, not knowing her time was short?

"Okay, we're coming up on the unauthorized road. It's going to be pretty bumpy," Officer Keoloha says quietly. The SUV slowly ascends a steep hill, and I let out a scream as a large truck comes barreling around the corner. Officer Keoloha curses under his breath, "Damn locals." We drive in silence for a minute; then Officer Keoloha begins again. "We think the accident happened just up here."

"What do you mean, you *think* you know where the accident happened? You aren't sure?" Beth asks.

"This part of the road is unpaved, so there aren't skid marks or other indications that James tried to stop the Jeep. It's impossible for us to know exactly where the brakes were applied."

"And you're sure they were applied?" I ask, and I hear Beth gasp quietly. I haven't told her that I've been wondering if something happened before the Jeep careened off the cliff. Something that caused them to crash. Something other than the road being narrow and dangerous.

Like an argument. And James, he had that temper. Especially toward the end.

I've been thinking a lot about a fight we had once—in the car of all places. It was New Year's Day. The day after I told him about the 20 percent. There'd been a party at his boss's house to watch the Rose Bowl. And despite the fact that we'd been up half the night arguing, he'd said we *both* needed to be there. He'd been angling for a promotion and thought it would look bad if *we* didn't show up. And I'd drunk too much. Like I often did when I was trying to forget something. And I'd said something stupid to his boss's wife. I can't remember what it was. But it had embarrassed him. He told me that much as we were leaving—as he stormed off to the car with me several feet behind him. On the drive home, he pounded his fist into the steering wheel and accidentally hit the horn. I laughed at him because I was buzzed. And he said, "You think this is funny? After everything you've done? What about *this*?" And he jerked the wheel, making our car swerve into the next lane. That obviously got my attention, and I sat up and looked at him, scared out of my mind, and he said nothing else. And neither did I. There were no words to describe what we'd become.

I can't help but wonder if something happened between him and Dylan. If they'd argued—maybe about the pregnancy?—and his temper had gotten the best of him, of them. Maybe he'd accidentally caused the crash because he'd done something stupid like swerve the car on purpose. I ask Officer Keoloha about this now, not mentioning our fight.

"Mrs. Morales, there's no reason to suspect this was anything other than a tragic accident. What happened between them in the Jeep before it crashed, we will never know. Could they have been fighting when it happened? Sure. But still. To be so careless while driving up here? When there are cliffs this steep? I'm just not sure why anyone would be reckless like that, no matter how angry they might be. I know this might be hard to hear, but like I've mentioned before, eyewitnesses who saw them picnicking said they looked happy. They purchased wine at that store, but we're certain James was driving, and there wasn't a way to test his . . ." He clears his throat. "Sadly, accidents on this part of the road are much more common than we'd like. There's a reason most car rental companies won't rent to people planning to drive this side. It's dangerous, especially as it gets later in the afternoon—the sun becomes blinding."

Beth interjects. "I agree with the officer, Jacks. I just don't think James would do anything to jeopardize another person's life."

"I'm sure you're right" is all I say, because that's what I want to believe. Even though I know James was capable of letting his anger outweigh his common sense.

"How were you able to pinpoint the time of day it happened?" Beth asks the officer.

"According to a police report that was filed by Dylan, her purse was stolen out of their Jeep while she and James were at the Seven Sacred Pools. She called in the theft at about four thirty and mentioned she'd been searching for it for an hour."

"You never told me this before now?" I ask. "Why?"

"Well, it wasn't relevant, in my opinion. It was her purse, her police report. I didn't consider it information you'd need or want."

"I guess it's not." I sigh. It wasn't relevant to me per se, but it was another piece of information that would always stick in my mind. More what-ifs. What if her purse hadn't been stolen? What if it hadn't been so late in the day?

The SUV hits several dips and potholes, and I grab the oh-shit handle again.

"Okay, Jacks, the area where we think the Jeep crashed is just up here, off a cliff that's about six hundred feet high," he says, letting his words settle in. I look through his window to the edge of the road, where the only thing separating us from the ocean below is a thick wall of tropical plants and flowers. I look behind me to gauge how steep this cliff is and grab the edge of the seat. It's high.

"There's no place to pull over, so I'm going to have to use my car to stop traffic both ways. There shouldn't be many vehicles on the road. But you'll still need to be quick."

"Are you sure you can do that?"

"You came all the way out here to see this; it's the least I can do," he says, parking the car diagonally and turning on the red-and-blue flashing lights.

"Okay," I say, feeling my heart collapse into itself as I open my door and look over my shoulder in case any cars are coming up behind us, still thinking about that truck that came barreling around the corner. I suddenly have trouble catching my breath—as if I've been running from something. But I haven't, I remind myself. I will finally be running toward something. Denial will have no place once I look over that edge.

Beth places a hand on my shoulder. "I'm right here, okay?"

It begins to rain again. As we start to make our way to the edge, Officer Keoloha stops us. "I just want to prepare you. It's a long way down. The lava rocks down there are sharp . . ." He trails off.

"You can talk to me about this like you would anyone else. Please finish what you were going to say."

Officer Keoloha gives me a long look before continuing. "Okay, the Jeep exploded and caught fire when it hit the rocks below. We found pieces of it scattered in the ocean in the bay we just passed. Some washed ashore. That's also where Dylan's body was found about two weeks after the wreck."

I find Beth's hand and grasp it but refuse to look her way. I can hear her crying softly, and I want to stay strong. I let myself go to that place, that awful, ugly place where I imagine James's final moments. The shock, then fear, and then searing pain. And the realization he was going to die. What did he think of in his last moments? Me? Dylan? And if he knew about the pregnancy, was he thinking about their unborn baby? I slide my wedding ring off my left finger and kiss it, then say a silent prayer that his death was quick and painless.

And then, even though I really don't want to, I say one for Dylan too before tossing my band into the ocean, watching intently until it disappears, imagining it cracking the surface of the water.

CHAPTER THIRTY-TWO

DYLAN—BEFORE

Dylan would never forget the moment she and James kissed for the first time. How, when it had finally happened, she realized she'd wanted it since the day they'd met. When James had waited for her after her shift, pressing a twenty-dollar bill *and* his business card into her petite hand. She could have thrown away that contact information and had no way to find him. But she hadn't. Instead she'd stared at it all night, turning it over in her hand, tracing the edges, wondering what his backstory was. How he'd gotten into software sales. Finally she'd buried the card at the bottom of her underwear drawer, debating whether to reach out.

Three days later, she was pulling out a pair of her favorite white lace panties when his card had dropped to the floor. She'd taken it as a sign that it was time to at least say thank you for his generous tip. And that would be the end of it. Because she had Nick. He was a good man. One she'd just gotten engaged to. And it was dangerous to toy with this idea that she hadn't actually found her future in the man she'd promised it to just days before.

James had responded within minutes. And Dylan had felt her heart flutter, her stomach tingle. They only dipped their big toes in at first, offering each other small scraps of their life through a daily email exchange. Maybe he'd send a funny meme of the latest political debate. Or she'd share a story from work, like when the executive chef got into a fistfight with the general manager over the very young and long-legged hostess they'd both been seeing.

But Dylan quickly found she wanted more. More than the challenge to write a witty email. More than the giddy excitement she felt as she opened his. More than the surface flirtation they'd been dancing around. She'd been staring blankly at the latest episode of *New Girl* when she got the courage to ask him about the one thing they weren't talking about: his marriage.

Almost twenty-four hours went by before she heard back. So long that she'd convinced herself she had scared him away. But then she'd heard the ding of her incoming email and saw his name. He told her he'd been married for eight years. And her name was Jacqueline. That things used to be good. But she had changed, he said. And he traveled a lot, and both the physical and emotional distance between them had driven them further and further apart. They were broken. And James didn't have any clue how to repair it.

Dylan wanted to know more—but she didn't ask. Because if she did, then he'd know she was interested. And she wasn't sure what exactly it was he wanted from her, or she from him. All she knew for sure was that she'd begun to feel differently about Nick. Like when she'd looked over at him on the couch recently—he was laser focused on the Lakers game, his body jutting slightly right and left with the players. She used to think that was adorable. But since meeting James, she'd feel a small prick of irritation when he did certain things—his quirks had begun to lose some of their charm.

Maybe it was the ring. The heavy oversize diamond that sat on her finger had begun to weigh down their relationship as well. Maybe it was because she knew now that *all this* was going to be permanent. The way Nick crunched his tortilla chips. The divide between her and her parents since she'd announced the engagement. The way he subtly tried to change her from the person she was to the one he thought she should be. More orderly (she was a self-proclaimed slob), more driven (she still felt a little lost), just more *everything*. Nick was incredibly decisive—it was actually one of the things she used to find refreshing. All of the other men she'd dated seemed a bit aimless, not unlike Dylan. But Nick had known what he wanted from the beginning. He'd wanted Dylan. And Dylan used to think she wanted a man like Nick.

Until she met James. He changed everything. She liked that he was older, more experienced, more worldly than Nick. And when they finally spoke on the phone, he made her laugh in a way that Nick never had—a laugh that would shake her whole body, a laugh that she would feel deep down in her gut. She quickly realized he could teach her things, show her things, challenge her.

They'd quickly graduated from emailing to texting and soon were in constant communication. Dylan's dull life suddenly sparkled when she shared with James the bits and pieces of it. She became addicted to their banter, which had become more and more flirtatious. So when he asked her to meet him for a drink, she knew exactly what she was doing. As she pulled on her favorite tank top and skinny jeans, she understood. Once she crossed this line, her life would never be the same.

She couldn't wait.

They'd met at a bar in Costa Mesa. Dylan sipped tonics with lime and James drank draft beers. They'd thrown darts and competed on the classic pinball machine in back that had flashing lights and a little Ferris wheel that would scoop up the metal ball each time Dylan used the right flipper to send it flying. Dylan teased James that he was so old he'd probably played it as a kid. (He had.) She'd brushed up against him, timidly at first, but as the night wore on, she became bolder. She was rewarded with his hand circling her waist. Rubbing her back. And then finally he pulled her in close for that first kiss, and Dylan arched her toes and tilted her neck so her mouth could easily find his. Dylan would play that moment back in her mind so often that she worried she might be obsessed, like that stalker woman in the Lifetime movie she'd watched. It was hard to explain (and she had no one to explain it to anyway, since no one else knew), but she'd never experienced a kiss like that, both soft and hard at the same time. Both right and wrong. It made her both incredibly happy and horribly confused. The only thing she knew for sure was that she'd do anything to feel that way again.

~

Dylan had made the short walk down to the pools after she parked the Jeep. She found James as he was coming out of the water, still smiling so wide the corners of his mouth practically touched his eyes.

"You have no idea—the adrenaline rush from that jump was insane. And then I floated in the water for a while; the temperature is perfect." She'd laid out a picnic on top of two towels she'd snagged from the hotel, and he sat down beside her and popped a piece of salami in his mouth. "I really wish you'd try it too."

Dylan glanced up at the bridge and held her breath as another person flew over the edge, this time a middle-aged bearded man, his belly jiggling as he jumped. "No, thanks," she said, and smiled. "I'm good just watching. That makes me nervous enough."

"You worry too much," James said.

"Maybe," Dylan agreed, thinking that James used to worry more too. But now he didn't seem to care. She used to be proud that she brought out that side of him—she'd feel a slice of satisfaction that she'd prevailed where Jacqueline had failed. But apparently now she was the one holding him back. Maybe the baby would change things.

"You ready to go?" James asked a short while later, after they'd finished the wine (Dylan had sipped lightly, wanting to please James). He'd fed her a piece of banana bread and then drew her to him, leaning her back and kissing her, causing the couple walking by to let out a low whistle. Maybe she'd imagined the shift in his demeanor. She'd pressed him several times to tell her what was on his mind, but he kept brushing her off, telling her it was nothing, seeming annoyed after the third request. That when he'd said that by *talk* he hadn't meant about anything serious.

But there was something in his eyes that made her question his words. Had he planned to tell her something important and changed his mind? Finally she gave up and accepted his answer as the truth— that there wasn't anything to talk about. Even though there were so many things to talk about. But how could she press him to reveal his secrets when she was keeping her own?

James stood up and held out his hand for Dylan to take. They packed up the remains of their picnic and walked to the Jeep.

"Damn it," James said. "The Jeep was broken into."

"Oh, shit. My purse was in here." Dylan looked inside, hoping somehow it was still there. But it wasn't.

"Are you sure you didn't take it with you when you set up the picnic? Or into the bathroom?"

Dylan thought hard. She'd been pretty sure she'd left it in the backseat on the floor, underneath a shopping bag. She had thought locking the Jeep would be enough. "I'm almost positive. What about your wallet?"

"I shoved it under my seat before I got out at the bridge," James said, reaching with his hand and retrieving it. "It's still here."

Dylan's stomach began to hurt. How was she going to get home? She'd have to call her roommates and have one of them overnight her passport. But still, they were supposed to fly back tomorrow. Dylan would need to change her flight too. Would James stay with her? And then her mind flashed to the pregnancy test sitting at the bottom of the bag.

"Come on," James called out as he headed back toward the pools. "Let's retrace our steps and ask if anyone saw anything. Then we can call the police."

Dylan's head was throbbing an hour later. They'd finally given up and called the police, filing a report over the phone. The officer who answered told Dylan it was quite common for that to happen, making her feel even more stupid. The police said they'd call if it turned up but gave her no confidence that it would.

James took her hand as they climbed into the car. "Don't worry, belleza. It's just stuff. It can be replaced." He'd initially been irritated with her as they searched, but as she became upset when they couldn't find any trace of her purse, he'd softened, using her special name. She loved when he called her that.

Dylan was exhausted, and that feeling in her gut had not dissipated. She still felt like something wasn't quite right. "Can we head back to the hotel now?"

"Can we keep going? Finish the drive? We're so close to the best part of the trip. Just lie back and close your eyes. Stop being so afraid. Let the curves soothe you." James leaned in and kissed her lips gently. "For me? I really want to see what all the fuss is about with the back road."

Dylan pointed toward the lowering sun. "But isn't it safer to drive during the day? It's going to get dark soon."

James kissed her again, this time more forcefully. "Do you trust me?"

Dylan met his gaze. For the past several months, they'd led a life that no one else knew about. They'd risked everything to be together. And now she was pregnant with his baby. Did she trust him? The truth was, she absolutely did. She just wasn't sure that she should.

"Yes," Dylan said.

"Remember on the way here—how we could smell the hibiscus and African tulips as we drove? How vibrant green the kukui trees were?"

Dylan nodded, recalling how he'd carefully studied the flora guide inside the case for the *Road to Hana* CD they'd purchased, then pointed out the trees and flowers along the way.

"Well, this . . . this is going to far surpass any of that."

Dylan bit her lip. She didn't want to go. But she wanted James to be happy. She wanted to be his number one, because sometimes, just beyond those beautiful eyes, she could see him thinking about his other life. About his wife. So she was going to continue on this road with him and help him forget. And she was also going to tell him about their baby.

CHAPTER THIRTY-THREE

JACKS—AFTER

When Officer Keoloha drops us off at the restaurant, our nerves as frayed as our hair from the strong wind, I'm not sure what we'll find—will the Jeep be here? Did Nick drive back to the hotel? Or go back to California? I try to ignore the hammering in my chest. My earlier anger toward him has subsided; my well of emotions has run dry. Reliving James's last moments was necessary, but excruciating and exhausting. Finally. All the questions that *could* have been answered were.

The challenge is not letting the ones that *couldn't be* haunt me.

But Nick is here. Waiting at the bar where we left him. Nursing a beer, staring into his glass like if he looked inside of it long enough, he'd find what he's looking for.

My heart leaps a little. He didn't leave. He didn't leave *me*.

"Hey," he says, his lips forming a slow smile. He doesn't ask us how it was. I don't offer any details. He doesn't need to. I don't have to. Because when he stands up and I reach him, I sink into his arms. And I know he can feel that I am emotionally lighter. That I've left a part of me back there on that cliff. I dig my head into his shoulder and close my eyes, and we stay like that for what feels like an hour but I'm sure is only a few seconds. Listening to each other without saying a word. Forgiving each other for our weaknesses. I can't make eye contact with Beth. I know what I'll see if I do. *That look.*

The ride back to the Westin is quiet, Beth finally giving in to her exhaustion once we reach Paia, snoring softly in the backseat.

"She's a good sister," Nick whispers.

"The best," I concur.

∾

Beth hugs me so hard the next morning that I have to fight to take a breath, and I gently wriggle from her grasp.

"Are you sure you're okay?" she asks me *again*—easily the fiftieth time since we returned from Hana last night. "I still have time to change my flight so we can fly home together." She looks at the cab that's waiting for her.

"I swear, Beth, I'm fine. Besides, I have Nick."

Beth gives me a look I can't quite place. If I had to guess, it's a cross between hope that I will recover and find happiness again and fear that I won't.

But "Be careful" is all she says. I nod, even though that's something I shouldn't be promising her. Because I've figured out a funny little secret about life: Even if you stay on the sidewalks and pay your bills on time and use hand sanitizer, bad things still happen. Yes, maybe you can cut your odds by playing it safe. By attempting to predict each and every possible pitfall. But your fate will still find you, no matter how much you hide from it.

∾

And now, just twenty-four hours—but what feels like a month—later, Nick and I are at the airport getting ready to fly back to an uncertain reality. The only certainty that I've learned is something about myself: I'm not the same person I was when I left California a week ago. The person who boarded that flight from LAX to Maui was weak. She was scared. Now I feel strong. Not quite indestructible, but much more durable. Like I used to be that crappy paper towel they show in the commercial, and now I'm the five-ply one. I used to break easily when there was a spill. Now I can mop up almost any mess. Pour that shit on me. I can handle it.

I drop my driver's license as we're making our way through security. It's raining again, the sheets of water hitting the concrete and making everything slick inside the open building that houses the Maui airport. "Would it kill them to put some doors on this place?" I had joked to Nick earlier as we stood in the long line to give the airline our bags.

"Here." Nick picks my license up off the ground and sticks it in the side pocket of my purse. "You don't want to lose this."

I smile at Nick and feel a memory flash through the back of my mind, one that I can't quite grasp. I pause, trying to reach out and grab the thought.

"What is it?" Nick asks.

I run through a mental checklist: wallet, phone, toothbrush. I haven't forgotten anything. "I just got a weird feeling for a second that something wasn't right. But it's nothing." I shake my head and put my canvas bag inside the white plastic bin on the conveyer belt, mentally rolling my eyes at the word stitched in black thread on the side of the tote: *Paradise*. I think of Beth, who bought it for me years ago as a birthday gift. Telling me that even if I wasn't traveling, carrying it would make me feel like I was on vacation. And I think of the irony now that I'm in paradise but not on vacation at all.

Once we get settled into our seats on the plane, I pull out the tabloid magazine I bought at the airport and start leafing through it.

It's time to get back to reality, and the first step is seeing what those Kardashians have been up to while I've been mourning. I look up to see Nick watching me, his face pensive.

"I'm sorry," he says.

"For what?" I ask, even though I know what for. But the thing is, I'm not sure he has anything to be apologetic about. If I'm being completely honest, as I'd stood on that cliff without him, just me, my sister several feet off to my right, I was happy I was doing it by myself. Because now I know I can.

"For bailing on you yesterday. My meltdown after we kissed. I was terrible."

I rested my hand on his arm. "No, you weren't. You were human. And that's okay."

"I need you to understand something. I've touched on this with you, but I haven't really gotten into it. Because it's hard to explain to someone who doesn't do what I do. But I see things at work. Terrible things. And to survive, you have to develop a shell. That's the only way you can go on a call where a six-month-old baby has been horribly burned by his crackhead mother and then come back to the station and not fall apart. Because the bells are going to sound again an hour later, and you have to pull on your turnout pants and get back out there.

"People need me, Jacks. I can't afford to fall apart. And I couldn't see where Dylan died. Because my mind would have clicked together all the parts that were missing from the accident report. I've been the first responder on calls exactly like that one. I know how she died. And I didn't want to *see* it. And I'm sorry I didn't figure it out sooner. That I wasn't smart enough to realize that was going to happen to me. I'm sorry I decided to put it in the box." He points at his chest, and I think I know what he means, but I wait for him to tell me. "It's where I put all the horrible things I don't want to deal with."

"I understand," I say. And I really do—because I have a box too. It's where I put the endometriosis. It's where I filed James's temper. It's where I put James's death. Until I realized that in order to be free of it all, I had to take the lid off and let it all out. And I hope Nick will be able to do that one day too.

Nick stares out the window as we taxi down the runway. "I was afraid if I didn't put Dylan and her accident in that box, the whole thing might come apart."

"You'd lose control," I say, and he nods and wraps his hand in mine—his fingers are warm and comforting.

When he turns back, tear streaks stain his face. "God, Jacks. I feel like you are the only person in this entire world who gets me right now."

"I feel the same way," I say, and hold my breath as he cups my chin and kisses me so softly, so gently that I almost melt into the seat, his salty tears escaping into my mouth.

"I don't want to fight this anymore," he says.

"I don't want to either. You don't have to be afraid of hurting me."

"I would never, ever hurt you. You know that, right?"

"I do," I whisper, and lean in to kiss him again before resting my head on his shoulder as the plane begins to ascend into the cloudless sky, both of us returning to a new life.

CHAPTER THIRTY-FOUR

JACKS—AFTER

"Okay, I'm ready." I point toward the cardboard box in the corner of the bedroom, the one Beth and I have been actively avoiding without discussion for the better part of two hours as she's helped me pack up James's things. The word *special* is scrawled across the top in thick black Sharpie.

I remember writing it like it was yesterday. James and I were moving from our tiny overpriced apartment in Newport Beach into this house that we'd been able to buy with his mom's help. What was going to be our starter home, but eventually became just *home*. At that time we hadn't accumulated a lot to put inside of the box. But I'd told James that we would as we created more special memories. I was planning to write that, *special memories*, but he grabbed me by the waist and threw me on our mattress—the last thing still in our otherwise-empty bedroom—before I could get to the second word. He laughed as he looked down at me. "I want *your* special box," he said suggestively as he undid the snap of my jeans, his bright-green eyes boring into mine.

As he yanked my pants down, he breathed that he wasn't going to use a condom. That he wanted to start trying.

My gut had clenched for a split second, but I pushed the guilt away. There was still a chance. I could get pregnant from today's quick, condomless sex. So I let my hope be stronger than my fear.

My sister slides the box across the hardwood floor, and I think I can read her mind. By the way her lips are pressed together, she's probably thinking, *What will happen to Jacks when she opens it?* Everything inside it is a fragment of my relationship with James, a moment in time we didn't want to forget. They're the items that made us an *us*.

"I want to do this," I respond to the question in her eyes. Whether this is true, I can't be sure. But I think it's what we both need to hear. And the fact that I was able to clean out his desk drawers without becoming hysterical I took as a positive sign. I'm accepting. I'm understanding. I'm adjusting. He isn't coming back. But guess what? The old Jacks isn't coming back either.

I've been home from Maui for three months, but I put this off until today. I knew there would be a day when I'd feel ready to go through James's things, and I let my heart choose when that would be. I woke up this morning at Nick's condo, his arms wrapped tightly around me. We've been sleeping like that, spooning, my back pressed up against his chest, sometimes even holding hands. Like we haven't wanted our bond to sever. And as I lay in his arms, his breath hot on the back of my neck, I knew it was time. That I needed to call Beth, get some boxes, and begin. To ensure I didn't back out, I even texted James's mom to let her know she could come by at the end of the day to pick up what she wanted to keep.

"I'm literally right here if you need me," Beth says as I pick at the edges of the packing tape.

I smile at her, thinking back to my conversation with Nick this morning, when I'd told him what I planned to do. His entire body instantly relaxed, as if the words had literally traveled through him. He had admitted early on that he wasn't comfortable here at my house, so he never stayed overnight. He'd said James's things—the framed college diploma in the den, his jackets still hanging in the front closet, his jeans and T-shirts still neatly folded in the laundry room—had always made him feel as if James's ghost were watching us. I'd tried not to take it personally—to understand how the very things that made me feel comfortable made him feel the opposite. And there was something about his point of view that had helped me realize that having James's aftershave in the medicine cabinet wasn't helping me let go. I'm not trying to erase James; I'm trying to find myself. And to move forward with someone else.

The morning after Nick and I returned home from Maui, Beth was on my doorstep with coffee. I knew it was her excuse to come over early so she could grill me about Nick. I told her I had developed feelings for him, because there was no other way to describe it. Was it more than that? Less? My body and heart said one thing (*Yes! Yes! Yes!*) and my mind chanted another (*Be careful!*). Beth warned me to take it slow, and I blushed before admitting it was too late for that—we'd already made love for the first time the night before.

She shook her head at me. "I hope this isn't a rebound. You're both definitely due for one."

Her words had stung, but I wasn't ignorant—I knew there was truth to them. But rebound or not, the way I feel about Nick is difficult to explain with words. It's more of a feeling, like maybe he's the silver lining in the dark cloud that's been hanging over me. Nick and I have been moving at a pace that both scares and exhilarates me. I've decided if I've learned one lesson in all of this, it's that life can be frighteningly short. So you might as well live it.

My phone vibrates. A text from Nick telling me he misses me. I scroll up. He's sent three since this morning. I can't help but smile.

I turn my phone on silent so I can focus. And I stare at the box again. I don't have to pull back the cardboard sleeves to know what I'm going to find inside the special box. I can already feel the lace of my garter that I wore on my thigh under my wedding dress—my "something new" that Beth purchased at a sex shop. It's hideous, red and black with silver fringe. Her intention. To remind me even vixens could wear white. I can see the pale-blue photo album, filled with snapshots of our history, the way we used to do it before those websites started creating them for us. I'm going to see pictures of James celebrating his twenty-ninth birthday, a shot glass filled with whiskey raised up high, me snuggled into the crook of his arm. I'm going to remember Beth's beautiful vow renewal at the Hotel del Coronado—how she'd famously cried happy tears as she walked down the aisle, her sassy short white satin dress flapping in the wind.

And when I dig deeper to the bottom, I'm going to touch the heart-shaped tin. The one that holds our letters to each other. The words we wrote when we were still so in love. The poem from our second anniversary. The proof that he loved me. That I loved him. That we were a *we*. The words that will continue to live on after him.

I watch Beth as she takes James's sport coat off the hanger and folds it neatly. She stacks it in the box marked with his mother's name. Isabella had texted me back with a list of what she wants, and I'm also putting additional things in that I know she'll cherish. I check my phone—it's nearly 4:00 p.m., and she'll be here soon.

I decide I need to rip the tape like I would a Band-Aid, and I find our wedding album sitting on top. "Will you put this in Isabella's box?" I hand it to Beth without opening it.

"Are you sure?"

I nod as a tear falls down my cheek. "She planned the whole thing anyway. And he looked so handsome that day. She'll love having it."

I sift through the box, taking deep breaths as I contemplate what to keep. I don't want to lose too much of James, but I don't want to lose myself either. It's a fine line.

I dig toward the bottom, my fingers feeling for the tin. I start tossing everything out: an envelope full of movie ticket stubs, a foam finger from our first Dodgers game, a program from *The Lion King*. The tears start to fall harder now. The dam has been broken.

"What is it? What's happening?" Beth crouches down beside me as I sob.

"It's not here."

"What?"

"Our letters. Our words. *His* words."

"Are you sure? Let me look." She leans over the box.

"I already did. It's not there, Beth."

Beth searches for a moment and shakes her head. "I'm sorry. I don't see it either. But I'm sure it will turn up. Maybe you moved it? Remember what a haze you were in after everything happened? Is it possible you took it out and didn't put it back?"

I don't remember taking it out. But Beth is right: the weeks after James's death were surreal, and many of my memories of that time are cloudy. Unfortunately, save for the pictures Beth boxed up right after James died and my favorite sweatshirt of his, this tin is the only thing I believe I can't live without.

Beth hugs me, and I cry until I can't anymore, amazed by how many tears I have inside me. That I keep believing they will eventually dry up.

"This sucks," I say into her shoulder.

"I know." Beth squeezes me.

The doorbell rings. I pull away and wipe my face with the sleeve of my sweater. "Shit. That must be Isabella. How do I look?" I say as I stand up.

"Like you've been bawling for hours," Beth says gently.

"It's fine. She's seen me looking even worse than this, I'm sure." But I wipe under my eyes and run a finger through my hair anyway.

I walk to the door, my heartbeat speeding up slightly. I haven't seen her since the memorial. Isabella had been somewhat stoic, thanks to the two Xanax I saw her sister slip her that morning. I suck in a long breath and open the door.

Nick grins and pulls a bouquet of red roses from behind his back.

"What are you doing here?" I ask, surprised to see him. He told me he was going to a new beer tasting room in Long Beach.

"Well, hello to you too."

"Sorry, I just thought—" I start, then stop. "These for me?"

"No, they're for Beth." He smiles, and I feel my chest warm.

"Thank you," I say, and cover his mouth with mine, trying to forget about the heart-shaped tin.

"Jacks?" I jerk back from Nick and drop the roses at the sound of my mother-in-law's voice.

I had planned to tell Isabella everything, eventually. But each time I thought about calling her and asking her to coffee, I'd imagine her face as I destroyed the version of her son that she'd thought she'd known. It's the same reason my mother still believes James had been in Maui for work. I know how it feels to question every memory you have of someone you love—I just wasn't ready to do it to someone else. And now, I'm forced to face Isabella, my heart banging inside my chest, a flush coloring my cheeks. I feel caught, even though technically I've done nothing wrong. But still, her eyes are full of questions I'm not sure I can answer. At least not with explanations she'll want to hear. I meet Nick's gaze briefly, and I can't quite read his expression—if I didn't know better, I'd almost think he were enjoying this. The drama.

I force myself to make eye contact with Isabella, who's standing there in her loose-fitting floral blouse and capri pants, a large tote slung over her shoulder. She looks out of place, like she meant to arrive at a farmers' market. And maybe it's that simple, that she no longer fits in here—into my life.

"Nick, this is my mother-in-law, Isabella. Isabella, this is . . ." I pause, not sure I can say the word. Not 100 percent sure what that word is.

"I'm Nick. Her boyfriend." Nick extends his hand, but Isabella steps back abruptly, as if he had a disease she didn't want to catch.

Boyfriend. It sounds so juvenile. But then again, what else is he? For a brief moment I see James leaning against the counter in my tiny kitchen wearing nothing but a pair of crisp white boxers. It's just two weeks after I'd met him, and he's grinning at me. And then I'm laughing and kissing him like I might never stop because he's just asked me not to sleep with anyone else ever again. "Because we're officially going steady. I'm your boyfriend now."

I give Nick a look, wishing he'd have let me handle it, and he mouths to me that he's sorry.

The three of us stand there in awkward silence, somehow all understanding it will be Isabella who speaks next.

"Jacqueline, please tell me this man is not really your boyfriend. That you haven't moved on. So soon," Isabella says shrilly, her brilliant-green eyes squinting just like James's when he was angry.

When I don't answer, her face registers understanding. He is exactly who he says he is. She shakes her head as if trying to toss away the information. She opens her mouth to say something, but quickly closes it. She stares at the ground, deep in thought. Finally she looks up at me. "Where are his things?" she asks. "I want them right now, and then I will leave," she says, every word slow and measured. I move to the side so she can get into the house.

Beth appears and gives me a questioning look as Isabella brushes past her toward the master bedroom.

"Can you go? I need to talk to Isabella alone. And tell Nick he needs to go home too. That I'll talk to him later—please," I whisper to Beth as I pass her.

I find Isabella sobbing in our closet, breathing in James's gray cashmere sweater. I start crying at the sight of her. At the grief I know she must feel but that I will never understand. The loss of a child.

"I'm so sorry, Isabella. I was going to tell you everything. I just—"

"You just what?" Isabella cuts me off. "Forgot to tell me you'd moved on?"

"No, it's not that. If I told you, then I'd need to explain who Nick is. How I met him. And that would hurt you."

"More than I'm hurt right now?" She continues to cry as she cradles his sweater.

"No. I mean, maybe. I don't know. I'm so sorry," I choke through my tears.

"It's bad enough you never gave me a grandchild. How could you? Did you even love him?"

Yes. I loved him more than anything. But I'm not sure that was enough.

The words bubble up inside of me, but I don't speak. I didn't want it to be like this—I had imagined this conversation going very differently, and certainly not starting off with her witnessing me kissing Nick.

But no matter how it started, it's time to tell her. Not to defend that I've begun to have some good days where James doesn't infiltrate my thoughts, but because she deserves to know the truth about how her son died.

"Isabella, I think you should come sit down. There are things you need to know."

"What could I possibly still need to know? After I've seen my son's widow making out with some guy in a motorcycle jacket just six months after his death?"

"James wasn't who I thought he was."

Isabella frowns. "What are you saying? Don't you dare slander him just so you can feel better about what you're doing here. My son loved you. No matter what I said, he always defended the things you did," she says, her voice rising. "James gave you everything, and you—"

I put my hand on her arm to interrupt her. "I don't know how else to say this, so I'll be blunt. James was having an affair. That's why he was in Maui. He'd been seeing her for months. And she was pregnant with his child. Yes, you're right, he may have loved me. But I think he loved her too."

Isabella lets out a cry, and I put my arms around her shoulders and hug her as tightly as I can. We stand like that for several seconds until Isabella pulls back, her mascara running down her cheeks. "You're sure?"

"Yes. I promise I'll explain everything."

She walks over to her tote and pulls out a package of tissues, removing one and dabbing each eye delicately. "I'm ready now."

I sit down on the bed and pat the place next to me. "Okay," I say. And because there's no room for lies in this version of my life, I start from the beginning and don't stop until every drop of truth is revealed.

CHAPTER THIRTY-FIVE

JACKS—AFTER

Nick's front door opens just as I'm about to turn the knob.

"Hey!" he says, a huge smile spreading across his face. "I didn't think I'd see you tonight—I was just heading out for ice cream."

"Ice cream?" I cock my head.

"Yeah—you got a problem with that?" He smirks. "I was stressed about your conversation with Isabella and thought I'd eat my feelings." He laughs.

I smile. "That's why I'm here—I wanted to talk to you about what happened at the house earlier today. It was pretty awkward."

"I know." He grabs my hand. "I'm sorry about the whole boyfriend thing. I totally overstepped," he says, and looks down at his cowboy boots. "It's just that . . . Jacks . . . I think I'm falling in love with you."

Suddenly I forget what had seemed so important as I'd driven to his house—the questions I had for him about how he acted. All I can think of is what Nick just revealed. Involuntarily I flash back to when James whispered that he loved me for the first time in my ear right before we fell asleep in his bed, his breath tickling my ear. I push the memory aside and let Nick's declaration sink in, let his words settle in my chest.

Thankfully he keeps talking. "And I know this is selfish, but I wanted her to know it." He looks back up. "I wanted *you* to know it." His gaze is so intense, it feels like he's looking through me.

The truth is, I've been falling too. I can tell by the way I rush to text Nick when something funny happens, like last week when I'd been in Starbucks and discovered a sock stuck to the back of my pant leg, the dryer sheet failing to do its job. I know by how my stomach flutters when his name comes up on my phone, and he's calling me sometimes four or five times a day—just to hear my voice. I was sure of it when I couldn't sleep at night and I'd think of him first, wishing he were beside me to wrap his strong arm around my waist. It's been a long time, but my heart still remembers the feeling of the first gasps of love.

I tilt my chin up and kiss him, deciding not to be scared. "For the record, I'm falling in love with you too," I whisper, the words feeling foreign as I say them out loud. James was the only man I ever loved until now. But James was the past. Nick is the future.

Nick pulls me in for a deeper kiss. I lose my balance, and he catches me before I stumble, causing the moment to pass. And I'm grateful, because I don't want to have the conversation. To dissect what it all means.

"Come on, let's go eat the shit out of our feelings," I say as I laugh awkwardly. "I could go for some mint chip—and let me guess, you're a rocky road kind of guy."

"Nope." He shakes his head, a smile playing on his lips.

"Chunky Monkey?"

"Try again." He closes his door and rattles the knob to make sure it's locked.

"Pistachio." I frown, and he gives me a blank stare. "What?" I ask. "Pistachio, really?"

"Fine, I give up."

"Vanilla," he says proudly.

"Vanilla?" I squint at him. "I would have never guessed that. It's so—"

"Boring?" he says, taking my hand.

"Maybe a little," I say.

"I like that it's predictable, easy, never disappoints."

I laugh. "Kind of like you?"

"Maybe," he says before kissing me, his lips soft.

As we're pushing through the front doors to go outside, Nick's arm slung over my shoulder, a woman with wiry short blonde hair and cut-off jean shorts nearly collides with us. "Sorry," she says, looking up from her phone and glancing from me to Nick, her eyes widening at him.

"No problem," I say, and she gives me a once-over, then hurries toward the elevator, her barely-there shorts rising up in the back with each stride, her pumps clicking against the floor.

"Did you see the way she looked at us?" I ask once we're out on the sidewalk. "Do you know her?"

Nick nods. "She was one of Dylan's roommates. They never got along very well." He frowns. "I haven't seen her in months."

~

After we order our ice cream cones and settle on a bench outside Baskin-Robbins, I recount my conversation with Isabella to Nick. He said he wanted to know how it went, and I decide that if we're going to have a *real* relationship, I need to share. But still, it feels weird, talking about my ex-mother-in-law with my new *boyfriend*. In between licks of my mint chip, I tell him how she fired question after question, some curious, some accusatory, and how I'd tried my best to hold my voice steady as I revealed the ugly truth about James. About me. About our marriage.

At first it seemed that she held me somewhat accountable for James's indiscretion. And I didn't argue the point—I had accepted that I wasn't an innocent party in our union. I hadn't cheated, but I'd betrayed him in my own way. But as I told her about my journey to Hana, how Nick had helped me find a bit of closure to fill the gaping hole James's death had created inside me, she began to soften.

She left two hours later. Her tears had finally dried up and were replaced by forced acceptance. "I'm sorry he did this to you," she said as she stood and grabbed her things. "I always prided myself on my close relationship with my son—I wish he had trusted me enough to come to me. Obviously I didn't know him as well as I should have."

"We all have secrets," I said as we walked to the door. "Some are just bigger than others."

"True," she pondered. "I have one more question."

"Anything."

"How do I move on from this? Because it's not like I can call and yell at him for being so irresponsible—for being so selfish! I feel like I have nowhere to place all this anger I'm feeling." She gave me a sad smile. "If I'm being totally honest, I had really wanted to direct it your way, but it's not as simple as that, is it?"

"No, it's not."

"So then, what?"

I thought for a moment before speaking. "I think you let yourself love him just the same. He was your son. And he loved you. That will never change."

"And you? Do you still love him? After all this?"

I thought back to standing on the cliff in Hana—the closest to James that I'd ever be again. In that moment I'd felt no anger, no resentment. Only love tinged with regret. I nodded. The next part I don't tell Nick, knowing it would bother him.

"I will always love him, Isabella. But I'm also ready to move on. I hope you can understand that."

"I can," she said softly. "You know, I was wrong about you, Jacks. You're much stronger than I ever gave you credit for."

I laughed lightly. "I think we may have both been wrong about each other."

Isabella hugged me one last time. "Take care of yourself," she said, grabbing the box of James's things I'd put aside for her, the wedding album sticking out of the top, and walked out my front door without looking back.

Nick kisses my forehead lightly after I finish telling him the story. "I know that conversation wasn't easy. But for what it's worth, I'm proud of you—I think you did the right thing by telling her the real story. She deserves to know."

"The truth will set us free, right?" I whisper as I rest my head on his chest, his steady heartbeat comforting me.

~

The next morning, the pressure of Nick's lips on my mouth prods me awake.

He moves in for a deep kiss that sends a shiver through my entire body. "See you later, sleepyhead."

"Can you stay a bit longer?" I pat the bed next to me. "Maybe do what we never got around to because I passed out. Sorry about that."

"I wish I could." He tugs at the bottom of the T-shirt he loaned me last night and raises his eyebrow. "But I've got to get to the station. The guys texted that it was a rough night, so I want to get there a bit early and relieve them."

I smile as I watch concern fill his eyes. "I love how much you love your job," I say, thinking about my classroom that I'd just returned to last week. How good it felt to take in each and every one of my new fourth graders' faces, to sit in the chair behind my desk and watch them as they read their textbooks, to let myself get excited about a field trip we were taking to the discovery museum. The school had offered to extend my leave of absence, but I needed to get back to teaching. It was what reminded me I was still me.

Nick kisses me again. "Stay as long as you want, okay? It's Sunday! Enjoy yourself. I set the espresso maker out for you. I know what a beast you are without your caffeine."

"I'm not *that* bad."

"Says you." He laughs when I swipe at him, and I watch him walk out of the room.

~

A few hours later as I'm leaving, I see the woman from the night before hovering in the hallway outside of Nick's front door. She flashes me a surprised look, then rushes away, but she abruptly stops and turns her body halfway around, as if she doesn't know which way she's going.

"Did you need something?" I ask. "Nick's not here . . ."

"I know. I saw him leave earlier." She stares down at her cherry-red wedge sandals, then looks back up. "I was coming to see you actually," she says as she takes a few tentative steps in my direction.

"Me?"

She rolls her eyes.

I think about the strange look she gave Nick last night. How she sized me up. "I know you must be upset about seeing Nick with someone so soon after Dylan . . ." I pause, remembering the conversation I had with Isabella. How hard it was for her to see I'd already moved on. "But it's complicated."

She crosses her arms.

"Listen . . ." I stop, realizing I don't know her name.

"Briana," she says.

"Look, Briana, I get it. You're upset about Dylan. My husband died too. They were in Maui together, having an affair. I'm not sure if you realize that. But that's how Nick and I met—we were both devastated to discover the people we loved weren't who we thought."

"You don't know what the hell you're talking about."

Her harsh tone stuns me. We stand there for a few moments, neither of us breaking eye contact, and finally, I speak. "Where do you get off coming here and attacking me? We're all upset. We all lost people."

"You really think Dylan was over there cheating on him when she died?"

"What else would you call it? They were engaged."

"Oh my God. You really don't know." Briana takes a step backward as if she suddenly needs to distance herself from my ignorance.

"Know what?" I ask.

"Dylan and Nick had broken up months before she went to Maui."

I feel as if the air is being sucked out of my chest. I struggle to take in a breath. They weren't engaged?

Briana seems oblivious to my shock. "Dylan dumped him because . . ." She doesn't finish her sentence.

"Because she wanted to be with my husband, James," I finish, almost instinctively trying to defend Nick.

"I think she hoped he would leave you," she adds, and I fight back my tears. Was that what James had been planning? To leave?

"Are you . . . are you sure they had broken up?" I ask, trying to find the logic in it. But my mind keeps drifting back to Nick, the sweet man who'd reached over and wiped a drip of ice cream off my chin, then kissed me where it had been just to make sure it was gone.

"She told me everything—the night before they left for Maui. She was so upset. Nick had started stalking her—he wouldn't accept that it was over."

Nick . . . a stalker? I shake my head.

"You don't believe me? Why would I make it up? I'm taking a big enough risk coming here."

"What does that mean? A risk?"

She looks past me as if she's worried someone might be coming. "After she gave him the ring back, he freaked out." She lowers her voice slightly. "She told me he followed her, threatened her. She thought about getting a restraining order."

Restraining order? Against Nick? Are we even talking about the same man?

I grab the doorjamb, thinking about James—how he'd lied to me for so long. How I'd been so oblivious. Nick can't be a liar too. There's no way I could be that wrong twice in a lifetime.

Briana stares at me for a moment, and I silently pray that she'll tell me she's mixed up, she doesn't have her facts straight, she's sorry she bothered me.

"I realize you don't know me," she says. "I could be some crazed ex-roommate making shit up. And you don't want to believe it. But it's true." She sighs. "I wish I still had her journal. It was all written in there. But it's gone—her parents have it."

"Journal?"

"I've said too much already." She makes a face like she's sorry. "Just be careful, okay?" She gives me one last long look, then hurries down the hallway, disappearing into the stairwell.

I call after her. But the door slams behind her, and this time she doesn't come back.

CHAPTER THIRTY-SIX

DYLAN—BEFORE

She didn't know what it was about this particular cloudy Monday morning, just three months after accepting Nick's proposal, that was giving her the courage to break up with him. All she knew for sure was that ever since the night James had invited her to Maui, her engagement ring felt even tighter, her chest even more compressed, her heart even less invested. She wiped the foggy bathroom mirror and stared at her reflection, wondering how she could've been so in love with Nick and could barely conjure that feeling now.

They'd met just eighteen months before, when she'd moved from Phoenix. The first time she'd seen the firefighter in her building was when he'd gotten off his motorcycle in the parking garage. She'd watched him guide his bike in and put his helmet away with such care, she was almost entranced. Another time she'd been behind him in the line at Peet's, staring at his dusty cowboy boots, never having known a man who had owned a pair. She found them sexy.

And then one day she'd been standing by the mailboxes, and she heard a male voice make a joke about all the junk mail in her hand. It turned out the voice belonged to the firefighter. She'd always had a thing for civil servants. Something about the uniform, about them protecting people, keeping them safe. Police officers. Paramedics. Even a security guard once.

He'd asked her out somewhere between small talk about how many trees the vast amounts of junk mail were killing and their mutual agreement that the hazelnut coffee at Peet's was their favorite. And even though when she told Briana about her date, her roommate had made a snide remark about not shitting where you eat, Dylan had just laughed. Because there was something about him. It might have been the way he cocked his ear toward her whenever she spoke, like she was about to say something important. Or maybe it was the way his eyes crinkled when he smiled, which was often. Whatever it was, she wanted to know more.

He'd taken her to the movies and to get ice cream after. She was home by nine. And it had been the best date of her life.

How things had changed.

She'd become tired of living two lives—the safe one she had with Nick, where he rubbed her feet after her shifts while guilt consumed her. And then there was the dangerous life she had with James—slippery and uncertain. But she had finally decided it was the one that she wanted.

She sat on the toilet seat lid and traced the word *journal* on the cover of her leather-wrapped volume with her fingernail. She'd spilled coffee on the corner and pages of the diary were stained a light caramel color, but that was one of the things she loved most about it. That it was flawed just like she was—just like the people she wrote about inside its pages.

She turned to the first entry, recorded just two days after she met Nick. She'd dashed into Laguna Beach Books and bought the journal, ready to write down everything about this man who was so different.

I've met someone. He's so incredibly charming! He makes all the others look like amateurs. Boys who thought they were men. Now I know the difference. Nick is a real man. I never want to forget the way it feels when he strokes my bare arm with his finger, like an electric charge is rushing through my body. And I'm trying to memorize the way he looks at me. Like he will never let anyone hurt me. Like he will always love me. It's little things, but they mean something so big—like when he takes my hand and guides me across the street. Or how he sprints in front so I never have to open my own door. I've never had a man do that for me before. I feel cherished.

She sighed at that memory. Feeling cherished had started out as something sweet because he always made her feel like the most important person in the world. But it had eventually turned to something more along the lines of compulsion or ownership. Like she *belonged to him*. A trinket that he polished then put away in a glass case so no one else could touch her.

To test the waters with James, she had recently thrown out the idea that she was considering ending things with Nick. She didn't get into the whys—that slope was too slippery to climb. She knew if she told James she only wanted him, he'd get spooked. His eyes had sparked slightly, but he'd made sure to let her know not to do it *for him*. Only to end things if it was best *for her*. She'd smiled and said, "Of course," in what she'd hoped was a tone used by a very confident woman dating a married man.

She turned to a fresh page in her diary. Maybe she couldn't tell James the truth, but she needed to be honest with herself. She needed to remind herself why it wasn't working with Nick. So she didn't lose her courage. She knew she'd be catching him off guard. Nick was always so invincible—never worried about things. Never anxious. Always so confident. She knew he'd try to convince her to stay, and he was so good at that—at making her believe he could take better care of her than anyone else ever could. That he loved her more than anyone else could. And maybe that was true. But James . . . it always came back to James.

I need to break up with Nick. But I'm scared—I know it's the right thing in my gut, but I don't want to hurt him. I also don't want to live this double life anymore, when it's James that I love and want to be with. Not that I can tell either of them that. That truth could make me lose everything. Since the night James told me he wanted to take me away to Maui, something changed inside of me. And something also changed with Nick.

Nick had been waiting for me in my apartment that night, the lamp casting a weird shadow across his face that made him look creepy. And he asked me where I'd been like he already knew. Maybe I was being paranoid. But he's been hounding me about wanting to meet this Katie that I'd been out with. And I'm out of excuses for why I can't introduce them. And I'm too afraid to put Katie in a position where she'd have to lie to Nick in person.

It's like Nick has tightened his grip ever since that night. He's always been possessive. But lately it's been different, more intense. He's had so many questions—way more than usual. Wanting to know everything from my work schedule to what I had for lunch. And he's been texting constantly. If I don't answer within a minute or two, he calls. It's to the point where I almost wish he'd ask me if I'm cheating on him.

I have to get out.

Dylan closed the journal and wedged it deep in the overnight bag she had brought to Nick's. "It's time," she said to her reflection, and walked out of the bathroom.

∾

She found Nick pouring a glass of orange juice. He leaned in to kiss her, but she moved away.

"What's wrong—did you wake up grumpy?"

"I can't do this anymore," Dylan blurted.

"Do what?" he asked, drinking his juice.

"This," she said, raising up her left hand and pointing to her ring.

Nick took a moment, as if registering what she was saying. Or rather what she wasn't. She knew she needed to bring herself to say the words *I can't marry you*, but they were stuck in her throat. The guilt from cheating on him with James was weighing on her. What if she'd never met James? Would she be perusing bridal magazines now?

"Are you breaking up with me?" Nick asked, setting his glass down on the counter with too much force, the juice slopping over the top.

Dylan nodded, but she couldn't look at him. She stared at her bare feet.

"I don't understand. This is so good. We are so good." Nick said, and tugged on the cuff of her robe's sleeve, forcing her to look up at him.

"It just doesn't feel right anymore," she finally said, tears perched in the back of her eyes.

"What doesn't feel right?" He was still gripping the pink fleece.

You're not James.

"Dylan, did I do something?" He tried again, his eyes pleading. She'd never seen him look so vulnerable. He had always been so strong and big—a broad chest, large biceps, the kind of man who protected you. In fact, she called him Paul Bunyan sometimes.

She eased away from his grip and watched his arms tense, the veins in his forearms bulging. "Nick, it's not just one thing—it's just the way I feel. Getting married is a huge commitment. We need to be sure. I'm not sure."

"I guess I don't understand what's changed. Dyl, we don't even argue! Did something happen? Because this doesn't make sense at all."

"I don't know how to explain it." *And I don't want to explain it.*

"Dyl, don't do this to me. I want you to marry me."

Dylan looked down at the ring. "I shouldn't have said yes." She flinched as she tried to slide the band over her knuckle. It was still too tight. She'd never gotten it resized. It was like deep down she'd known it wasn't just the ring that didn't fit.

The look on his face crushed her, and she almost reached out and hugged him. She almost changed her mind, told herself James was never going to leave his wife anyway. And would eventually end things with her. That was what married guys usually did. Got tired of the mistress. Figured out the wife wasn't so bad after all. But she stayed strong. She decided that James would see this as sign of loyalty. Maybe not at first. But eventually.

"I thought you loved me the same way I loved you . . ." He paused, and she knew he was waiting for her to say that she did love him that way—but she couldn't. Even as she eyed her ring and thought of his proposal, she didn't think she ever had—loved him the way he needed her to, anyway. "Is there someone else?"

Dylan's head shot up, and she locked eyes with Nick. She knew she could tell him right then. That it would be out in the open *finally*. But there was something about the way he was looking at her . . . she knew he wasn't ready to hear it. And she didn't want to be cruel.

"No."

He narrowed his eyes and pressed his lips together. And she wondered again if he already knew. If he'd known all along, since the night he'd waited for her in her apartment—or even before.

"You have to give me something here. If I've done nothing wrong and there's no one else, then what?" He threw his hands up in the air.

Dylan decided she had to say it. The words she knew would devastate him.

"We don't fit together." She took a deep breath and didn't stop until she'd said it all. That she didn't love him the way he loved her. That she was doing him a favor, that he deserved someone who would love him more. She told him he deserved passion. But she stopped there. She didn't say that what she had with James was thrilling, exhilarating, spontaneous. That she felt more passion in her fingertip for James than she did in her entire body for Nick.

But then he started crying—giant tears that didn't look right streaming out of his eyes. "You're wrong, Dyl," he said through his sobs.

"I'm sorry." She reached for his hand, but he stepped backward.

"So that's it then?" he asked.

She didn't know what to say.

"This isn't you, Dylan. You're fragile. Delicate. You need to be taken care of. Remember how lonely you were when I met you? You'll never find anyone who will take care of you better than I do."

She didn't know if James would be that person, but she wanted to find out.

After that, he refused to talk to her. Became sullen. She decided she should go. She worked the ring off with some Vaseline and set it next to her set of keys to his condo. Then she grabbed her bag and walked out the door. She knew she needed to start looking for another place, that it would be awkward to run into him. She hoped eventually he'd come to realize this was for the best and that they could be friends.

❧

But Nick didn't let go. He didn't give up. The calls started. The emails. The texts. One day she had fifty-six missed calls from him, and twice as many text messages. He said he wanted her back. That he would do anything. The way he said *anything* into her voice mail made her heart hurt. She had to change her phone number.

Then he confronted her in their building. Once when she was getting her mail. Another time as she was stepping out of her car. She screamed that time because he scared the hell out of her. He came out of nowhere. The look on his face made her feel so bad. "It's just me, Dylan," he said.

This behavior went on for over a month. Jimmy from work offered her his couch, but she didn't know how to explain to James why she was sleeping at some guy's apartment. She worried he'd see it as baggage. And then he might never leave his wife. So Dylan started to do everything she could to avoid running into Nick, leaving her place super early and coming home late.

When she didn't see or hear from him for almost a week, she started to breathe easy again. She was leaving for Maui the next morning and was lost in thought about the trip. As she pushed through the back door of her restaurant, she was going over her packing list, remembering that on the way home, she needed to stop at Walgreens for some travel-size bottles for her shampoo and conditioner.

"Dylan."

She jerked her head to the side and saw Nick leaning against the wall by the dumpster.

"Hi," he said when their eyes locked.

But Dylan's lips wouldn't move; her feet were frozen in place. He smiled at her, and she felt her arms prick with goose bumps. It was his flashy grin, as she always called it. The one that could charm anyone from a baby to an eighty-year-old woman. Why was he smiling at her like that? Like nothing had happened? Something didn't feel right. She wanted to call out, to race back inside, but she was worried he would get angry. Chase her. Cause a scene. But she was just as scared to stand there.

"Dylan, why won't you say something, my beautiful girl?" He laughed—it was the one she'd heard when they were watching *The Tonight Show* or he was telling her his latest firefighter joke. But he looked different—his facial features contorted by the shadows. "Dylan?" Nick tried again.

"What are you doing here?" Dylan tried to keep her voice from shaking, her car keys making an indentation in her palm.

"I've been so lonely, Dyl. My life is empty without you in it. And you're lonely too, I know it. I can see it in your eyes. That's how we both felt when we met, remember?"

He took a step toward her, and she stiffened.

"We've already talked, Nick. There's nothing more to say."

"You look upset. Don't be upset with me."

"I'm not," she lied, hoping the shadows were concealing her racing heartbeat. She was sure it was visible through her T-shirt.

"Good answer." He grinned. "Because this can all be resolved right now. Now that you've had some time to process everything—to realize you do want to be with me." Dylan watched with disbelief as he dug into his pocket and pulled out her engagement ring. The diamond caught the light behind him. "Here, put it back on." He held it out to her. "You're my soul mate."

"Nick—"

He put his hand up as if to stop her from disagreeing. "You are, Dyl. You are."

She took a small step backward, slipping slightly on a puddle of oil. She tried to calculate how far she was from the door. Maybe she could reach it, then lock it before he followed her inside. But then what? She willed one of her coworkers to walk out. Where was Margo with her cigarette or Eric with the trash?

"Take it, Dyl, and we'll put all this behind us. We'll fly somewhere—anywhere—and get married tonight!"

Why was he acting as if she could be so wrong about her own feelings? As if they could just pick up and move forward? She stared at the ring—the one he *knew* didn't fit her. Didn't he?

She couldn't shake the uneasy feeling in her gut, her instincts telling her something was seriously off with Nick.

Why hadn't she seen it before now?

CHAPTER THIRTY-SEVEN

JACKS—AFTER

As I drive home, Briana's accusations about Nick are trying to clog my thoughts. But I'm choosing to think of the Nick I *know*—the one I've known for *months*—instead of the man presented to me by a woman I met one day ago. I'm focused on the Nick with the perpetually mussy hair, the scuffed cowboy boots he wears rain or shine, the dozen different smiles. That's the Nick I spent last night with. The one who made me laugh so hard when he told me a joke about a firefighter's hose that I nearly spit out my ice cream. The one who told me he was proud of me.

The one who told me he loved me.

I pull into my driveway and try calling Beth for the second time, but she doesn't pick up. I send her a text that I need to talk ASAP, but I already know what she'll say because it's what I'm feeling too. That this roommate is just angry. Grieving. Jealous. Whatever it is. That she's trying to hurt me the way she's been hurt. What other objective would she have in telling me these crazy things about Nick?

I chew my cuticle as I stare at the screen of my phone, trying to push Briana's image out of my mind. The way she didn't blink when she said she'd taken a risk coming there.

Hi, beautiful. What are you doing?

Nick's text pops up, and I smile.
     A sign. Take that, Briana!

Hi! I just got back to my place.

I see the bubble that he's responding and wait, my stomach fluttering.

Miss you! Do you miss me?

Of course!

Ok just wanted to say hi! Gtg—cat stuck in a tree ;)

When Beth's text comes in next, I start to feel silly for trying to get hold of her so many times.

You ok? Saw two missed calls from u. I'm in lame-ass PTA meeting with horrible reception. Will be done here in 15. Can we talk then? Or is this a 911?

All ok! Meet you at your place in thirty?

Perfect!

I decide to walk to Beth's. The fresh air will do me good—the best way to put this crazy morning behind me. To focus on what *I* want to focus on—that I feel happy. *Finally. Thankfully.* It's late morning, and there's still a cloud cover, so I open the closet for something with long sleeves to put on over my tank top and jeans. I stop when I see James's sweatshirt. I forgot it was in here. Slowly I reach out and finger the gray cotton fabric, remembering the first time I wore it. We were watching fireworks on the Balboa Peninsula, and he gave it to me when I started shivering. He didn't have a shirt on underneath it, but he didn't care. He stood there shirtless in the sand as the sky blazed with light. He explained that he'd had it since college, hence the tiny holes in the sleeve and the frayed band around the waist. And somewhere along the way, it became mine. I'd claim it before he could, and he'd just laugh and shake his head, not understanding I loved it because it was his.

I step closer and bury my nose in it, hoping for a trace of his smell, of him. I tug it off the hanger, and something falls out of the pocket and slides under the sofa. I pull the shirt over my head, feeling instantly better to have a piece of James wrapped around me, and bend down, slipping my hand under the couch until I touch what feels like a credit card.

I pull it toward me, and for a moment, everything around me is hazy—the edges of my thoughts blurry as my mind tries to rationalize what I'm looking at: Dylan's face.

In the palm of my hand is her driver's license.

Instantly I recall the thing that bothered me when I dropped my own driver's license at the airport. The piece of information I couldn't remember. It was this. Her ID. It had been in this pocket since the day I ran to Beth's house and showed it to her. I forgot all about it.

I study it, remembering the day I first met Nick. I see his scuffed cowboy boots. His shiny motorcycle. His gray eyes squinting at me as he waited for me to process who he was. Then his calloused hand as he handed me this. As proof that he was her fiancé.

But had he been?

If he wasn't her fiancé, he would have never been the one to receive her personal things.

But wouldn't this driver's license have been in Dylan's purse . . . which Officer Keoloha said she'd reported stolen while she and James were at the Seven Sacred Pools?

Did he lie to me when he said it was mailed back to him?

There must be an explanation.

I think about Briana. The restlessness I've been feeling since we talked. I pace in front of the closet, James's sweatshirt hanging midway down my thighs. Maybe Dylan had traveled with a passport and left her license behind—and Nick had simply used it to lie about being engaged to her? Nothing more. That was possible, wasn't it?

Fuck.

I'm squeezing the driver's license so hard that it makes a red mark on my palm. A terrible feeling starts to spread through me—I try to stop it, but it's moving at lightning speed.

Did Nick stalk James and Dylan? Follow them to Maui?

I think about Nick's text just moments ago. That he misses me. A joke about a cat in a tree. That guy would never track his ex-fiancée to Maui!

I keep tightening my hand around Dylan's license, questioning everything. Hugging James's sweatshirt as close to my chest as I can. A big part of me wants to cling to another explanation. One where this is all a big mistake. One where I didn't simply move from one man with a secret life to another.

I'm in the car, throwing it in reverse before I can talk myself out of it. I have to find my answers.

CHAPTER THIRTY-EIGHT

DYLAN—BEFORE

Dylan couldn't believe Nick had shrugged and told her he wished her only the best. "Can't fault a man for trying," he'd said, then flashed *that smile* at her as he squeezed the engagement ring between his fingers. She watched him walk—no, *saunter*—down the alley. Then she heard the distinct sound of his motorcycle roaring to life. The noise had cued her to leave—she was still standing on the same slick oil spill behind her restaurant. She considered going inside and asking Johnny to walk her to her car. But he'd have questions—she'd never wanted an escort to the employee parking lot before. And she didn't want to get into it. Plus, she wasn't sure she could explain Nick's strange behavior if she tried. Or if he had even been acting as oddly as she'd thought. What if his behavior was in her head? If she was making it worse than it was because of her guilt over leaving him for James?

Still, she hurried to the parking lot just in case, trying to shake off what had just happened. How Nick had gone from smiling to melancholy to almost jubilant in the span of just minutes. Once inside her car, she locked all the doors, glanced in the backseat to make sure no one was there, and backed out onto South Coast Highway. She turned on the radio; the song "Shake It Off" was playing. *It must be a sign,* she thought, and began to sing along with the lyrics.

Midway through her duet with Taylor Swift, she saw him in the rearview mirror. She tried to tell herself it wasn't Nick, just another motorcyclist with a similar bike, but she recognized the deep-red mud-guard and matching helmet that reflected the streetlight. She changed lanes, and he followed—still several car lengths behind, but each direction she took her car, he paced with her. Dylan tried speeding up, slowing down, and turning quickly, but she couldn't lose him. Her heart began to pound, and her palms were wet from perspiration. She wiped them on her black pants and kept driving; she could stop at a gas station or somewhere and ask for help. But help for what? She had no proof of anything, and she knew Nick would deny her accusations anyway. He seemed oblivious to his behavior—not understanding he was acting like a stalker.

So when she saw the light up ahead turning yellow, she made a split-second decision—she slowed her car as if she were stopping and then gunned it, slamming her foot into the gas pedal and blowing through the intersection. Horns blared, but she made it across safely. Then she checked for Nick and was stunned as she watched him barrel through, barely missing a shiny silver Mercedes SUV—the rolled-down windows in the backseat revealing tweens in matching soccer jerseys, screaming when their driver slammed on her brakes. A shiver passed through Dylan. She had put those lives at risk.

Nick was riding her bumper—revving his bike's engine. Why was he following her? He'd given up so easily in the alley. Or had he? She replayed how he'd twisted the engagement ring on his finger, how he'd left with almost a spring in his step. He must have known then that it wasn't over—that he was going to follow her—that she'd never suspect because she was gullible. He had manipulated her. Dylan tightened her grip on the steering wheel, mad at herself for being so stupid. So believing. She wondered if this was her penance for cheating on him. If she deserved this.

Dylan heard honking and looked over her left shoulder. Nick was riding right next to her—too close to her car—motioning wildly for her to pull over. She debated what to do. But then she saw the young faces of the soccer players in her mind and knew she had to stop. She turned on the first street she could and parked. She thought about calling the police, but her phone was in her purse in the backseat. And she didn't know what she'd say—*my ex-boyfriend is following me?* She knew now that he wasn't going to give up until she gave him what he wanted.

But what he wanted, she couldn't give him. He wanted her back.

She watched as he stopped his bike in back of her car. She felt a scream in the base of her throat, but when she opened her mouth, no sound would come out. Helplessly, she stared at him as he got off his motorcycle and removed his helmet, running his fingers through his hair.

Then he gave a smile, one so sad Dylan returned it reflexively.

"Hey, Dylan, roll your window down, okay?" He stared at her, then tapped on the glass with the engagement ring. "Knock, knock!"

Dylan shook her head; his face changed so quickly she wondered if she'd imagined the somber smile. His lip curled; his cheeks reddened. She started to get really scared. He kept asking her to open the door, and she kept shaking her head. She watched him make fists with his hands and punch them against his sides.

"Dylan, come on!" he yelled, then hit the window with an open palm.

Her body jerked backward, her heart ramming against her chest; she had no idea what to do. She looked around her, but the street was empty. Her stomach dropped as she noticed the "Dead End" sign at the end of the road. Nick rattled the door handle, then turned and flailed his arms in the air in frustration, like she'd seen children do at the restaurant.

Dylan shivered. Could he pry the door open? Was he strong enough to break the glass? Would he take it that far?

"Dylan, you are my soul mate. Don't you see that?" He flattened both of his palms against the glass, the diamond ring pressed between his right hand and the window. "This is yours. You belong to me."

He thinks I'm his possession. That he owns me.

After that, it was as if Nick was moving in slow motion: As he put one leg in front of the other, his distressed jeans grazing the ground, the tips of his boots peeking out. As he turned his back to her, his leather jacket catching an air pocket. As he walked toward his bike, his arms out in the air like he was about to take flight. A panicked feeling coursed through her. She felt behind her seat for her purse, then reached around to grab it. She had to get to her phone. She had to try to get help.

Suddenly there was a thud against the roof of the car. Dylan screamed and dropped her purse. She was staring into Nick's abdomen, his belt buckle pressed up against her window. Then he stepped back and lifted his arm over his head, and she saw it. A tire iron. He yanked it over his shoulder. Dylan ducked and covered her head, bracing herself for the blow against the glass. Tears poured out of her as she lay against the seat, praying for her safety, trying to make sense of what was happening to her. Trying to understand how Nick could turn into this man.

But the window never shattered. Instead, she heard sirens. She hadn't called the police, but maybe he thought she had, because he ran to his bike and took off so fast she wondered if she could convince herself he'd never been there at all.

Then she saw the tire iron on the pavement.

~

I'm finally home and in bed, and my heart still won't settle. Each heavy beat reminding me of what a fool I am—how blind I was to who Nick really is. My skin crawls when I think of the look in his eyes as he pressed the ring against the glass. Like nothing was wrong. Nothing was out of the ordinary. Like me getting back together with him would have been the most natural thing in the world. It makes me think my relationship with James isn't so unusual. He might be married, but at least he's sane. And we're leaving for Maui tomorrow— something that I need now more than ever.

CHAPTER
THIRTY-NINE

Jacks—after

Breathe, Jacks. Just breathe.

My gaze falls on Dylan's driver's license resting in my cup holder as I pull into Nick's parking garage, my breaths shallow. I let my car idle and scan the area for Nick's bike just in case. But it's not here. A ripple of guilt snakes through me. Sneaking into his place. Going through his things. James had been a liar. Telling me he was in one city when he was in the middle of the Pacific Ocean. Was my behavior now only a symptom of being deceived by my husband? I really didn't have much proof—other than the ID. Was that enough of a justification to lie to Nick and go into his apartment without his consent? I look at Dylan's face again—her pouty lips. Her rosy cheeks. But the thing is, I need to figure out the truth. If we have any future, I have to know.

My phone dings. It's Beth.

Where are you? Thought we were meeting here.

I glance around. There's no time to explain to her what's going on.

At Nick's, looking for something. Call you after.

I park and push the button for the elevator, remembering my first time here when I tentatively entered through the lobby, noticing the Peet's coffee shop, the dry cleaner's.

I had been a widow, still so raw from everything I'd learned about the husband I thought I knew. I never predicted I'd return here in a very different role—a girlfriend with questions about another man she thought she knew.

When Nick showed up on my doorstep the first time, I never asked him how he knew how to find me. Had he stalked me too? Or had digging into Dylan's double life simply led him to me? Looking back, I don't see Nick ever acting obsessed with her. He'd just seemed like a man grieving for the woman he loved, the same way I had been dealing with losing James.

As my finger hovers over the number for Nick's floor, I think about getting off on the one below and trying to find Briana. Ask her more questions. I could show her Dylan's driver's license. Ask her what she thinks it means that Nick has it. I shake my head and punch the button for the floor that Nick lives on, worrying my own insecurities may be causing me to jump to the wrong conclusion.

So I head to Nick's place. I walk down the hall and stop at his door, staring at it. Fumble for my key in my purse, remembering him giving it to me on a keychain with a red heart. I'd been wide eyed at first and asked, "Are you sure?" Then he nodded and said, "Of course, you belong here." I giggled in response, twirling the key around my finger.

I think about how I never had any of James's passwords, not even to his cell phone. Nick wouldn't have given me a key if he had something to hide.

I run my thumb over the red heart and slide the key into the lock. "Nick," I call out, just in case he's home. I wait to step inside. "Nick?" I say again. Slowly I make my way into the condo and let the door close behind me. I stand in the middle of the living room, waiting. For what, I don't know. Despite my plan to give him the benefit of the doubt, to let him be innocent until proven guilty, his place looks different with Briana's accusations swirling inside of me. The Ikea furniture now seems too sterile. The stack of magazines on the coffee table looks too perfect. The glow of the time on the microwave is eerie. The hair on my arms shoots up, and I feel a strange sensation, as if I'm being watched. As if I'm not alone. If he is a stalker, he could have cameras set up. I shake my head. I'm being ridiculous. That's something Beth would say after watching too many episodes of *Law & Order: SVU*.

I finger Dylan's ID in my pocket, making sure it's still there, which somehow makes me feel sane. Like I have a reason to be here. To make sure everything is okay. That I didn't go from one liar to another. I glance around me. The espresso maker parts are rinsed out and in the dish rack where I put them, the magazine I was reading still open to the page I stopped on—an article about how to make a face mask out of avocado. I'm standing here, not sure not where to start or what I'm trying to find, when a booming sound rips through the condo, and I scream.

I realize it's just the air conditioner kicking on. My racing heart settles. And I roll my eyes. What's got me so jittery?

I almost leave, deciding to simply ask Nick about the ID and take it from there. But then I think of James. How hard it had been to make sense not only of his death, but of the whys—the affair, the deceit, the other woman. And I decide I have to search Nick's place so I can prove to myself that he's not James.

I start in the kitchen, opening cupboards, pulling out drawers. I move to the linen closet in the hall, but I only find towels and a surplus of soap, deodorant, and body wash.

Maybe his biggest flaw is that he's too clean.

I open the medicine cabinet in the guest bath, look under the sink. But there's nothing suspicious.

I hesitate outside the threshold of his bedroom. Somehow looking in here feels worse, more invasive.

Nick's bed is still just as I left it, the comforter longer on one side than the other, the pillows thrown on top of it casually. I've never been a great bed maker. James used to laugh at me because I struggled with the whole process—especially the fitted sheet.

Inside his bathroom, there's also nothing out of the ordinary, his smell still lingering from his morning shower. I'm feeling foolish for snooping on him. What did I think I was going to find? I'm standing in front of his walk-in closet, debating what to do, and finally decide I might as well finish what I started. Then I'll talk to him face-to-face so he can explain the ID. I check the time on my phone and see two missed calls and several texts from Nick.

Hi, my love!
Just got back from a call and thinking of you and missing your gorgeous face.

The last message has a picture attached. I click on it. He's wearing his navy-blue Long Beach Fire Department T-shirt and hanging from a pole. His lopsided grin makes me feel even guiltier. I send a quick text.

Sorry, just got these. Miss you too!

And I do miss him.
Three dots instantly appear as he types his response.

Where are you?

At my house.

I hate lying to him, but he can't ever know I was here. That I questioned his integrity. Quickly I start to slide hangers to the left and right, the same four or five flannels and T-shirts he rotates hanging from them. I open drawers and gently search behind his socks and boxer briefs. I move a stack of jeans and look behind it. Nothing.

I stand on my tiptoes and peer over the shelf with his baseball caps. I reach my hand up and feel the side of a box. I pull out a drawer and step on the edge, careful to not use all my weight so I don't break it off its track. I slide the box toward me, and it tips over the edge and falls against my chest, knocking me off balance. It hits the hardwood floor with a thud.

I pull it open, and it's just bunch of old T-shirts. I grab one and almost laugh at the absurdity of what I'm doing as I stare at the logo from a 5K from a couple of years ago. I breathe for the first time in what feels like minutes. Just shirts.

Beth will tell me I was nuts for coming over here. That I ransacked my boyfriend's apartment for what? To prove to myself that not all men are liars? I catch a glimpse of my reflection in the mirror on the wall. I do look a bit dazed. My hair is falling half out of its ponytail; my eyes have large bags under them. I wipe a smudge of mascara from my right lid. It's time for me to stop listening to secondhand gossip and letting my mind take me to crazy places. I need to talk to Nick about the driver's license. Let him give me his logical explanation. He more than deserves that.

I push the T-shirt back into the box, and my hand hits something that feels like a rubber strap of some kind. I pull it toward the top and remove the T-shirt above it, blinking several times at what's dangling from my fingertips.

Dylan's purse.

CHAPTER FORTY

JACKS—AFTER

I'm holding the same purse Officer Keoloha described when he told me the story of Dylan filing the police report. It's a straw tote with a rubber handle and a bright-pink-and-green jeweled pineapple on the side.

I pull the purse open slowly, trying to make sense of why it's here, in Nick's closet. I squeeze a dried hibiscus flower between my fingers, picturing Dylan plucking it from a bush and smelling it. Or maybe James had picked it and given it to her, and she'd tucked it behind her ear? I find a banana lip balm and remove the cap and inhale it. There's a map of the road to Hana folded neatly. Had she been following along as they drove? Guiding James to each viewpoint? And then I find her wallet. I hesitate before unsnapping the small turquoise billfold, praying there's something inside of it that will explain everything. Because there has to be a reason her purse is here. I open it and see various cards—ATM, Vons, library. There's also a five-dollar bill and a pay stub from the restaurant where she worked.

But there's no driver's license. No passport. No identification of any kind.

I think of her ID in my pocket. Was it once here, wedged between the grocery store card and the bank card?

I close the wallet and notice some tissue at the bottom of the bag. I unwrap the Kleenex, and I'm staring at something I've had in my hands more times than I can count.

A pregnancy test.

The only difference is hers was positive.

I stare at the jeweled pineapple on the side of the purse cradled in my arms—wanting to understand why it's here in Nick's walk-in closet.

The hairs on my arms stand on end again, and sweat trickles down my back. I keep thinking I hear a key in the lock.

I check my phone again, which I had set to silent mode. More texts from Nick.

Hey!

I tried calling you. Are you still at your place?

Hello?

Quickly I shove the box back up on the shelf. I remove James's sweatshirt and wrap Dylan's purse in it and hurry to the elevator, pushing the button over and over, but it won't come.

My thoughts unfold one by one.

Nick has Dylan's purse, which was stolen less than an hour before she died.

I take the stairs two at a time, lose my balance, and grab the handrail, the purse flying, its contents spilling.

He could only have her purse if he'd been the one to steal it.

I scoop up Dylan's things, shove them back into the bag, and wrap it in the sweatshirt again, my hands shaking. Finally I'm in the parking garage standing next to my car. I push the button on my fob and hear the click of the doors unlocking.

Which means Nick was in Maui when they were. That he'd been inside their Jeep just before they died.

I gasp for air as the realization sinks in.

"Surprise," Nick says from behind me, his breath on my neck.

CHAPTER FORTY-ONE

Jacks—after

I freeze, squeezing the sweatshirt, the purse beneath it pressing into my ribs. "Nick . . . you scared the shit out of me—" I try to swivel around, but his lips are still pressed against the back of my neck, his arm around my shoulder.

He plants a light kiss on my cheek. "Aren't you happy to see me?" he asks.

"Yes, even though I can't exactly *see* you," I say, his hot breath tickling my ear.

My mind is racing, the strap of the purse poking me. It won't let me forget what I now know. That he was there. Inside their Jeep. Was he a stalker, a jilted lover who had spun out of control?

Or more?

I release a long breath. There has to be an explanation. Maybe Officer Keoloha didn't mention that the purse was found. And maybe Nick has it because it was sent back to him because he *had been* still engaged to her. His touch feels like the Nick I know—the Nick who could never have lied to me. "That feels good," I say, and he spins me around.

"I tried calling you about thirty minutes ago to let you know I got off work early . . . why didn't you tell me you were here?"

"I . . ." I was so focused on not getting caught ransacking his place, I hadn't decided what I'd do if I did. I feel my cheeks redden as I try to think of a reason. "I came here to surprise you actually. When you got off your shift. Funny, we were surprising each other!" I force a laugh.

"Well, it's kismet then—us surprising each other. I decided something today, you know," he says, shoving his hands into his pockets.

"Oh? What's that?"

"I'm a pretty lucky guy." He smiles.

I smile back and take a deep breath. There's going to be an explanation. There has to be.

"Hey, so where were you going just now? It looked like you were leaving."

He furrows his brow.

I stare at him for a beat, searching his eyes, looking for the assurance that he's not questioning me because he knows I was up to something. That it's all in my head, and it's *my* Nick I'm looking at. "I took the stairs to get a little cardio in," I say, the sweatshirt feeling like a neon sign pointing toward my lie. "And I got hot while I was running—so I was about to throw this in my car," I add. I hate drawing attention to James's sweatshirt, but I can't think of any other reason I'd be holding it.

"I've never seen that one before," he says.

My heartbeat speeds up again. "I found it in the back of the closet today. I'd forgotten I had it."

"You okay?" He squints at me.

I nod.

"Hey . . . let's get out of here—go for a drive. There's supposed to be a beautiful sunset tonight. I know a spot where we can watch it on the cliff in Newport Coast. It'll be chilly, but you have that." He motions toward the sweatshirt, and I think I see a flicker of something—doubt?—cross his face.

I hesitate, because I need time to think—to talk to Beth. To figure out how I'm going to explain why I have the purse. But I already told Nick I was surprising him.

"C'mon, let's go. Gorgeous sunset. Me. What more could you ask for?"

Nick's eyes are lighting up. He's *him*. The funny one who sent me a hilarious cat meme yesterday. The sexy man whose eyes almost disappear when he's laughing hard.

"Okay," I say, and open the back door, gently putting the sweatshirt on the seat as I calm myself down.

"Good answer!" Nick says, and gets in the passenger seat.

"What do you think is the best way to get there?" I ask, starting the car.

"Head down the one thirty-three; the place I'm thinking of is in Newport Coast off PCH—best views ever."

We head toward the beach, and Nick rolls his window down, resting his arm on the top of the door. Then he turns to me. "You want to stop for ice cream first?"

I think about last night. How we toasted our love with our cones. Mint chip for me. A double scoop of vanilla for him. I remember thinking it was the first time I'd really felt peaceful in as long as I could remember. And I'd love to have that feeling again. Because I know once I ask him about the purse and the ID, there's no turning back.

"That sounds nice."

~

We eat our cones at a table outside the parlor and watch the waves slowly roll in. It's peaceful, hypnotic—almost enough to let me pretend I wasn't in Nick's walk-in closet just an hour ago. He talks mostly about his last shift—and I try my best to listen. But I can only go a few minutes without thinking about the ID and the purse. And how he will explain them. *If* he can explain them. Beth would tell me I'm crazy to be sitting here eating ice cream when I should be confronting him. But—and there are so many buts. Because either way, someone is going to get hurt by what is said. And I'm tired of being hurt. I think back to when I'd glanced through my peephole that day the police came to tell me James was dead. How I would have loved to have just a few more moments of not knowing! Just one more day of having my biggest problem be a leaky faucet. I ponder those last moments more than I should—wishing I could go back and be the naive girl behind that door.

"You were on my mind today," Nick says when we get back inside my car.

"Oh?" I ask as I turn the ignition and back out of the parking space.

"I think about you *a lot.*"

"And?"

"Well, I don't want to scare you away by saying this—in fact the guys at the station told me I'd be nuts to admit this to you right now. But I'm going to take a risk and do it anyway . . ." He runs his fingers through his hair. "I realized that you're my soul mate."

I let the words sit there for a moment, turning them over in my mind. I've never believed there's just one person for everyone.

"Too much?" He laughs lightly, searching my face.

"No," I say, and pause before adding, "I'm just taking it all in."

Taking him in. Wondering if I know him at all.

"I realize it's probably too soon when we've just said the *l* word, but it's different with you."

"Wow . . . I'm . . . flattered."

"Flattered?" he asks, and I cringe.

"Sorry, I didn't mean flattered. I don't know. I'm a little caught off guard is all."

Nick stares at me, almost as if he's looking through me. And I feel pressure to say something to take the weight of his gaze off me. "I love you," I say, but my stomach knots at the words. They feel wrong. Like they're the last thing I should be saying right now.

"But that's not the same thing, is it?" he asks, sounding hurt. "Do you believe you're my soul mate?"

His phrasing of the question throws me off. Am I understanding him right? That he isn't asking if he's mine? Just if I think I'm *his*?

Dylan's purse and ID are practically screaming at me from the backseat, and I know I can't ignore them for much longer—hiding the truth no longer seems like a viable option. Could Nick have lied to me about how he came to have her purse—but be telling the truth about thinking I'm his soul mate? Were things with me really different than they had been with Dylan? I'm going to ask him about the purse as soon as we get to the hotel. Until then, my instincts tell me to be agreeable. "I do. I do think we're soul mates," I say.

"Do you think you're mine?"

"Yes, that's what I just said."

"Not exactly," he says.

Why is this so important to him?

Before I can respond, he continues. "Because the thing is, Jacks, for this to really work between us, we need to be on the same page."

"We are on the same page—I love you." I feel squeamish after I say those words. There's something off-putting about his tone, his demeanor, his needing me to say this a certain way.

"But do you love me more than you've loved *anyone* else?"

His question feels like a punch in the stomach, because I know he's asking about James. "You're two different people. I can't compare you," I manage, judging the distance to Newport Coast Drive in my mind. I ask, judging the distance to it in my mind. My heart thuds in my chest as I calculate; it's still several minutes away. I know I need to ask him, but I'm so scared. Maybe I should turn the car around. Drive to Beth's. Have her there when I question him.

"Yes," he says. "And you're probably going to need your sweatshirt. It will be chilly once we get outside."

Nick reaches into the backseat to grab the shirt. "Wait," I say, but he's already unbuckling his seat belt.

"What the—"

He doesn't finish. But he doesn't have to. His face freezes as he sees the purse. "What are you doing with this? This doesn't belong to you."

"I—"

"You went through my things?" He raises his voice. "Is that why you were in my place?"

"Nick, I—"

"You don't trust me?" he asks, like it's the most inconceivable thing in the world.

As I look into his eyes, my first instinct is to say that I do. Because he's been there for me through the worst time of my life. I've confided in him. He's listened. But the purse. The purse doesn't make sense.

"I don't know what to say."

"You know, I love you more than I *loved* Dylan. But you obviously don't love me more than you *loved* James," he says, and I feel myself getting defensive. My love for James isn't in the past tense. I'm not sure it ever will be. Or if I ever *want* it to be. That love is deep. With roots. It is complicated and quirky and now he's gone, but it's still ours. And that can't be measured. But before I can respond, Nick dives in again.

"*He* cheated on you. I would never do that to you. But yet it's *my* home you snoop through?" Nick says, and when he puts it this way, it does seem wrong.

"Nick, I was going to tell you. Because obviously we need to talk about what I found and why you have it—"

Nick turns away, and his shoulders start shaking.

"Nick?" I say his name a few times, but he doesn't respond. Finally he turns, and there are tears streaming down his face. There's something about his overwhelming emotion right now that warns me not to reach out to him. Like he's deliberately creating a wall between us with his tears.

"I thought you understood me, because you'd been through the same thing. It's like you don't care about me the way you should. And neither did Dylan. And I hate it when I give, give, give and get nothing in return. When I lose."

"What do you mean?" I ask, a slow chill traveling up my spine. The red flags are becoming impossible to ignore. My gut tells me I already know the answers to my questions about the purse, the driver's license, the stalking. The realization runs its way through me, quick and sharp.

"She gave herself to him, but she *belonged* to me." Nick turns toward the window again.

There's something about that word that pushes me to confront him. "Nick, were you engaged to Dylan when she died?"

He jerks his head around and stares at me. I grip the steering wheel tighter, bracing myself for his answer.

"Yes, I was," he says slowly, and I let out a long breath.

So maybe there is an explanation for the rest of it.

After a beat, he says quietly, "In my heart I was."

My stomach drops. "What do you mean, *in your heart*? You either were or you weren't."

He doesn't directly answer me; instead he starts telling me about how she used Vaseline to get the ring off, that she told him it had never fit quite right. "I told her we could get it resized. Or I could get her a different one. But she didn't seem to hear me. She just told me she had to go." He rubs his hands on his jeans, lost in thought for a moment.

"Nick, did she break up with you?" I ask again, my frustration mounting.

"She said that's what she wanted, but she didn't have a reason. I knew she just needed time to think. That she'd be back."

"Did she come back? Change her mind?" I press, sitting up taller in my seat.

"I was working on that," he says, then shakes his head.

"What do you mean?"

"I needed to know how she was spending her time without me. I figured it wouldn't take long for her to figure out she was making a mistake. So I followed her." He chews on his lower lip. "I never expected to see her cheating on me with *him*."

"But was she cheating if—"

He cuts me off and launches into a story. He tells me how one night she headed north toward Los Angeles. She took a downtown exit he didn't recognize. His heart was hammering so hard, and his hands were getting numb—he thought he might be having a panic attack. Then he pulled his bike to a stop and watched her pull up to a hotel.

"That's when I saw him for the first time." He grits his teeth. "Your husband. He leaned down and kissed her. And she held him there against her mouth for too long. They were in front of people—in front of *me*. I almost rushed James right then—I wanted to beat the shit out of him. But I couldn't move."

I try to push the image out of my mind that he's created, but I can't. I see James's eyes light up, him scooping Dylan up in his arms, covering her mouth with his. Where had I been that night? At home folding his underwear?

"I couldn't stop imagining them up in a hotel room doing God knows what!" He stops, balling his hands into fists at his sides. "I didn't sleep at all. I went to the gas station and got coffee to stay awake, and finally, early the next morning, I saw your husband come out, and I followed him."

I can't bring myself to stop him. Because he's filling in the blanks. Blanks that I haven't realized have been there for far too long.

He tells me James led him to our house. A few Google searches later, he had answers: His name was James Morales. And he was married to a woman named Jacks.

Me.

"I followed you. I watched you at Trader Joe's as you loaded up your cart with frozen orange chicken and spring rolls. As you debated between the low-fat and the two percent milk. That was cute." He laughs. "As you tried to fit everything in that clown car of yours."

Goose bumps prick my arms as the real Nick becomes clearer to me. He stalked Dylan, then James, then me.

Nick describes trailing me through the aisles of the grocery store, then out into the parking lot as I struggled to shove my bags into tiny trunk of my Mini Cooper that James always chided me for buying because it wasn't practical. Then to my home. Is that why Nick had seemed familiar when I first met him? Because I subconsciously remembered seeing him?

Rage burns inside of me as the weight of what Nick is saying hits me. He took advantage of me.

"I followed you for weeks. I realized we were kindred spirits, you and me. Even though we never spoke, I felt a connection. Because of what we'd both been through—"

I pound the steering wheel with my fist and accidentally hit the horn. "You lied to me!" I burst out.

Nick doesn't react. "I never lied to you."

"Yes, you did! What about when you came to my house? You acted like that was the first time you had seen me."

"I never said that. I never told you I'd never seen you before."

He was right. He hadn't. I realize I'm speeding and ease my foot off the gas pedal slightly.

"But you just said you'd followed me for weeks. Why didn't you mention that?"

"Jacks, don't you understand I came to your door to help you? And *that's* what I told you I was doing."

"To help me? Is that what you call it?" My voice is shaking.

"Yes. Absolutely. I had information, remember? Like when I figured out Dylan's email password and printed out all her emails to James. And showed them to you. It was so you could see what was going on between them. So you could know what he'd done to you."

I think back to how much it hurt to read them. Had he really been trying to help me by making me read their loving thoughts to one another?

"Nick, you misled me. You said she was your fiancée."

"She *was* my fiancée!" He lets out an exasperated sigh. "I didn't agree to the breakup."

I pound the steering wheel again. *Fuck. Fuck. Fuck.* "How could you do this, Nick? How could you misrepresent everything?" And how could I be so stupid?

"Calm down, Jacks. I never lied to you. I told you I loved her, and I did."

My head is spinning. I try to calm my breathing, but it's hopeless. I'm panting like a dog.

"Going to Maui together was to help us get over them. That wasn't a lie either. And it did help—you even said so yourself."

I think about the time we spent asking questions Nick already knew the answers to.

"But you weren't honest. You'd already been there."

"That's true. But I never told you I hadn't been." He folds his arms across his chest. "I went because I needed to know."

"Know what?" I whisper fearfully.

"Why she'd chosen James over me. Why he'd *won*."

Won? My God. He's delusional. I cover my hand with my mouth.

"I followed them to Maui, yes. And then I watched them on their excursions. They were so giddy. And I just kept getting more and more angry. Thinking about you, at home. So oblivious."

That word is like a slap across the face. Because I was. Blind to it all. Pushing my stupid cart through Trader Joe's, trying to pick the perfect fucking milk. Thinking my husband was where he said he was. Having no clue he was swimming with sea turtles with his lover, being trailed by some—

"And then they decided to drive the road to Hana. I saw them kissing by some store. Dylan was wearing this little dress—one I'd never seen before. That she'd clearly bought for him."

"Stop it! Stop it right now!" I yell.

"No. You need to listen to me." He holds up the purse. "I'm going to explain!"

But I don't want to listen. I don't want to know. I just need out of this car. I picture Dylan and James having their picnic, saying what would be some of their final words. Had James whispered that he loved her, told her how happy he was that he'd now have the family he'd always wanted? Or had my shadow been in the back of James's mind, our tattered love still a placeholder in his chest?

"Once I was in Maui with you, it all made sense. Why they had the accident."

Accident? I shake my head, tears rolling down my cheeks.

"The brakes giving out right when they did—at the cliff where there were no guardrails, where so many other accidents have happened—that was fate. When I pricked a tiny hole in the brake line, I had no way of knowing when or *if* James would lose control of that Jeep. That was between *him* and God. Everything happened the way it did because you were meant to be with me."

I see James's smile. His bed head. His lanky body. His sea-glass eyes. I glance at Nick's profile.

He really doesn't think he's responsible for killing them.

One man dead. Another responsible. I gave my heart to both of them.

A wave of nausea cascades through me, and I swallow the bile in my throat.

"What about the pregnancy test?" I whisper. "What did you think when you found that in her purse? Because you didn't already know, did you?"

He shakes his head. "That was a surprise. But they'd made a fool of you. Of both of us," he says. "It worked out as it should. Those two didn't deserve to bring a baby into this world."

"Nick! You can't mean that!" I stare at him in disbelief. How could someone do something so horrific and not *see* it?

How could I have loved a man like that?

His arms go rigid. His jaw tightens. "I love you, Jacks. Don't you get it?"

The sob I've been holding in finally escapes my throat. "Why aren't you upset about what . . . you did to them?"

"What *I* did?" He's yelling now.

"The brake line didn't prick itself! You killed them!" I scream, my voice shaking with emotion.

He shakes his head. "That's on him."

"No!" I yell the word so loudly I don't recognize the sound of my own voice. I yell at him for taking James. For Dylan. For that baby. "No! No! *No! You* killed them. Oh my God. How did I ever love you?" I'm sobbing so hard I can barely see the road. Fear and anger are swirling together inside me, and I'm not sure which feeling is more powerful.

"How can you say that?" He slams his hands on the dashboard. Dylan's purse falls off of his lap onto the floor.

A sign. That I need to get out of this car. *Now.*

He looks at me, a rage in his eyes I have never seen before. I let out a startled yelp when he punches the radio, his knuckles covered in blood when he draws them back. I wipe my tears. We're on a high stretch of highway that overlooks the beach, which is several hundred feet below—if I stop now, I'll need to outrun him while dodging the traffic on the curvy road. I know I won't get far.

Suddenly he lunges for the steering wheel, and I turn it sharply, narrowly avoiding an oncoming car. "What are you doing?" I scream.

"Why couldn't you just love me? Why doesn't anyone love me the way they're supposed to?"

He gives me a long look that I can't read, then grabs the wheel before I can stop him. He yanks it, and I fight to regain control, but he's too strong. I scream as we slew off the road, the car smashing through the guardrail and sailing toward the sharp rocks that separate the canyon from the ocean.

In the next strange moment of sudden silence, I think about James—the day he proposed. The goofy grin on his face as he waited for me to answer. I picture my sister, the tears glistening in her eyes when I held up my college diploma. I see my parents on my wedding day, smiling widely through their apprehension, their love for me stronger than their fear I might be making a mistake. I listen to Nick's screams bleeding into my own and realize that no one will ever know the truth—that he killed James and Dylan. That we are both going to die with his secrets and his lies.

CHAPTER FORTY-TWO

JACKS—AFTER

The first thing I hear is an incessant beeping sound.

Ding. Ding. Ding.

Where am I?

Ding. Ding. Ding.

My foggy mind tries to take inventory of my body. There is pain. So much of it. Everywhere. In my legs. My arms. My chest. Especially in my head. I try to open my eyes, but they won't cooperate.

"Her eyelids just fluttered! Call the nurse!" I hear my mom's voice, more high pitched than normal, and feel someone squeeze my fingers. "Jacks, can you hear me?"

Yes, I want to say. *I can hear you, Mom.* But my mouth won't open. I want to tell her I can hear the tears in her throat. She's been crying.

Where am I?

"Doctor, she's trying to say something!" It's my sister's shaking voice now, and the urgency in it gives me the push I need to force my eyes open. Beth is by my side—dark shadows under her eyes. My mom's are swollen and puffy. Dad's are filled with relief. He smiles at me.

I look around, my pulse quickening. I see monitors. An IV drip attached to my arm. A thin hospital gown covering me. A cast on one leg. A scratchy sheet rubbing the other. I try to move, but the pain is too severe. I try to talk, but no words will come.

A man with thinning gray hair rushes in. "I'm Dr. Turner." A nurse follows him, and he says something about checking my vitals. They start to examine me, flashing lights in my eyes, checking my pulse, looking inside my mouth. They ask me questions that I struggle to answer, not because I don't know what my name is or what year it is, but because my mouth is so dry. The nurse hands me a cup of water and tells me to sip it slowly. Finally Dr. Turner pulls up a stool, gives me a sympathetic smile, and asks me what I remember.

I can feel a memory sitting in the periphery of my mind, waiting for me to grab it. I think hard. Force myself to recall what happened. What brought me here.

I close my eyes, and it comes to me like an electric shock.

Nick. The lack of remorse. The refusal to accept what he'd done. His ambivalence. My rage. His rage. The fight for the steering wheel.

"A car acc—"

I start to say *accident*, but stop to correct it to *crash*. Because it wasn't an accident at all. Just like James's wasn't. Tears stream down my cheeks at the horror of what's happened—the memory of Nick's words, his justifications—hitting me all over again. I fell in love with the man who killed my husband. *James.*

He's gone. Oh my God. It feels like the wound has been torn open all over again. As if he's been ripped from me all over again.

Beth rushes over and wipes my tears, having no idea how much pain I'm actually in. What's really happened.

Dr. Turner continues. "You are at Hoag Hospital in Newport Beach. You have several lacerations from the impact," he says, giving me a moment. I reach up and feel a bandage around my head. "We had to put eleven stitches in your scalp and three over your right eye, so you probably have a pretty nasty headache." The nurse comes over and adjusts my IV. "You've been unconscious for almost twenty-four hours."

Almost a full day? It feels like I was in the car just moments ago. I can still hear his voice.

"On a scale of one to ten—ten being unbearable—how much pain are you in?"

Emotionally or physically?

"Five," I finally say, choosing the first number that comes to mind. How could I explain that the pain in my heart is far worse than the one in my body? I'd give that pain a fifteen.

"Janet just gave you a dose of Percocet," he says, nodding at the nurse. "So you should feel relief very soon."

Will I?

"You also broke your leg," the doctor continues. "In two places." He taps the cast just below my knee and also by my shin.

"You're lucky to be alive." Beth says, squeezing my hand.

"Thank God," my mom sobs. "First James and his terrible accident, and then you. When I got the call, I was outside of my own body, thinking I could not lose you, my baby. Thank God. Thank God." My mom presses her face into my chest, and I wince from the pain, but don't let her know how much it hurts.

"The police asked to be called when you're feeling up to it. They have a few questions for you," the doctor says.

I feel the rush of the car swerving out of its lane, my head slamming against the window.

The police.

The last time I talked to two officers, they told me my husband was never coming home because he'd died in a car crash. And now they wanted to talk to me about *my* car crash. But there was so much more to tell them.

The ID, the purse, Nick.

"How is Nick?" I find my sister's eyes, and they tell me the answer I both feared and hoped for.

Beth and my parents exchange a look, and the doctor and nurse silently leave the room. Beth is still holding my hand, gripping it harder as she talks. "He was ejected from the car. He didn't make it," she says softly.

"Nick is dead?" I ask, needing to hear it again. To be sure.

"Yes, I'm so sorry." Beth says, not realizing my tears are flowing faster and harder not because I'm sad, but because I'm relieved.

CHAPTER FORTY-THREE

JACKS—AFTER

A month later, the sound of Nick's screams as we flew over the cliff aren't quite as deafening. I don't see the flash of the guardrail every time I close my eyes. I don't remember my head hitting the driver's-side window each night when I lay it on my pillow. The memories of the crash have subsided *slightly*.

But the vivid details of Nick's words, *those memories*—they could live with me forever.

Beth was horrified when I told her the story in the hospital—then enraged. She said she would've killed him if he hadn't already been dead.

"You knew something wasn't right with him. You tried to tell me," I said to her.

"I was being protective, but I had no idea what he was capable of. My God. No one could have known that."

Then I told her what I couldn't reconcile no matter how many times the thought passed through my mind. "He said he did it for me—that he killed them for *me*," I said. "How am I supposed to live with that?" I whispered.

"I don't know," Beth said. "I wish I did, but I don't. But I will be here for you as we figure it out."

"Why couldn't I see it?" I blinked through my tears. "Am I that much of an idiot?"

"No, you were mourning James."

"Who was dead because of Nick! I wish I had made different choices—if I hadn't ruined things with James, he would still be here."

"Jacks . . ." She trailed off, the skin between her eyes gathering as she thought. "At some point you're going to have to let yourself off the hook."

"I can't do that." I said. "James is dead because of me."

"I could never pretend to understand what you're going through, but I can tell you this—it is *not* your fault. And hopefully, after some time, you'll see that—that you weren't in control of what happened. That you didn't make James have an affair. Or make Nick do what he did," Beth said, her eyes filling with tears.

I shook my head gingerly. "No, you don't understand. I deserve this. To live with what I've caused." I rolled over, my back to her, and cried silently until I fell asleep.

And now, thirty days later, I'm still working to believe what Beth said. Intellectually, I understand I didn't kill anyone. But my actions started a ripple effect that ended with three people dead. My therapist tells me if I stop blaming myself, if I stop being mad at myself, that I will have to deal with the real pain. The real loss. And that's what I'm hiding from. But my therapist also says that I will come to terms with what's happened—with her help, but also at my own pace. And that's okay. She helped me talk to the police about what happened. She sat with me while I recounted the story for what I hoped would be the last time for a while. And she listened to me sob hysterically after they ended their investigation and told me that, after talking with Briana and some of Nick's coworkers, and looking at flight records and talking with people in Maui, that Nick had, in fact, been there during the exact dates Dylan and James were. And, although they couldn't prove he'd pricked that brake line of the Jeep, they believed he had.

I took a leave of absence from work. And I'm in the process of putting my house on the market. My therapist also warned me not to undergo too much change at once, but I've found that it's helped me take my mind off things—at least a little bit. And she does agree a fresh start will be good for me.

I'm searching James's desk for some paperwork the real estate agent needs when I see it.

The heart-shaped tin.

It holds our letters. The ones James and I wrote to each other in the beginning of our relationship. The ones I couldn't find.

I thought it was gone.

I slowly remove the lid. I exhale when I see James's messy handwriting jumping off the pages. "I wonder why he had these?" I say to myself as I read the one on the top of the stack—the first note he ever sent me, when his love for me radiated off the page in deep waves, making me laugh and cry at the same time.

> *Jacks,*
> *I should start this letter by telling you that you're like a fine wine—you know, because of how we met. But you'd just call my bullshit, I know it. So I'll tell you something else, something I haven't been able to stop thinking about since that day. You're unlike anyone I've ever met, and you are going to change me in amazing ways. I can't wait to see what happens next with us. And yes, I am writing US, even after such a short time together. Because there's no going back to my lonely Lucky Charms life now. The only life I want is the one with you in it.*

I feel a warmth run through my body, realizing he had read this one recently too. Had he sought these letters out to dispose of them as he began his new life with Dylan? Or had he been rethinking his choices? Rethinking us—his life with me in it?

I'll never know for sure. But I'm choosing to believe he knew we had simply lost our way, that our love wasn't the kind to disappear. Like the sun behind a cloud, it would still peek out from time to time.

ACKNOWLEDGMENTS

Writing *The Good Widow* was an amazing experience. (And we aren't just talking about the research trip we took to Maui while crafting it!) Suspense is something we've been wanting to write for a long time. And we are incredibly thankful to Danielle Marshall at Lake Union for giving us the opportunity to spread our wings with something new. And Dennelle Catlett, your publicity support has been amazing. And Kathleen Zrelak at Goldberg McDuffie—you are always a huge cheerleader. And to our editor, Tiffany Yates Martin—your smart observations were spot on and made this book better than we could have imagined! Thanks to everyone at Amazon Publishing for making us feel special.

Elisabeth Weed! Your unwavering belief buoys us. Your notes on this novel made it shine, and as always, you steered our career in the right direction. Thank you for all of your awesomeness. Dana Murphy—we are so appreciative of everything you do!

To the wonderful bloggers and reviewers who tirelessly champion books and literacy in general—we hope you realize the tremendous positive effect you have on authors and readers alike. Thanks to each and every one of you. You are making a difference. And a special shout-out to Andrea Katz for being one of our earliest readers. Your feedback was invaluable.

And of course, we can't forget you—the readers. The ones who generously read our novels. We hope you come with us as we try something new. We are nothing without each and every one of you. Thank you!

The island of Maui is one of our favorite places in the world. We've vacationed together with our families, and when we took the trip to Maui and drove the road to Hana, we didn't do it just for the fruity cocktails and gorgeous beaches. We wanted to make sure we got everything exactly right. Thank you to the lovely Hawaiian people who helped inspire this book.

To our friends and family—you are the best! Thank you for attending our book events and listening to the same stories dozens of times. We promise to come up with some new material soon!

To our husbands, Mike and Matt—you have both been so patient, especially when we tell you we want to book a research trip to Hawaii two weeks before we do it. (Oops.) Now is probably the time to tell you the next book is set in Mexico . . . You let us ride out this dream, and for that, we are forever grateful. We love you guys.

ABOUT THE AUTHORS

Photo © 2016 Debbie Friedrich

Liz Fenton and Lisa Steinke have been best friends for more than twenty-five years. They've survived high school, college, and the publishing of three novels together. Liz lives in San Diego, California, with her husband and two children. Lisa, a former talk show producer, now lives in Chicago, Illinois, with her husband, daughter, and two bonus children. Visit Liz and Lisa at www.lizandlisa.com.